MW01129269

DIAMONDS FOR DIAMOND

A JACK DIAMOND MYSTERY

KAY NIMITZ SMITH

A JACK DIAMOND MYSTERY
BOOK 1

Copyright

For my Harry

who taught me that the only way to eat an elephant
is one bite at a time.

Chapter 1

THE SUDDEN SILENCE startled him. It echoed in his mind, erasing all but the lingering ringing tinnitus in his ears and the pounding of his racing heart. He squeezed his eyes shut, willing his eyes to work better, futilely trying to see something in the darkness before him. His hands reached out instinctively, zombie-like, probing the blackened space before him, protecting his body from the unknown, the unseen. The complete sensory deprivation shocked him. Every time. He knew what to expect. He'd done this countless times before. But the deafening silence and the absolute blindness never grew mundane. Never became routine.

A trickle of frigid water kissed his neck and edged its way down the back of his suit. He could only blame half his shivers on the rapid drop in his body temperature. He focused his energy on unclenching his fists, releasing the tension in his taut muscles, forcing his body to relax. He couldn't let the sudden influx of fear grip his heart. Fear led to panic, and panic led to mistakes. He couldn't afford to make a mistake. Not today. Not now.

Taking a deep breath, he focused on the task at hand. He turned on his flashlight, equally disappointed and relieved when the light's rays penetrated only a few inches before his face. He found the rope floating in the water above him, and tugged once, sending a signal to his team up above that he was ready to begin his search.

He adjusted his buoyancy compensator and felt the bubbles swirl around him. His feet rose behind him, and he kicked with his fins once, twice, allowing his body to flow through the murky water. He pointed his flashlight down, seeing nothing but the silt floating around him. Searching in near zero visibility seemed like an impossible task. But someone had to look. Someone had to find her.

He dipped his head, pointing himself downward and kicking once again. His heart lurched when the sandy bottom of the river jumped into his view. His gloved fingers inadvertently swept through the silty bottom, stirring muck and debris into his already limited line of vision. Frustrated, he chastised himself. Such a rookie mistake. He knew better than that. He allowed his body to float, slowly propelling along the bottom, his stomach clenching every time he came across a plant waving its arms in the water or a boulder firmly planted on the river's bottom. He'd found a peaceful joy in his training. But the clear, near perfect visibility of scuba diving in the local swimming pool could never come close to comparing to the eerie other-worldliness of scuba diving in the Willamette River.

He tugged once more on his search line, letting his team on shore know of his whereabouts. He had no idea how far he'd swum or how long he'd been down there. His team kept track of his stats.

Theoretically, he should be doing that too. But for now, he had time to wonder at the peculiar experience opening up before him.

His eyes grew wide as he came across a strange metallic object, shining in his meager light. Not until he had swum nearly right on top of it did he realize it was a French horn. How a French horn got buried in the bed of the Willamette River, he didn't know. Frankly, he didn't want to know. He pulled his wrist up to his face, pressing the light close to his dive computer. Peering through the murk, his clock blinked twelve minutes, thirty-two seconds. His eyebrows shot up. He thought for sure he'd been under much longer. Time slowed down under water.

He tugged on his search line twice to get more line, and let his body move further in the dark depths. He kicked his fins, spanning his light to the right, spying nothing, absolutely nothing in the waters. He turned his head to the left and her arm smacked his face.

Jack shrieked like a little girl. His arm flew up in defense. He grabbed the woman's arm, instinctively trying to shove it away from himself, and then blinked in horror when her skin started to slough off in his hand. Fighting the urge to gag, he took a deep breath, not wanting to lose the woman — or what was left of her skin — in the murky depths. Tugging three times on his line, he signaled his find to the team waiting up on land.

Taking a deep breath, he closed his eyes and let the stillness around him reach his heart and mind. He'd seen this before. Dozens of times. Hundreds.

But no matter how many times he'd been in this position, no matter how many times he'd done this before, seeing it up close and personal still took a moment of preparation. He steadied his breath once more and opened his eyes. Focusing on his breathing, he slowly pointed the flashlight up and to his left, his mind bracing itself for the horror movie about to come to life.

And there she was. Hanging upside down like trapeze artist in a stunt gone awry, the woman's long hair flowed across her face, her arms floating freely in the water. He realized, upon closer inspection, that her skin hadn't peeled off when he'd grabbed her the first time. He had merely caught a handful of her sweater, twisting it around her arm. His imagination must have married his nightmares, creating the illusion of sloughing. He swallowed his nausea and relief and turned his flashlight up. The woman's legs and feet were tangled in the mess of weeds and branches above them. No wonder she'd drowned. A wave of grief washed over him. The poor woman. Her life had ended before she'd even had a chance to start living.

Jack had seen her children, shivering and dripping wet up on shore, huddled beneath the firefighter's blanket. Their father had been pacing, obviously distraught. Evidently, he'd only been gone for a short while. They'd left the mustard at home. His wife had died because they'd left the mustard at home. The man's distraught voice echoed in Jack's head. He had left his boys and their mother to go buy mustard, of all the most inane things. And now she was dead.

Jack had heard bits and pieces from the other witnesses as he had set up his dive gear. One of the boys had waded into the river and slipped. Panicking, he had called for his brother to help. Neither had been wearing life jackets. Neither knew how to swim. She must have seen the boys flailing about in the water, must have heard them calling for help. One of the witnesses said she had managed to get the first boy back onto sure footing quickly. But then her other son had started making his way into deeper waters. She had reached him just before his head went under, he said. She had passed him off to one of the kind strangers who had waded into the water to help. She'd smiled, he said, relieved that she had eluded her own personal tragedy. She'd been right there, he said. And then she wasn't.

Jack praised the woman's efforts to save her children. She had sacrificed her life to save her son's — an act of courage his own father could never have, would never have even remotely considered. A surge of jealousy clenched his heart, and he felt the sting of tears prickle the back of his eyes. Jack had brought the woman home to her family. A family that had loved her. A family whom she loved enough to give up her life in exchange for theirs. He smiled then, as a lump formed at the back of his throat. Man, he loved his job.

Chapter 2

Jack Diamond smiled and waved at the records clerks as he buzzed himself into the back offices of the Hansen Building. A flurry of gossip fluttered through the glassed-in office as the women blushed in response, huddling their heads together. One of the women, stuck filing in the back, dropped her manila folder, rushed through the narrow aisle between the floor-to-ceiling walls of files, dashed toward the front desk, trying to get a better look before the heavy door closed behind him. She slumped down into the nearest chair, disappointed at having missed out on the best view.

Jack chuckled to himself as the door closed behind him. Just to his right, he noticed a new plaque had been hung, naming Lieutenant David Kent the State Sheriff's Association Manager of the Year. Jack raised his eyebrows and nodded his approval. Lieutenant Kent was a good boss. He deserved that kind of recognition. He turned, took three steps down the hallway, glanced up, and stopped dead in his tracks. There, leaning up against the door frame to his Sergeant's office door, stood Claire Wilcox. He'd recognize that ass anywhere.

His heart stopped. Stuttered. Stopped again. And then began galloping at an alarming rate.

As the blood rushed to his face, and then just as quickly emptied out and left him looking like a ghost, settling embarrassingly elsewhere, Jack panicked.

Turning to the right, he made a mad dash down the hallway, out the next door, down the stairs, and headed straight for the men's locker room where he could stop and breathe for a minute. Why now? Why today of all days?

Jack fought the urge to scream. Or punch something. Or vomit. Or run back upstairs and plead with her to take him back. To pull her into his arms and beg her never to leave him again. To hold her close, stroke her hair, kiss those sweet, sweet lips and make love to her until her toes curled and she cooed beneath him, curling up in his arms afterwards and sighing as she drifted off into a contented sleep.

Desire settled into disappointment, then transformed itself into dreariness. Today of all days. Why did the love of his life have to show up today of all days?

Jack washed his hands, ran them through his dark, wavy hair and rubbed them across his face. He avoided his reflection in the mirror, making his way back out into the break room to grab a bottle of water before heading back out on the road.

How long had it been since he'd seen her? Twelve years? Thirteen? Jack started up his patrol car, and headed out the back lot. He waited for the electric gate to open completely before leading his car toward the road, hanging a right onto Glisan.

His mind filled with memories of her. The way her smile reached all the way to the twinkle in her

7

eyes when she laughed. The way her voice sounded when she whispered in his ear. The feel of her hands when her fingers entwined with his. The smell of her hair. The arch of her foot. The shape of her breasts.

Memory after memory came flooding back. All through college he'd been enraptured by her, had admired her from afar, in awe of her intellect and her beauty. He'd counted it as one of the best days of his life when she'd agreed to go out on a date with him. And one of the worst when she walked out his front door.

He'd assumed too much. He'd taken her for granted. He'd always thought that she would come running back.

He had admired her dreams of becoming a pediatric plastic surgeon, wanting to make the world a better place. Her dreams had matched his own need to right the wrongs in the world, to protect those who couldn't protect themselves. He thought they'd conquer the world together, working hand in hand. He never fully grasped her need to leave in order to make her dreams become a reality.

With a haughty arrogance, he thought he could let her go, and she wouldn't want to leave. Or, that after she left, she'd find success in her accomplishments, and then she'd come running back victorious, sensational, sated in her glorious triumphs, and most importantly, wanting to share it all with him.

His arrogance had cost him, dearly. Her departure had nearly torn him in half. Even to this day, his heart ached with the love he felt for every single ounce of her very being. And it had been his own damned fault. He had, after all, let her go.

Like a fool.

And now she was married.

To an even bigger fool.

A rat bastard that couldn't possibly understand her dreams, her needs to make the world better. The bastard's intellect couldn't possibly ever fathom the amazing gift he had in the gem he had married.

And there was nothing, nothing at all he could do about it.

Because, to make matters worse, and just to rub a little salt into the wound, God's ironic sense of humor had aligned things just perfectly so that the bastard could now loosely be called his boss.

Ron Wilcox.

How a man like Ron Wilcox ever managed to become a sergeant in charge of a Patrol Unit at the Multnomah County Sheriff's Office was beyond Jack's imagination. Yes, he technically met all the requirements — the four year degree, the eight years of service as a Deputy at the Sheriff's Office. He'd done his time doing Court Security, Day Shift patrol, then a short stint in Detectives. No one really knew why it wasn't longer, although plenty speculated. He'd botched his way through a summer at River Patrol. Then, just two weeks ago, after one too many close looks at the bottom of a whiskey bottle, he landed himself on the dreaded graveyard shift patrol, with Monday, Tuesday,

Wednesday nights off. The worst of the worst at shift sign ups. It wasn't "technically" a punishment. His shift Lieutenant couldn't do that. However, Jack had walked in on the patrol deputies joking around that their new graveyard shift sergeant was in the penalty box for his latest assignment. How Ron had managed to save his job irked Jack to no end. But how the drunken bastard had managed to keep his wife just pissed him off.

Jack flipped on his turn signal, and steered his patrol car right onto 242nd. He kept his eyes on the road, but his mind didn't travel with him.

At least he didn't have to work with the jerk any more. He'd just received his orders that he would be transferring over to the Detectives Unit, effective immediately. Jack cocked a smile, his dimple poking through his stubble in the dark. He'd spent weeks preparing for the Detectives Oral Boards. The whole experience had been equally as stressful, if not more so, than the process he'd had to go through to get hired on as a Deputy. And it had all paid off. He'd finally climbed the ladder to Detectives. Detectives! Jack's smile deepened.

Jack turned left onto SE Stark, smiling as the cars around him all began to drive meticulously at the speed limit, and not a mile over; suddenly using their turn signals, and waiting patiently for pedestrians to cross the roads. He kept his car pointed toward the old Historic Columbia River Highway, edging his way toward the quiet solitude of the back roads.

The real feather in his cap came from his new sergeant, Larry Moore at the Detectives Unit. Larry had given Jack the okay to stay on the Sheriff's Dive Rescue and Underwater Investigations Team even after he moved to Detectives. Larry Moore was a harmless place-filler, serving as the Sheriff's Office Sergeant in charge of Detectives. He did what he was told, followed his orders, did his job to the minimal requirements necessary, and acted more like a lap-dog yes-man to his own boss, Lieutenant Manny Rodriguez. As much as Jack wasn't particularly looking forward to working for Larry, he was excited about the prospect of working with, and learning from, Manny. Better still, he was thrilled at being able to stay on the Dive Team. And, better yet, he would no longer have to work for Ron Wilcox.

Jack glanced down at his MDC, his patrol car's mobile data computer. A new message popped up, indicating that Ron Wilcox — speak of the devil — was calling in sick for the rest of his shift. Jack's smile blossomed into an outright grin.

Jack turned right onto SE Hurlburt Road, and peered out into the thick black road winding before him. The tops of the trees swayed gently in the night's breeze, moving to the moody lyrics of Pink Floyd playing quietly through the radio in Jack's car. Man, he loved his job. Where else could you drive through the pristine Columbia River Gorge in the middle of the night and get paid for it? Claire had loved the Columbia Gorge, the beautiful border separating the states of Oregon and Washington. Jack smiled, his brain flashing back memories of necking in her car along darkly lit roads, then later watching the elegant beauty of the sun rise from Crown Point.

Jack's phone chirped, waking Jack out of his reverie. The MDC had been awfully quiet tonight. Not much had been going on in East Multnomah County this evening. He glanced down at the caller ID on his phone and answered the call.

"Go ahead, Sam."

Deputy Sam Neely's voice shook with laughter over the air. "Diamond. Quit day dreaming and switch your radio over to "Love Talk" with Dr. Savannah. You've got to listen to this. We're talking some seriously kinky shit."

Jack shook his head. "All right, fine. I'll switch over. But this had better be good, Sam. They're playing 'Dark Side of the Moon' in its entirety." Reluctantly, he reached his hand underneath his MDC and flipped the radio channel. Sure enough, he tuned in to the middle of a young man's delineation of some of the most bizarre sexual fantasies Jack had ever encountered. And after having worked more than enough sex crime scenes while on patrol, Jack had heard, and unfortunately, born witness to the negative impacts of, more than his fair share of bizarre sexual fantasies. Jack rolled his eyes and chuckled.

"Dude, you need to go wash your ears out with soap."

Sam's laughter came through with a loud crackle. "Stay safe out there, Diamond."

"You, too, Sam."

Jack flipped the station back to the music marathon. As far as he was concerned, life was too short to listen to stuff that was truly none of his business. Or stuff that reminded him too much of the seedier side of his job.

Before he could stop it, his mind started to replay scenes in his head: flash after flash of crime scenes; random snippets of teary confessions; spittle spraying out of a man's mouth as he screamed in protest, forcefully dragged toward an awaiting police car; the sharp bark of Trojan, the K-9 dog, as he cornered a bad guy in a tree; tears running down a child's face with the words, "Daddy! Daddy!" pleading through the rain; the bloody mess on a baseball bat, lying perversely innocent on the kitchen floor next to an ever expanding pool of blood; the flash of his mother's mangled fingers flitting toward his brother's bloody face pressed up against the filthy orange linoleum. Jack blinked, willing the scenes away. Echoes of his memories washed over his heart once again, and he rubbed his face clean, turning up the radio to tune out the memories.

The wind shifted, and a flutter of sound tickled his ears. Instantly alert, Jack's hand slid to the left side of his duty belt and he turned down the volume on his portable radio. Driving through the isolated back roads of East Multnomah County truly stunned the senses with its breathtaking beauty during the daylight. But out here in the middle of the night with no one around for miles, and the

13

dark so pitch black you couldn't see anything past the stretch of the car's headlights, sometimes gave Jack the willies. More often than he cared to admit. It didn't take much to send his heart racing, flashes of horror movie scenes racing through his head.

Leaning forward, he turned off Pink Floyd, peering out into the pitch black, his eyes darting across the road, seeking out the disturbance. He slowed to a crawl, allowing his patrol car to creep forward. At this time of night, there was very little traffic up on Larch Mountain. No real need to worry about oncoming cars. He shook his head, and reached forward to turn the music back up when, once again, a strange fleeting noise came to him from across the way.

The hairs on the back of his neck stood erect and instinct took over. His eyes searched the dark as he reached for his radio mic. "County 55."

"55 go ahead." The dispatcher's smooth, sexy voice cut through the night air, reassuring him, and the rest of the graveyard patrol, that someone was always there, always listening, always at the ready to send help and coordinate operations.

"Can you please create a suspicious circumstances call for me? I've got a situation up here on Larch Mountain Road. I'm hearing some strange noises from the woods." Jack looked around, still seeing nothing more than the road in front of him and the trees around him. He would have felt foolish, if not for the gut instinct he had learned not to discount. He clicked back into the mic. "Can you please start 53 to cover me until I figure out what's going on? I'm just east of Brower Road."

"Copy, 55. County 53, do you copy?"

Sam's voice boomed over the handset. "Roger that. It'll take me a few to get up there, I'm just clearing from I 84 at Troutdale."

"Copy, 53. Twenty-three forty-seven." The dispatcher's sultry voice could make even the notation of the military time of day sound sexy. Her voice faded into the darkness outside.

Jack allowed the patrol car to creep along slowly, his ears pricked, his mind slowly second guessing his instincts. Damn. Sam was a good twenty minutes away.

His MDC beeped. An incoming message from another deputy, working across the county, awaited him. Jack glanced down as he pulled up the message, asking him if he had found Sasquatch. He chuckled nervously and deleted the message that didn't warrant a reply. Jack edged further along the dark road. A dreaded sense of unease washed over him as he realized, for the hundredth time, just how isolated this part of the county was, particularly at this time of night. Just as he was about to make a u-turn for one more pass, he heard it again, this time, louder, and more desperate. A woman's cry. He flipped on his rear blue flasher lights, turned his search light toward the woods, twisted his whole body toward the side window for a better view, and felt — then heard — the undeniable sickening thump of an impact. Whipping his head around, he caught just a glimpse of her horrified face as a woman's body flipped upward and onto the hood of his patrol car.

Chapter 3

JACK JOLTED HIS patrol car to a halt. He was already half way out the door, his gun unholstered before the woman's half naked body even had a chance to roll off the hood and land on the ground with a dull thud.

She sat up, slowly, brushing the gravel off her shoulder and arm, her hand coming to rest in her hair. Jack had her in his sights, assessing the situation as quickly as he could. After no more than a few seconds, he re-holstered his gun, and reached up to his mic.

"County 55."

"55, go ahead."

"Yeah, I need medical up here Code 3. I'm east of Brower Road, just past milepost 4. I've got a pedestrian versus auto, female, late 20's, early 30's. She's got a head laceration, and her elbow's in bad shape, but I don't know yet the extent of her other injuries. Stand by."

"55, I've got medical on the way. Twenty-three fifty-eight."

When she turned her head to face him, Jack's heart stopped. "Claire?"

The woman shielded her eyes from the patrol car's blaring lights and looked up. Not Claire. Jack started breathing again. "Ma'am, try not to move. You've been in an accident."

The woman glanced down at her body, only just now seeming to realize it was attached to her. Blood trickled down her legs, the skin having been torn from her knees by the asphalt. One of her shoes lay askew, the other missing entirely. She looked at her elbow, gingerly tiptoeing her fingers along the joint, and wincing at the barest touch. A twig snapped in the woods beside them, and she jumped, awakened once again to the terror that had flown her into the middle of the road, desperate to seek help.

"Help me up!"

"Ma'am, you've been in an accident." Jack kept his voice calm, despite the twitching of his instincts, which urged him to pay more attention to his surroundings.

"Help me up! He's coming! He's coming!"

The woman's frantic ravings started Jack's heart pumping faster. "Who's coming?"

"The man who did this to me! He's coming! Help me up! Help me up!!" The woman shifted her weight around, trying to find a way to get her feet underneath her, without scraping her knees further, and without moving her injured elbow.

"Ma'am," Jack started, using the voice he reserved solely for calming injured children and overactive downy-furred yellow lab puppies, "it's really best if you stay put until the ambulance gets here. We need to make sure nothing is broken or otherwise seriously injured." His eyes flitted toward her temple laceration, and her clearly dislocated, or broken, elbow.

Another twig broke in the woods. She shrieked. "He's *coming*!

The woman scrambled up, and Jack rushed over to half carry, half assist, her toward the back seat of his patrol car.

"Stay." His voice was no more than a whisper. Jack pulled out his gun, and flipped on his mic simultaneously.

"County 55, I need back up here Code 3."

"Copy, County 55." Jack tuned out the rest of the dispatcher's message, calling all available units to come and assist.

Jack knew better than to head into the woods without backup. Even with his mag light and his car's search light panning into the trees, he could see nothing, hear no one. He kept his gun and his mag light panning the area for a good ten minutes before he heard the sirens in the distance.

Doubt settled in to his bones, and he re-holstered his gun, then pressed the button to turn off his heavy duty flashlight. Keeping his eyes toward the woods, Jack headed back to the woman shivering in the back seat of his car.

"Ma'am?"

"You didn't find him. Oh, God, you didn't find him." Her shivering increased tenfold.

Jack walked to the back of his patrol car and unlocked the trunk. Pulling out a blanket, he pressed his mic again. "County 55. What's the ETA on that ambulance?" He slammed the trunk, and headed around to the side of his car.

"County 55, they're about two minutes out."

"Copy that."

"Zero eleven."

Jack draped the blanket around the woman's shoulders. Then he reached into his pocket and pulled out a small stack of folded tissues. He peeled one off, and handed it to her.

"It's wrinkled, but it's clean."

She nodded her head, reaching out a shaky hand. As she began to staunch the flow of tears, Jack pulled out his notebook, squatted down beside her, and began to jot down a few notes.

"Ma'am, can you tell me what happened?"

She just shook her head, and continued to mop the tears off her face. She glanced over her shoulder, but could see nothing.

"Okay, let's start with something easy. Can you tell me your name?"

"Heather. Heather Allen."

"Okay, Heather, can you tell me how you came to be half naked, running into the middle of the road right into the front of a police car?"

At first she shook her head, crumpling up the tissue and blotting at her face again. Jack reached into his pocket and pulled out the rest of his stack, handing her the whole pile. She nodded, sniffed, and then peeled a fresh tissue off the top. She wiped her nose and gulped. Jack wrote a few notes into his notebook, listening to the approaching sirens, praying for them to come faster. When, at last she began to speak, her voice shook so badly, he had to lean in. Once they started coming, the words came out in a jumble, confused, quick, and all at once.

"We met in a bar. He seemed, you know, kinda nice. I thought he might be the one, you know?" She sniffed at her tissue, and then started up again. "We had a few drinks, and then I thought, okay, he's a nice guy, kinda sweet, maybe I'll go for a drive with him." She looked up at Jack, as if seeking out reassurance. Jack did his best to hide his, "stupid, stupid woman" look from his face as he quickly took down her statement. "So we went for this drive. And I thought, you know, this is pretty. This is real nice. And I thought, okay. So I reached over and grabbed his hand and put it on my lap and, you know..."

She paused for a moment, looking at Jack to see if he caught her drift, but he kept his eyes firmly facing his notebook. He was finding it harder and harder to keep his "stupid, stupid woman" look off his face.

"So I put his hand in my lap, you know, and I let his fingers, you know, kinda roam around like. It was nice. All dark and stuff."

"Do you know where you were headed? Know where he was driving you?"

"Oh, you know, I don't pay attention to that kind of thing. I don't usually ever need to know, you know?" She sniffled, and a new round of tears started slipping down her face. Jack gritted his teeth. When would people stop being so incredibly stupid?

"So anyways, we were, you know, driving around, and the next thing I know, he's stopping the car. And I'm thinking, okay, we're getting close to his house or something. Or maybe we'll do some necking or something."

She looked down for reassurance, confirmation, and Jack just nodded his head, continuing to write notes. "So then he gets out and says he has to get something from the trunk. And I start thinking, 'Why? What's in the trunk that you can't get right here?' so I asked him, 'Why?' and he says he thinks we have a flat tire or something."

The woman stopped talking as the sirens grew louder. Jack looked at her, making sure he had her full eye contact, before he went on, "Heather, let's get through the rest of this quickly so we can get you all patched up and taken care of."

Heather sniffled again, and reached up to touch the back of her head, wincing once again at the ever expanding throbbing bump. Jack urged her on. "So what happened after he said that you had a flat tire?"

Heather gasped, and said with a more indignant voice, "So the guy, he pops open the trunk and heads to the back of the car. So I get out, and I start checking out the tires. Neither of them on my side were flat. Not even close! And as I'm standing up to tell him so, I look up, and he's got this metal bar thingie, you know, like, um, a crow bar. Or a tire iron! And he's holding it over his head! You know, like raised up? Like he's going to hit something with it. And then all of a sudden, he's bringing it down, and he's hitting me!" She reached up and touched her elbow, wincing once again.

"So I whap the hell out of him with my purse and his arm kinda, swings back, you know? Like he's out of balance? So then he staggers a little onto the car, so I slammed the trunk lid down, and it kinda bounces off his arm or something. Now he's mad! And he roars! Like I've hurt him or something? And I'm thinking, 'Good, that'll show you, you smarmy bastard!' And then he starts yelling all sorts of obscenities at me! And I just take off! And I grabbed inside my purse and pulled out my pepper spray, and he reached out to try and grab me! And I sprayed the hell out of that pepper spray can and he screamed! And he clawed at his eyes, and kinda fell? Like to his knees? And I ran flat out into the woods, screaming for someone to help! And then this tree jumped out and smacked me in the head!"

Her fingers slid up and gingerly touched the sore spot on her forehead. She winced and pulled her hand down, looking at her fingers. She jolted, suddenly remembering where she was. She looked up at Jack and took a shuddering breath.

"So then, I saw a house, and there was a dog, barking, and I pounded on the door, but no one would come! No one would answer! And so I ran. And I thought I heard him running after me! And so I ran some more, and I followed the long drive way out to the road, but then I heard a car coming, and I couldn't tell if it was his or someone else's so I hid behind a tree kinda along side the edge of the road until I could see the car, and then it was you! And you had your flasher blue lights on! And thank God you were there! And you saved me! And I ran out, and there you were, and you're here! And you saved me!"

The last few words came out all in a whoosh. Heather took a deep shuttering breath and smiled up at him, just as two of the Sheriff's Office patrol cars came flying up the road, the ambulance right behind.

Chapter 4

IT WASN'T LONG before the paramedics had patched her up as best as they could. Her left arm was in a sling, her right hooked up to an IV. She had large bandages on both knees, one on her temple, and she was pressing an ice pack against the back of her head. Before she headed out, Jack managed to get a very brief description of the man who had attacked her, along with a sketchy idea of what kind of car he had been driving, as well as her contact information. In all likelihood, he'd have to reinterview her in the morning, after the shock and the meds had worn off. He was glad that the gravity of the evening's events had begun to settle in to her soul as the paramedics began to pack up. The last words he heard her exclaim were, "Oh God, I should have been paying more attention!" as the ambulance drivers slammed the doors and headed off toward Mt. Hood Medical Center. She definitely could use a dose of common sense to go along with the pain meds.

The evening grew long as he and the other deputies began their investigation. Jack put in a call to the K-9 unit, hoping the well-trained tracking dog would have better luck finding something. While he waited for the K-9 unit to arrive, Jack put out an APB to the local hospitals, to keep their eyes open for someone seeking medical treatment from a trunk lid injury and/or extensive pepper spray burns to the face and eyes, in case the fool wimped out enough, or was stupid enough, to seek out medical care.

When Trojan the K-9 and his handler finally arrived, Trojan immediately went to work. Behind three separate trees, all within easy view of Jack's patrol car, Trojan scented something. Clearly, the bad guy had hunkered down, even for a short while, behind the trees to get a better look at Jack and his victim. Jack shuttered. Thinking someone might be out there, hiding in the dark, scoping him out, waiting for the right time to attack was a nightmare. But *knowing* that someone was out there, hiding in the dark, scoping him out, that just plain old frightened him. Jack shuttered once again.

Trojan set off through the woods, his handler right behind, tracking the scent in a hurry. Two of the deputies began scoping the areas around the trees Trojan had identified, searching for evidence the bad guy may have left behind. One of the deputies set off at a trot behind Trojan's handler, acting as the cover officer, in case Trojan sniffed out the bad guy. Jack, itching to go along, stayed behind, knowing that his own scent would cloud Trojan's hunt. He forced himself to begin writing notes, again. Jack's heart raced as he heard the dog's footsteps tearing through the tinder in the woods. He wondered if the bad guy had the common sense to leave before the big German Shepard made his way through to his hiding spot. He'd seen Trojan capture a bad guy before. He'd heard the dog's fierce bark from a distance. Even from the safety of the inside of his own patrol car, he'd been terrified of the vision of the dog's formidable crouching stance, ready for his handler's permission to attack and pull down the bad guy. He couldn't imagine how fiercely terrifying it must be to be on the receiving end of Trojan's attack. The dark of the woods soon swallowed the noise of Trojan's footsteps. The beam of light from the dog handler's flashlight grew ever smaller as the forest enveloped them completely in the darkness.

Jack felt, more than heard, the dog's sharp barks only minutes later. He'd found something. His heart began to pump in earnest, the adrenaline kicking in with the hopes that the bad guy was cornered up a tree. Jack jumped when his phone chirped seconds later.

"Jack. We're done up here. He's gone"

Jack frowned at his phone, knowing that Trojan's handler wouldn't call off the search unless there truly was nothing left to be found.

"Copy that. What happened?"

"We ended up on the other side of the woods, about half a mile away from you off a small gravel road or driveway. I'm guessing this road hooks up with Alex Barr road. It'd be easy for him to make it down to the scenic highway and out to I 84 without your guys seeing him. Looks like after the guy followed your vic out to those trees by your patrol car, he backtracked round to the other side of a house tucked in back here. Then he headed straight back to his car. Trojan hit on the guy's scent really hard around the side of the road, evidently where the guy'd parked, then sat down. Clearly, whatever Trojan detected is long since gone."

"Copy that." Jack couldn't help but feel the disappointment wash over him. He'd hoped that the jerk who had dislocated the woman's elbow and was intending to do her more harm, would be cowering in a ball right now, with Trojan's sharp teeth clasped firmly around his jugular.

Jack and the other deputies caravanned to meet up with the dog, his handler, and the cover officer. They searched the area where Trojan sat, patiently waiting to be dismissed, but none of them found any evidence of the assault. Not so much as a cigarette butt. The guy'd been careful. All too soon Trojan and his handler headed back on patrol. Jack called his Acting Sergeant and filled him on the latest updates of the investigation. The other deputies cleared the area, and Jack returned to his patrol car. Slipping his car into gear, Jack began the long drive down to the Wood Village field office, his thoughts turning back to the rather lengthy report he would inevitably be finishing up well past the end of his shift.

So much for the sexiness of law enforcement work — all he seemed to do these days was jot down notes for the endless piles of reports and paperwork that had to be completed for each and every case. Paperwork. Yet one more reason he was glad to be done with patrol, and headed for Detectives. At least then the paperwork seemed to actually mean something.

A lot of the other guys in Jack's class at the Academy had aimed for undercover drug investigations. Other guys simply wanted to be on the road, hitting the swing shift with all the action. But not Jack. He wasn't interested in the drug unit or undercover work. Nor was he interested in car chases, accident investigations, or handing out tickets to lazy ass bastards who couldn't bother to follow the laws. Most of all, Jack had no interest whatsoever in Internal Affairs, investigating internal complaints against his own colleagues, jerks like Ron Wilcox, who also couldn't bother to follow the laws. Nope. Not his cup of tea.

Jack wanted to be a part of the Detectives Unit, investigating the Big Ones. Murders. Assaults. Domestic Violence. Child Abuse. Sex Crimes. He wanted to find enough evidence to prosecute the bastards that beat up their wives. He wanted to be responsible for putting away the sons of bitches who shook their babies to death, who raped women and children, who murdered in the heat of their anger, or, much worse, in the cold, calculated plans of their sick and twisted minds. He wanted the satisfaction of knowing that people like his father could never, ever see the light of day because he, himself, had found enough evidence to put them in jail for the rest of their lives. He wanted to be able to give the victims, those people under his care and protection, the security and relief in the knowledge that he had protected them. He had rescued them from their

29

worst nightmare, and put the bad guys away where they could never hurt them again. That's what he wanted. That's what he'd always wanted. And that's what he would always want, as long as he worked for the Sheriff's Office.

The lights of the approaching city pulled him out of his mood. In a heartbeat, one could turn the corner and come from the pitch black of rural woods and head straight into the lights and sounds of a small city. That's one of the things he loved the most about living in Portland. An hour away from the breathtaking Pacific coast. An hour away from the magnificent mountains. Gorgeous waterfalls, the Columbia Gorge, and a large enough metropolitan area to acquire just about anything you could possibly need. The urban sprawl had spread all the way out to Fairview, Troutdale, and Gresham, and one day all too soon, it would suck up Sandy and the rest of the small towns up the side of the Mount Hood. Jack sighed.

He stopped at the flashing red light and glanced around. Not a car in sight. For now, thankfully, even in this day and age, the city of Gresham seemed to sleep in the middle of the night. As it should be, he thought. Too often these days small towns and cities were becoming more and more nocturnal, the seedy part of life trying to struggle through the cracks like unwelcome weeds.

"County 53." The dispatcher's voice reminded Jack of Lily, the radio talk show goddess who hosted the midnight long sets of classic rock. Smooth and sexy, like dark chocolate on a hot summer's night.

Jack listened to Sam's voice boom through the air. "County 53, go ahead."

"I've got a suicide gone awry at the Super 8 in Troutdale. Medical is already on route."

"53, copy that. I'm on route."

"We've got a male, aged 48, who apparently believes he's OD'd on Anise seeds. He's worried that he's taken too many. Victim sounds distraught."

"53, roger that. Can you send County 55 to cover?"

"Copy. County 55 can you cover?"

Jack pressed his mic and replied. "Copy that. I'm on my way. Coming from Stark Street Bridge." So much for getting his paperwork done.

"Copy that County 55. Three forty-two."

Sam's car was already parked by the time Jack pulled into the motel's parking lot. He watched Sam make his way to the front office to retrieve the room key. Jack waved, parked, then headed straight for the paramedics.

"Hey Jenn, Kevin."

They answered in practiced chorus. "Hey, Jack." Kevin Liu and Jenn Lake had been working together for so long that they'd morphed into a single, cohesive unit. It's what made them such an incredible team, saving hundreds upon hundreds of lives each year. They always reminded Jack of Fitz-Simmons on "Agents of Shield."

"Last night on patrol, eh?" Kevin leaned against his rig and gave Jack his undivided attention. Jenn stayed on task. She was more than half way through her prep to head in, awaiting clearance. The paramedics had long since learned the value of the policy that they wait for deputies to clear all suicides, assaults, and homicides before entering, in case the area turned out to be part of a crime scene investigation. Jenn made sure she was always prepped and ready for entry before she'd been granted clearance, to keep the patient's wait for medical assistance as minimal as possible.

"Yeah." Jack's sheepish grin pulled the dimple out of his cheek.

"We sure are gonna miss seeing you around."

"Aw, thanks!"

"Well, it's not like he's dying!" Jenn's snarky comment seemed almost out of character. She rarely, if ever, deviated from her assigned task, always focused, always on alert.

"Well, if I was, you'd be the ones I'd want here to fix me up."

Jenn stopped writing on her clipboard and looked up.

Jack winked at Kevin and flashed Jenn a grin. Kevin smirked, ducked his head, and pulled his red medical kit out of the back of the rig.

Jack scratched the stubble on his chin. "So what the hell is Anise seed? And why would someone take it? What's the OD limit? What should we be looking for before you guys head in?"

Jenn looked up from her clipboard, and recited from memory, "Anise seed is usually taken orally to stimulate breast milk in nursing mothers. Some say it also helps with bad breath and eases stomach gasses." She frowned, glancing down at her clipboard. She scanned her notes quickly, and then looked back up at Jack. "But in men? I'd say he probably took it as an aphrodisiac."

"An aphrodisiac?" Jack snorted. "This'll be interesting." Jack sidled back up to Sam and they headed to the room together.

Sam pounded on the door with his mag light. Jack kept his hand on the butt of his gun, just in case. "Mr. Gerbrowski? This is the Multnomah County Sheriff's Office. You called for assistance?"

They heard a muffled response.

"Mr. Gerbrowski, are you able to come and answer the door? Or should we use the key?"

Again, only a muffled response.

Sam looked at Jack, and nodded. Jack unholstered his gun, Sam unlocked the door, and they burst into the room.

Jack cleared the entrance while Sam surveyed the room. The room reeked of black licorice. Jack shivered. It couldn't have been more than 43 degrees, the bitter chill of the air conditioning blasting the room with frigid air. With short quick steps, they'd quickly cleared the bedroom, bathroom, and closet, noting that only two occupants filled the room: Mr. Gerbrowski and his obviously well-loved blow up doll.

"Mr. Gerbrowski, can you hear me?" Sam made his way over to the troubled man, who through an

33

amazing feat, had managed to wrap himself, naked, from head to toe in bubble wrap.

The man nodded his head, not quite enough in his right mind to be embarrassed by the hilarity of the room spread out before them. Sam tended to Mr. Gerbrowski, helping him to uncover his ears and chin from the bubble wrap, while Jack went in search of illegal drugs, weapons, and paraphernalia. Jack discovered the bottle of Anise seed on the bedside table next to the telephone, and cleared his throat, "Sam."

Sam nodded, and focused his attention back onto the bubble-wrapped man. Jack called Jenn and Kevin to join them to haul the man away for medical and psych evaluations.

As the paramedics made their way in and took over the care of Mr. Gerbrowski, Jack caught Sam's eye and together they put on their gloves and assessed the rest of the room. The pillows, all four of them, had been wrapped completely in bubble wrap. Jack flipped down the comforter and sheet and discovered that the entire mattress had also been covered in bubble wrap. Sam's eyebrow quirked up. He leaned down and swiped his finger along the plastic only to discover that the entire surface had been coated with a greasy substance — something that looked a bit like Vaseline. Or some other type of lubricant. He looked at his glove-tipped finger, his face a mask of disgust. His eyes met Jack's. Jack quickly looked away, biting the inside of his cheek to keep from laughing.

Just as the paramedics began to push Mr. Gerbrowski's gurney out the door, he screamed. Jack and Sam reached for their guns, adrenaline pumping.

"Betty! Don't forget Betty!" He grabbed the door jamb and with surprising strength refused to let go. "Please! I need Betty!"

The paramedics looked around, worried that perhaps they had missed another patient. Jack, panicked for one sick moment, afraid he might have missed an unconscious victim, knelt down on the floor and looked under the bed, fearful of what he might find.

Sam snorted.

Jack looked up, startled, only to follow Sam's gaze. Mr. Gerbrowski stretched his whole arm out toward the corner of the room, where his blow-up doll, which had bee-bopped across the floor, bounced up and down in the flow of the air conditioning.

Jenn injected a full syringe into the man's IV and softly spoke in Mr. Gerbrowski's ear. "Betty'll be just fine, Mr. Gerbrowski. The nice deputies will take good care of her."

Mr. Gerbrowski did not seem convinced. His arm reached out frantically, his thin fingers clasping with fierce strength upon the door jamb as he continued to call out for "Betty, sweet Betty!" The medicine must have kicked in rather rapidly because soon the man's eyelids began to droop. His hand lost his grip, sagging slowly to the side of the gurney. The paramedics lost no time in getting the man out the door and into the awaiting ambulance.

Jack stood up and turned to grin at Sam. "Hell of a way to end my last shift on patrol!"

Sam laughed. "You know you're gonna miss this shit when you're in Detectives."

Jack grinned, heading toward the front office to return the keys to the night manager.

Through the crisp night air, Sam's falsetto voice carried through the air behind him. "Betty! Don't forget Betty!"

Chapter 5

"Mr. Diamond."

Jack looked up from the piles of paperwork in his hands and smiled. "Heya, Sheriff. How're things?"

"Let's go for a walk."

Jack's eyes flitted down to the paperwork in his lap, and then over to the Human Resources manager, and back up to the Sheriff in less than a heartbeat. The Sheriff didn't miss a thing. Jack cleared his throat and cocked a sheepish grin.

"Absolutely."

The Sheriff flashed his signature smile at the HR manager. "Thomas, you don't mind if I borrow him for a minute or two, do you?" Thomas smiled and shook his head.

"Not at all, Sheriff. As long as you don't forget to send him on back when you're through with him." Thomas gave Jack a quick appreciative once-over, and sighed — almost inaudibly — then turned his body, but not his attention, back toward his computer screen.

Jack stifled a grin and grabbed his jacket off the back of his chair. He apologized to Thomas for leaving in the middle of their discussion regarding changes in the health benefits package. "I'll just leave these here."

Thomas smiled up at him and took the file from his hands. "Fine, fine. I'll be sure to give you a call when the paperwork comes through." He twiddled his fingers in a wave, and leaned his body slightly out of his cube, not missing the opportunity to watch Jack walk away. A file slid to the floor, spilling papers across the aisle between the cubes. The woman in the cube across from Thomas' looked up, catching Thomas' gaze. She blushed, picked up the scattered papers, and quickly scooted her chair back into her cube, having been caught red-handed also staring at Jack's walkaway. Thomas tut-tutted the woman, winked at her, checked to see if there was one last view, and then headed back to work, another sigh escaping unawares.

Jack led the Sheriff through the maze of cubicles toward the hallway doors. "Where are we headed?" Jack's eyes flitted over to the ongoing chess game on the long counter in front of the door. Everyone who wanted to play was allowed to move the chess pieces, as long as the chess moves were legal, and as long as they didn't forget to change the sign in front of the board when they were done. The placard in front of the chessboard indicated it was black's turn. Jack scanned the chessboard out of habit, but did not stop to make his usual chess move. He lengthened his stride to grasp the door the Sheriff was holding open.

"Oh, I suppose a little walk upstairs to the garden would do just fine."

Jack nodded, pressing the button for the elevator and looking up at the arrows above the elevator doors, waiting not-so-patiently for one of the white triangles to light up. The Sheriff, in his ever gracious and warm manner, greeted the flotsam of staff, deputies, County workers, and attorneys that flitted into the busy hallway and out of the elevators as he and Jack waited for their elevator to show up. He leaned his ear down toward a short statured Internal Affairs investigator, and answered her questions in his soft voice, his eyes frequently making direct contact, making sure that he'd addressed her concerns to her satisfaction.

Jack marveled at the man's ability to keep people at ease, to encourage them to be better deputies, to work toward making the County a safer and better community, all the while having the stiff backbone required to face the County Commissioners on a monthly basis to fight for every penny he could squeeze out of their tightfisted budgets.

The good citizens of Multnomah County had elected Matthew O'Brien as Sheriff on the heels of several scandals and unpleasant negative press that had plagued the Sheriff's Office over the past decade. Having been wildly successful as the Washington County Sheriff for the last sixteen years, Sheriff O'Brien's deeply ethical and moral background righted the keeling ship that had been the Multnomah County Sheriff's Office.

He commanded respect and authority over his officers and staff, often rubbing his hand across his bald head while mulling difficult decisions, or running his fingers through his thick red beard while contemplating budgetary crises. The Sheriff always had time to listen to his deputies, addressing their concerns with as much fairness and grace as he could muster, all the while keeping his eye on the bigger picture. His staff and his deputies sometimes grumbled when they were asked to tighten their belts to reduce their budgets, or when he transferred them to different departments, ever seeking to keep mediocrity at bay, ever striving for excellence by keeping his deputies on their toes, challenged both mentally and physically.

The Sheriff demanded nothing but excellence from each and every single one of the deputies under his command. And because of his belief in their abilities, the Sheriff's Office had never been so strong a force as it had been in the few short years he'd served in office.

Jack stepped out of the elevator and onto the pathways of the eco-roof that led around the side of the building, facing downtown Portland. Jack had wondered if the additional cost of the eco-roof really justified its installation, but he'd heard that the additional insulation of the garden on the top of the building helped to reduce water run-off, and helped to reduce the air conditioner's workload in the hotter summer months. It didn't really matter, he supposed. The view was unparalleled. And the privacy provided the Sheriff with the opportunity to hold conversations without being interrupted by the daily operations of the Sheriff's Office in the most populated county in the state of Oregon. Jack sat down on the bench and waited for the Sheriff to speak his mind.

"Jack. You've been working for the Sheriff's Office now for what, twelve years? Thirteen?"

"Twelve and a half, sir."

"And you've been working in the Detective's Unit for a few weeks now?"

"Yes, sir."

"And how are you liking it?"

Jack grinned. "I love it, sir!"

The Sheriff nodded his head and looked out toward downtown. "What is it you love the most about it?"

Jack furrowed his brows together, wondering what the Sheriff was hinting at, but supposed he'd best be honest. "I love getting the bad guys, sir."

The Sheriff nodded his head and looked away again. "I need you to be careful, Jack."

"Careful, sir?"

The Sheriff nodded. He sighed heavily before speaking again. "Sometimes, when you're working Detectives, you've got to get inside the minds of the bad guys. You've got to figure out what they're thinking. Why they're thinking it. You've got to act like you're one of them when you're interviewing them, to convince them that you understand, that you see their point of view. That you agree that what they did was justified. What they did was perfectly normal, fine, okay."

41

Jack looked at the Sheriff, wondering where this was coming from. He nodded his head, and the Sheriff went on. "That way, they'll talk to you. They'll open up. They'll share their deepest, darkest secrets with you. That way, they'll own up to what they did. And you'll nod your head and tell them that you understand. That sometimes you feel like doing the same thing. And then maybe they'll tell you some more. There's always more. Remember that, Jack. There's always more."

The Sheriff looked at Jack, his eyes piercing straight into Jack's soul, searching to make certain that Jack understood the wisdom that he was imparting.

"Those are the easy ones, Jack. Getting those guys to confess, that's the easy part. Then using their confessions against them to get your convictions, that's the icing on the cake." The Sheriff smiled briefly, but then looked away again.

"But sometimes, Jack, you meet a bad guy, and his mind is so sick, so twisted, you just can't see how someone like him could really exist. They're the scary ones. They just want to get inside your head. They want to mess with you, to mangle your mind into the sick and twisted mess that theirs has become. Those you gotta be careful with. Don't take those cases home with you. Don't let their mind games twist your soul into worry and keep you up at night. You get what you can get from them, and you rely on the evidence that's out there, and you get out. Don't let them get inside your head."

The Sheriff searched Jack's eyes again. Jack nodded, wondering why he suddenly felt afraid. Then the Sheriff blinked, then turned to look toward the view in front of him. A seagull cried overhead, and Jack wondered for the second time why the Sheriff was advising him so.

"Everything else going okay for you?"

Jack blinked. "Yes, sir."

"Dive Team doing all right this year?"

Jack marveled at the knowledge that the Sheriff knew that he served on the Dive Team. With so many people working at the Sheriff's Office, how did he possibly find the time to run the Sheriff's Office, and keep tabs on all of his deputies? Clearly, that's what made him such an outstanding and beloved Sheriff.

"Yes, sir. We had a challenging recovery last week."

The Sheriff grinned this time, his smile reaching all the way up to his eyes. "That's what I heard. And a rescue the week before. You've had some good stats this year."

"Yes, sir."

"And your brother, is he doing okay?"

Jack flushed. He cleared his throat and looked up into the Sheriff's eyes. "About the same as always, sir."

Again, the Sheriff missed nothing. "Good. Glad to hear it."

The Sheriff stood up and brushed off the seat of his pants. "Well, I'd best get back down to work. Francis will be hunting me down by now, wanting me to sign something or other."

Jack chuckled, still confused and wondering why the Sheriff had brought him up to the roof. The two rode back down the elevator together in silence. They alit on the third floor. The Sheriff headed through the doorway, but held the door open for a moment behind him. For a second, Jack wondered if he was supposed to follow the Sheriff down the hall toward the inner sanctum of the Sheriff's Office, but then the Sheriff turned and looked at Jack, holding his gaze for a long moment. "It was good to talk with you, Jack. You stay safe out there."

"You, too, Sheriff." And with that, the Sheriff turned and left Jack standing in the hallway wondering what that whole conversation had been about.

Chapter 6

JACK JERKED UPRIGHT, his heart racing. He blinked, trying to adjust his eyes to the dark. Three-sixteen. Too damned early to be getting up. He flopped back down on the bed, his head sinking into his pillow, his arm coming to rest across his eyes. The chirp of his phone jerked his heart. So that's what woke him. Jack reached his left hand across his nightstand and answered, his right arm never uncovering his eyes.

"Diamond. Go ahead."

"Jack, sorry to wake you. This is Pete. We've got a floater out by the Ankeny Street Dock. Can you take the lead on this one?"

Jack wiped the crusty gunk out of the corners of his eyes and scrubbed the stubble on his face. "Yeah." He cleared his throat, changing his voice's reply from a bass back up to a baritone. "You get hold of Max yet?"

"Yep. She's on route."

"Who else is coming?"

"I've got Shea and Hank on the way. Still trying to get hold of Mason."

"Sounds good. I'm on my way."

Jack pulled on sweats and a Dive Team shirt, grabbed his gear and headed out the door. Scooping out a dead body, a floater no less, was not Jack's idea of a great reason to get out of bed this damn early in the morning. He yawned, pulling his County rig out of the driveway, and headed straight for downtown Portland and the Willamette River Boat Dock. At least Pete and Max would already be there by the time he arrived.

Pete Spencer and Maxine Goertzen had joined the Sheriff's Office at the same time. They were in the same graduating class at the police academy and had become friends through an easy process of elimination. Being the top recruit at the academy, Pete was the obvious choice for the Victor Atiyeh award, an honor given to the recruit with the highest academic scores and best leadership skills in the class. Pete's intelligence made the daily examinations a breeze. His physical skills, however, left something to be desired.

Max, on the other hand, easily outstripped all her competition on the ORPAT, the Oregon Physical Agilities Test, an obstacle course designed to test the physical capabilities that are associated with being a police officer. A natural athlete, Linfield College's Athletic Department had given her a full ride scholarship. She ran both track and cross country, and still held the school record in the 10K. Despite her short stature, she also played basketball all four years. She may have been tiny, but she was quick on her feet, and could block a pass, grab the ball, and dribble it half way down the court before her opponents knew what had happened.

Pete paired up with Max on the second day of tactics training and gladly took the bruises and body slams in exchange for her private tips and tricks to outmaneuver his opponents. The two rapidly became fast friends. Peter's kids now called her Auntie Max, and she spoiled them rotten.

Jack parked his car next to the Dive Team van, and headed inside to grab his scuba gear. Pete and Max both glanced up and grunted their hellos. The rest of the Dive Team suited up quietly in the back. Pete had already donned his dry suit and was hooking his tank and regulator up to his buoyancy compensator. Max gathered up the ropes and the rest of the gear they'd need.

"So, what've we got?"

Both Pete and Max replied at the same time,

"We've got a floater."

"River Patrol called."

Jack laughed and the two deputies looked at each other, grinning. "You first," replied Pete, as he nodded to Max.

"River Patrol got a call early this morning that there was a floater in the water near the Burnside Bridge. Some drunk was taking a piss off the side of the seawall when he caught sight of her. He ran screaming across the street to the Fire Station. They came over with flashlights and peered over. Sure enough, the drunk was right. According to them, she's wedged pretty good under the Ankeny Street Dock." Max flashed her lovely smile at Jack, knowing that he was the lucky duck who would be

47

retrieving the dead body from under the dock, and not she. She prided herself in not allowing her jealousy to be perceived in a negative light. The next one was hers. She loved that everyone on the Dive Team took turns. No one got all the good jobs, and no one got stuck doing the less pleasant jobs every week. They were all in it together. She grinned. The next one was hers.

Pete took over the story. "Portland Fire & Rescue sent out a boat to verify she's a recovery, not a rescue. River Patrol," he nodded his head down toward the water, "has Boat One ready for us."

Jack finished gearing up, and they all headed down to the dock. The trip up the river went relatively quickly. Miles and Ju-Tau, the two River Patrol deputies, kept their eyes peeled for floating debris, while the Dive Team members set up the rest of their equipment, preparing for the recovery. As the boat slipped under the Burnside Bridge and slowed to a crawl, edging toward the Ankeny Street dock, Max pointed her flashlight into the swift moving waters of the Willamette River. Her gaze followed the path of the River Patrol boat's ray of light streaming into the muddy water. All too soon her eyes came to rest on the eerie scene. A woman's arm floated out from beneath the dock, her blond hair a tangled mess in the filthy water.

Jack hooked the search line up to his chest harness, sat on the edge of the boat's dive platform, slipped on his fins. He rubbed his face before pulling on his full face mask. Jack spoke through the voice-activated communication link, "Alright Max, I'm good to go."

Max adjusted her headset, and pressed her mic. "Copy that, Jack. Hang on a sec, and we'll get you in the water." She stifled the jealous twinge once again, and concentrated on doing her job. Being the head of com ops was, in her opinion, the next best thing to recovering the bodies.

"Pete, you ready to go?" Max glanced over at Pete, Jack's safety diver for this mission, and waited for his okay sign. Safety always came first.

"Yep, indeedie."

Pete's face, in complete contrast to his light-hearted words, held a more grim outlook on the upcoming adventures. If he never had to recover another dead body, he'd be more than happy. He volunteered to recover the corpses as infrequently as he could get away with, and only recovered bodies when Jack informed him that his turn had come up. Everyone on the Dive Team took their turns, but some of the Dive Team members had less of an issue with recovery than others. Pete shivered. Being on the boat, running the lines, head of com ops, he loved those positions. But the dead bodies? Not so much a big fan.

Max turned to the River Patrol deputies. "Alright, we're ready to splash a diver."

"Boat's in neutral. We're good to go."

She clicked on her headset. "Jack, hit the water."

Jack patted the top of his head out of habit. "Goin' in."

Jack glanced back at Pete's face, noting for the millionth time the relief in Pete's eyes. Jack wondered if it was about time he should have a talk with Pete. See if perhaps he might need to take a six month leave from the Dive Team; get some new, fresh blood onto the team and give Pete a bit of a break. Pete's distaste for recovering dead bodies had slowly, over the years, migrated into a near phobia. He'd seen Pete's revulsion at the sights and smells of a floating corpse one too many times. Jack couldn't afford to have a member of his Dive Team be afraid to do one of its main functions, no matter how good he was at being a safety diver, driving the boats, monitoring the com channel, or tending the search lines. He allowed the idea to wash over him as he slipped into the water.

The blackness enveloped him. Diving in the Willamette River always gave Jack a bit of the creepies. He never knew what he'd discover when he dove down here, particularly this close to the seawall. People threw all sorts of crap down there, and his disgust with the human race never seemed more perturbed than when he was diving the Willamette. Particularly with zero visibility. Even with his heavy duty diving flashlight, he couldn't see more than a foot in front of him. It reminded him of horror movies.

Max's voice entered his thoughts. "Jack, you're about thirty feet away."

"Copy that."

Jack headed upward, allowing his head to clear the water. He swam on the surface of the water, his line tethered to the boat behind him. Jack kept his eyes trained on the dock, his mind racing to the possibilities of what the body could be caught up on.

"Jack, can you see her?"

"Stand by."

Jack's heart began to pound a bit harder. No matter how much he knew he was about to come upon a dead body in the water, it still startled him, every time. Within seconds, the woman's mass of tangled hair entered his line of vision. Jack braced himself, and pointed his flashlight at her body. He avoided her face. He made it a point to always avoid their faces if he could.

"Max, I'm at the body. Stand by while I check her out."

"Copy that."

Jack fought the instinct to hold his breath. Floaters, inevitably, reeked. The gasses from their rotting bodies create a natural buoyancy, and the stench increased with every hour of their decomposition. Jack thanked the grant committee, one more time, for providing them with the funding for the new dive gear. The full face mask communication system enabled Jack and the rest of the Dive Team to protect themselves at least a little from the hazardous materials in which they dove. The com system eliminated odors, as well as provided the divers with the ability to communicate with each other verbally, rather than relying on simple hand gestures or line pulls.

He aimed his flashlight down her body. Her leg pointed at an odd downward angle into the depths of the eerie darkness below. "Looks like it's her leg that's hung up on something."

Jack dumped some air out of his buoyancy compensator, and pointed his body downward, following her leg into the depths. He kicked his legs, urging himself closer, trying to see what had entangled her as he kept his light trained on the mess before him.

The hem of the woman's jeans had somehow caught on a piece of metal chicken wire. Jack adjusted the air in his buoyancy compensator again to allow himself to hover horizontally near her feet. Then he hooked his flashlight to his D ring on his chest harness to free up his hands. "Max, can you give me a bit more slack? Looks like she's caught on some chicken wire, and I've got to try to cut the bottom of her jeans out from the mess."

"Copy that."

Instantly, Jack felt the tension on his search line slacken off. He kicked his fins, heading a little lower into the water. His eyes followed the chicken wire down further.

"Looks like the chicken wire is caught up on something else, a shopping cart maybe? I can't tell. I'm not going to be able to bring up the chicken wire without another set of hands, but I think I can free up her leg by simply cutting off the bottom of her jeans."

"Copy. Do you think you're going to need wire cutters?"

"Stand by."

Jack unsheathed his dive knife, and situated himself by her foot. In a few short moves, he had her jeans freed from the wire, and her leg floated up toward the rest of her body. "Okay, she's freed up."

"Copy that."

Jack sheathed his knife and started kicking up toward the surface. With a shock he realized that she was floating away. Jack swore.

"Jack! You okay?"

"Stand by. Damned floater is getting away." He kicked harder, trying to reach her, as the newly freed body bobbed up against the underside of the dock, and began to meander along with the current, away from the seawall, away from Jack.

Jack cursed again, berating himself for not tying her body off to a second line before cutting her loose from the chicken wire. He wondered what type of evidence would now be floating off her body while he chased her in the current underneath the dock.

Jack kicked with as much muster as he could manage, grateful for his frequent trips to his gym and their saltwater lap pool. Within a few strokes, Jack had managed to catch up to her. He stretched his gloved hand out and snagged her jeans. He reached up and secured his grasp around her waist. Thank God she was a new floater. If she'd been in the water a couple of weeks or a month, half of her skin would have sloughed off when he'd reached his arm around her. He shuttered, grimacing at the unpleasant thought.

Jack began the laborious task of lugging her back to the dive platform and onto the boat.

"You got her?"

Pete nodded, grimacing at the odor, fighting back the urge to vomit. Even though she'd only been in the water a couple of days, she still stank. Jack smirked, grateful at the one advantage to being the primary diver on this mission. With his full face mask, the dead body smell didn't penetrate. He wouldn't have to smell her until he got out of the water.

Pete and Max took over, getting her body situated into the body bag, and ready for the medical examiner. Jack slipped back into the water to check for any remaining evidence. He hoped he'd be able to recover the woman's purse, or cell phone or anything else that might belong to her. Identifying bodies became infinitely more simple when they carried their own identification.

Unfortunately, visibility was nil. Jack grew tired. The efforts of having lugged the woman's body through the water coupled with the lack of sleep brought a weariness that seeped into his bones. The cold of the water and the squeeze of his dive suit began to make him uncomfortable, but Jack pushed those thoughts aside. The risks of scuba diving in the Pacific Northwest — drowning, running out of air, nitrogen narcosis, air gas embolisms, the bends — those risks were bad enough on a good day that he didn't need to add exhaustion to the mix. At least down here in the Willamette he didn't have to worry about octopi, wolf eels, jellyfish or urchins like he did when he was diving up in the Puget Sound.

Shining the light down into the murky darkness, Jack followed the chicken wire down, spotted a shopping cart, then the wheel of a bicycle, and then arrived all too soon at the bottom. This was where the real dangers lay. The murky underbelly of the Willamette River teemed with endless quantities of used needles, used condoms, used tampons, shopping carts, bicycle parts, chicken wire, fencing material, fishing lines, and the occasional raw sewage leaks. Jack marveled at the copious quantities of detritus found at the bottom of the Willamette River, flowing right through the center of Portland. Jack shook his head and took a deep breath. He sifted his hand through the silt, hopeful to uncover something useful, but remained wary, given the fear of used needles and other unpleasant debris. Nothing.

Jack turned, swimming along the bottom for a few minutes, allowing his hand to sift periodically through the silt, but nothing productive came out of his search. Resigned, Jack headed back to the boat and the mystery surrounding the dead body that awaited him.

Chapter 7

AS THE BOAT pulled into the dock, Jack's face split into an enormous grin. "Wee Willy? Is that you?!?"

Jack abandoned ship and bounded onto the dock before the River Patrol Deputies had even begun to tie off. In three long strides, he had overcome the distance between himself and the lone person on deck.

"Jack? Jack Diamond?!? Oh, my, it's good to see you! What in the name of High Heaven are you doin' here?"

Jack swooped up the tiny woman, and spun her around in a circle, landing a wet and sloppy kiss on the nape of her neck. The woman walloped him upside the head with her medical bag and screeched, "Put me down, you big lout!"

Jack eased her feet back to the dock, but kept his large hands around her tiny waist as the dock began to rock with the incoming wake waters. The diminutive woman couldn't have been much taller than four feet ten or eleven, and didn't weigh more than ninety pounds. Jack beamed down at her once again. "How long has it been, Willy? Six years? Seven?"

"Closer to nine, I'd say." She grinned up at him, craning her neck to see into his face.

Pete and Max clamored off the boat and hovered behind Jack. The two River Patrol deputies finished tying off the boat, and stepped around the rest of the Dive Team members as they gathered their gear and headed up the gangway toward the Dive Team's van. Pete cleared his throat, not wanting to intrude, and yet wanting to be rid of the over-ripe corpse waiting patiently for them on the boat.

Jack turned at the sound, and grinned. He slid his hand easily to the small of the woman's back, and led her over to the last two of his Dive Team members still on the dock. "Pete? Max? I'd like you to meet Willy, otherwise known as Dr. Monday Elizabeth Willner, the best damn medical examiner this side of the Mississippi."

The tiny woman glared up at Jack, her death stare could have melted steel. She was most definitely not amused that he'd used her Christian name. The nickname, she could stand. But no one, not a single person on this Earth save her mother and Jack Diamond ever dared to call her Monday. "Don't you mean the best damned medical examiner on *both* sides of the Mississippi?" He looked down into her face, and grinned, crushing her against him for another bear hug. She punched him in the arm to loosen his vice-like grip, and turned to her new colleagues, holding out her hand. "Hi. I'm Dr. Liz Willner."

"Pete Spencer."

"Maxine Goertzen. Everyone calls me Max."

Liz smiled at them both and shook their hands. "Nice to meet you. So, I hear you've got a body for me. Care to get me up to speed?"

Jack's eyebrows creased, wondering why she'd left North Carolina, where'd she'd served as a well-renowned medical examiner for the last ump-teen years. Jack looked down, and read a world of hurt and what? resignation? in her eyes. He quirked up his eyebrow, and she smiled.

"We can catch up after I get this one," she nodded toward the body bag, "back to my morgue and into the cooler."

Jack nodded, his mind slipping back into the memories of his past. Jack and Monday had attended Duke University for their undergraduate degrees a lifetime ago. They had become instant friends in their Taekwondo class their sophomore year when, on the first day of class, Monday had easily flipped Jack's six foot two inch, one hundred eighty pound frame onto the flat of his back with one swift move. He never again underestimated her strength. And after slugging through Organic Chemistry, and watching her breeze through with straight A's, he never, ever doubted her intelligence. He watched over her like a hawk protecting its hatchlings, ever ready to come to her defense. But she'd only needed him one time in all those years. Jack had never gotten over his school-boy crush. But then Claire came along, and that helped. Monday never did feel the same way about Jack. She only had eyes for her Harry. Jack's jealousy twinged a bit, even now, when he imagined the two of them together, blissfully married for these past fourteen years.

Jack watched Monday going over the cursory review of the corpse, only half listening to Pete and Max filling her in on the specifics of the recovery. His mind filled with myriad questions. When Monday zipped up the body bag, Jack woke up out of his reverie and began to help Max and Pete unload the Dive Team gear. They met the transport folks half way up the ramp, slowly making their way down to the dock with the morgue's stretcher. Jack, Pete, and Max pressed themselves against the railing, holding their gear aloft, the ramp barely wide enough to allow the stretcher to pass.

Jack stashed his dive gear in the van, and waited for the ten minutes it took for the transport folks to load up the body and bring her back up to the awaiting van. Monday, lost in thought, jumped when Jack called her name.

"Can I ride back with you to the morgue? I can shower up while you get her prepped, and then I can come take notes."

"Get in!"

They buckled themselves in and made their way to the morgue, easing their way through the city streets, the early morning traffic still light. "So, do you want to start at the beginning? Or would you rather start somewhere in the middle, and have me fill in the blanks for you?"

Monday stopped at the yellow light and turned her head to give Jack a good once over. "You look good, Diamond. Life seems to be treating you well."

"Quit avoiding my questions, Wee Willy."

She snorted. "Stop calling me that." Her grin didn't quite reach up to her eyes. Jack noticed. Few things slipped by Jack when it came to Monday.

"Then start answering my questions."

The light turned green and Monday eased her car back into traffic. She sighed lightly, and then dove in. "It's not that complicated, really. Harry wanted a change."

"Harry wanted? Since when do you worry about what Harry wants? Harry would walk to the moon and back if you asked him to, and wouldn't stop to ask for a glass of water."

Monday turned to look at Jack again, letting his dimple tease a smile out of her tired face. "It's Mom. Okay?"

"Your mom? She alright?"

Monday tilted her head to the side, back and forth. "Not sure. It's been a bit rough these last few months. She's had a few, well, not-so-great moments with the other mentally challenged folks in her home. Been acting out a bit. It's just so out of character. I guess it just made sense to move closer."

Jack's heart clenched for his friend. He reached over and squeezed her hand. "I'm so sorry." Jack swallowed the lump in his throat. "Is she still working up in the San Juan Islands?"

Monday smiled. "Yep. And the assisted living facility she's been in for the last few years has been a really good fit for her up there." Monday slowed the car down, and let it come to a rest at the traffic light.

"That's why it's been so challenging, with her acting out. She's not usually like this."

"Next time you go and visit, let me know. I'll tag along with you and Harry."

Monday's smile grew. "I'd like that." She turned right, narrowly avoiding a bike messenger who had guts of steel and an obvious imperviousness to traffic lights. "So how are things at home?"

"Good. Very good. Things are good."

"Hmmmm." She turned her head and gave him a hard stare. He cocked his eyebrow at her and she grinned. "All right. So things are good at home."

Jack laughed.

"And how's GranNini?"

"She's doing great. Just published another book."

"Which was wildly successful?"

"Yep! Just like all the rest."

Monday took a quick peek at Jack and liked the looks of the blush across his handsome face. She took a gamble, and dared broach an often forbidden topic. "Anyone special in your life?"

Jack cleared his throat. "No one in particular."

Monday checked her rear view mirror, trying to seem nonchalant. "How about that E.R. nurse you were seeing a while back?"

Jack made a noncommittal grunt and looked out the window. Monday grinned. She patted his leg, and then turned her attention back onto the road in front of her. "So, how long have you been with the Dive Team?"

61

Jack stretched out his long legs and spread his arm out across the back of Monday's headrest. Now that they were in much more comfortable conversational territory, he relaxed. "Goin' on eight years now."

"Get a lot of recoveries?"

"More than my fair share. Most of 'em are teenagers in the summer, jumping off the rocks up on the Sandy River. I swear they have no common sense. Do they honestly not realize that they're jumping into shallow water? Great way to break their necks. And don't even get me started on the stupid parents who let their kids wade out into the water, because the temperatures finally got above 90 in Portland. They don't even think about where that water came from — that just hours ago that same water was snow up on the mountains. And the water's too damned cold for their kids to be in for any length of time, even if it is 90 degrees outside. Or the kids go out without life vests, thinking they're only wading — not thinking about how strong the current is, how fast it moves. They get swept away. The guys on River Patrol and a lot of us on the Dive Team go out and try to educate people, but I swear half the stuff we say falls on deaf ears. They just want to be in the cool water when they're hot. They don't even think about the dangers."

"Stupidity kills more and more people every year, Jack."

Jack nodded, looking out into the city park blocks.

"Jack," Monday pressed her hand onto his, "recovery of a loved one's body gives the family a sense of closure they so desperately need in the tragic, senseless drowning deaths."

He nodded, staring fixedly outside the window, refusing to meet her eyes. Her voice grew quiet and soft, making a lump form in the back of Jack's throat. "It takes a very special person to recover and take care of the dead, Jack."

Jack turned and met her eyes. Her eyes that had seen more death than a thousand people would see in their lifetimes. He squeezed her hand and she smiled, turning her head back to examine the traffic in front of her.

Monday glanced up at the traffic light as she slipped through the intersection. "How many hours do you spend training?"

Jack laughed. "Loads. We train pretty hard throughout the entire year. Gotta keep current with our certifications. Keep our divers safe. We also spend hundreds of hours each year training for swift water rescue and recovery. We've got to be careful out there."

"I bet the rivers can be pretty treacherous, particularly when the snow runoff from Mt. Hood raises the rivers to flood levels."

"Absolutely! Diving in flood levels is pretty dangerous work. But then of course, so is diving in and around the waterfalls."

Monday's eyebrows shot up. "You actually rescue and recover victims from waterfalls?"

Jack's grin smirked. "Absolutely. Some of our best recoveries were off the waterfalls. People go off the marked trails, and then slip and fall down the cliffs into the waters below. Some people try to commit suicide. You name it, we've seen it."

"Do you have a lot of rescues? Or is it almost always recovery?"

"We rescue people all the time. The River Patrol helps people when their boats are in trouble, but when people are in the water, we're on it. One time, about three or four years ago now, there was a nasty water skiing accident. Pretty horrific, actually. Woman was water skiing, she fell down. Husband turned the boat around to pick her up, but ran her over instead. Her leg got chopped off by the prop. Thank God the Sheriff's Office River Patrol was right there. They scooped her up, got her into an ambulance. Our Dive Team got in the water immediately, and, honest to God, I swear it was a miracle, but I actually found her severed leg."

"Good Lord! Were they able to get it to her? Reattach it in time?"

Jack's grin spread from ear to ear. "They did indeed! She still sends me Christmas cards every year to thank me."

Monday swatted him with the back of her hand, sharing in his joy. "Good for you, Jack!"

"We're also in charge of all the underwater crime scene investigations."

"Investigations *under* the water?!?"

"Absolutely! You'd be amazed at all the number of dumped, stolen vehicles that end up in the Columbia and the Willamette Rivers. People steal cars, go for joy rides, then drive the stolen cars down boat ramps hoping to permanently hide their crimes in the river."

Monday looked over at Jack, slack jawed. "You actually go under the water to investigate?"

"You look so surprised!" Jack grinned. "Underwater crime scene investigations have come a long way in the last ten years. Our Dive Team has recovered hundreds of stolen cars. Tons of knives and guns thrown into the rivers by bad guys. Nowadays we can even recover fingerprints, blood samples, and all sorts of evidence bad guys leave behind."

"Blood samples that have been underwater for hours?"

"Days even."

"Good Lord. I had no idea. And they're not deteriorated samples?"

"You'd be amazed. And the more evidence we can recover, the more bad guys we can put away."

"Ah, well, right there's job satisfaction at its finest."

She pulled her car into her reserved parking space and the two of them got out and headed toward the morgue. The van had already backed into the loading dock, and the two of them walked in behind the body.

"I've got to tell you, Jack, I feel sorely behind the times when it comes to underwater evidence recovery. I honestly had no idea it had become so involved, so successful. I'm going to have to do a lot of research when I get home tonight."

"That's what you get," Jack grinned, "for being virtually land-locked for the last umpteen years."

Monday swatted him again with her medical bag.

"You'll catch up in no time! It's *you* we're talking about, remember?"

Monday grunted.

"I can set you up with some of the latest research if you'd like."

"Thanks. I'll take you up on that."

Jack smiled. "I'll meet you in the Autopsy Suite. Which one are we going in?"

Monday walked up to the computer, typed in her password, and looked at the room schedule. "Looks like I'll take her in Suite 3."

"Groovy. I'll meet you there in a few minutes."

Almost half an hour passed before Jack meandered into the autopsy suite, suited up from head to toe in scrubs and booties. His hands were still tucking in his thick black hair under the hairnet and tying the scrub cap straps around his head when he stepped into the cold room. Monday was already hard at work.

Jack's fascination with the surgical process behind autopsies battled with the unpleasant smells that filled the room. His surgical mask did nothing to ease the stench. One time, during his first autopsy, he'd tried to put Mentholatum under his nose. But instead of smelling dead guy, he just ended up smelling minty-fresh dead guy.

Jack pulled out his digital camera and began to take the necessary photos of the victim's face and body to document the autopsy. Then he rolled her fingers for prints. Hopefully someone would recognize her, making the identification of Ms. Jane Doe significantly easier. Monday took blood samples for a DNA match. She also called in the forensic dentist to have the teeth x-rayed for comparison to aid in identification.

"Why don't you just wait to have the DNA sampled for her ID?"

"When there is adequate dental evidence," Monday explained, "forensic dentists can compare dental anomalies, resulting in an identification faster, and cheaper, than DNA analysis." Jack nodded, watching in awed reverence and respect as Monday methodically and easily made her way through the procedure.

Two and a half hours later, Jack stripped out of his scrubs and headed back to the Detectives unit with just a few interesting tidbits to go on to help solve his case. The victim, a late twenties to early thirties blonde female weighing 137 pounds, had never been pregnant. Boring. She'd had the usual dental work done. Boring. She'd eaten a meal consisting of sushi and a couple of beers with lime. Boring. She took pretty good care of herself, her fingers and toes both professionally manicured, and given the look of what few clothes she had left on her body, Jack could assume she wasn't a low-end prostitute. Hmmm. Less boring. Her body showed signs of recent sexual penetration, a bit rough, and no semen — he'd worn a condom. Again, intriguing.

Monday had said that the tox screen results wouldn't be ready for another week or so, but that given the amount of alcohol in her belly, she'd consumed enough during her last meal to make her at least a little drunk. The good condition of her liver suggested that she didn't make a habit out of getting drunk, and her lungs were clear — making her a non-smoker. Boring.

Faint ligature marks around her neck indicated a preliminary cause of death as that of strangulation by garroting. Less boring.

But the interesting finding of the day wasn't what Monday had found, but what Monday discovered to be missing. Carved out of the woman's chest, about three or four inches above her left breast, was a flap of skin in the shape of a diamond. Nope, nope. Definitely not boring.

Chapter 8

JACK CLICKED ON his bluetooth ear piece, and started making his phone calls on his way back to the office. No sense in making the investigation wait while he commuted in traffic. His first call went out to Vice, confirming that they weren't missing any of their usual prostitutes fitting Jane Doe's description. They couldn't think of anyone off the top of their heads, but promised to call back by the end of the day after they'd checked their records.

Next up, Jack called over to the Portland Police Bureau's Missing Persons unit. He'd only been working the Detectives Unit for three months, and already he knew many of the key players outside the Multnomah County Sheriff's Office who could help make his life a whole lot easier. Sharmila flirted with Jack shamelessly over the phone, her Indian accent making her words run together like water over a brook. Jack passed along the general description of Ms. Doe, noting that she had probably been missing since Friday night or Saturday afternoon at the latest, given the condition of her body and the approximate length of time she'd spent in the water. Sharmila took copious notes, and said that she'd put Jack's request at the top of her pile for the day. Jack asked about GraceLin, Sharmila's newly adopted

Chinese daughter, and Sharmila chattered on for a few minutes about how cute she was as she learned how to walk, and what a blessing it was to have GraceLin in her life. Jack smiled through the phone, always pleased to hear about the positive side of life. Particularly when he found himself knee deep in a homicide investigation.

Jack parked his car, made his way through the throngs of cubicles back to his desk, and took a deep breath. The office noises overwhelmed him some times. He could hear snippets of conversations around him — detectives talking to parole officers, sergeants passing along information to the detectives. Nick Buchanan, Jack's partner at the Detectives Unit, with the cubical right next to Jack's, slurped up coffee, trying to wake up from the late night he'd spent on last night's domestic violence investigation. Jack sat down, his body suddenly weary from the long night. His voice mail light on his phone blinked furiously at him. But he couldn't quite face the messages just yet.

Instead, Jack ran Ms. Doe's fingerprints through AFIS, not truly surprised — but still disappointed —when he didn't find a match. He called the Clackamas County Sheriff's Office to see if his Jane Doe was one of theirs who had simply floated downstream. Next, he spoke with the Portland Fire Department, and talked with the officers who had interviewed the drunk guy who'd discovered Ms. Doe while peeing over the seawall. He had just finished adding his notes to his ever-expanding notebook, when his stomach growled. Loudly.

Nick popped his head around the side of his cube and laughed, covering the mic of his headset with his hand. "Jack, when your stomach makes that funny noise? It means that you need to eat something, dude." Nick smirked, then nodded, his attention focused back on his headset, and began talking to the person on the other end of his conversation.

Jack laughed, grabbed his water bottle, and headed to the break room, hoping he still had a tub of yogurt left, stashed in the back of the fridge. The date on the strawberry yogurt was somewhat questionable, but Jack's stomach growled in protest at the thought of waiting until he could pick up something for lunch. He refilled his water bottle from the filter, pausing to take a long gulp. Then he grabbed his maple pecan granola from the cupboard, snagged a spoon from the community drawer, peeled off the top of the yogurt, sprinkled on the good stuff, and dug in. His ritual never varied when it came to his yogurt. Actually, his rituals regarding food in general rarely changed. For that matter, his rituals regarding anything rarely changed. Jack liked to do things a certain way, and when that way turned out successfully, he simply continued to do it that way forever. Or until a better way presented itself. Which, on rare occasions, he supposed, it actually did.

He reviewed his notes from the autopsy, trying to formulate an idea about his Jane Doe. The missing skin from her chest intrigued him. What had the bad guy tried to remove? Had the bad guy tried to stab her, but slipped? Had he bitten her and tried to expunge his saliva from her skin? He made a note in his book to ask Monday whether she'd found any saliva off the cut. Had he tried to cut off a tattoo? He wrote another note to inquire about dyes that may have been left behind. Did she have a funny birth mark that the bad guy wanted to eliminate? Jack pondered the idea. Why had he removed a piece of skin, but not cut off her fingers, thus eliminating her fingerprints? Why had he not cut off her head? Jack made mental notes about the bad guy, wondering if perhaps the bad guy's time with Ms. Doe had been limited, or if, perhaps, he wasn't quite as bad of a bad guy as some of the sick and twisted freaks Jack had come across in all his years on the force.

Most bad guys, Jack thought, weren't as bad as the ones on television or in movies. Most bad guys were simply folks who didn't always follow the rules, who didn't think the rules applied to them, or who simply took things ever so slightly too far. There were always bad guys out there that lived in the extreme. The terrorists who got on airplanes and flew them into buildings. The child molesters who stalked children on their way home from school. The bastards who beat up their wives and children with their fists or their belts or their baseball bats when they'd had too much to drink and couldn't, or wouldn't control themselves.

Jack's stomach clenched, and he dropped his spoon, his appetite destroyed. He threw his garbage in the trash, and headed back to his desk, his mind replaying memories he had no desire to revisit. He rubbed his eye with the heel of his palm as he made his way back to his cube, wanting, needing to get something else, someone else, into his head.

He dropped his notepad on the desk. He plugged in his earbuds and pulled up an iTunes playlist, cranking up the music too loudly to be able to hear his own thoughts. He still needed to write up his notes into a report from the dive recovery mission. Jack pulled up a blank Dive Team mission report form off the computer and began to type. He'd created a bunch of blank report forms, outlining the basic information he needed to incorporate for each separate type of report during his third week at the Detectives Unit. Once he realized his Lieutenant required the same types of forms to be completed and filled out over and over again, he'd spent the better part of a few days creating several basic forms. He'd tailored each form to include the necessary information so that he wouldn't forget and leave out any important documentation. He frequently updated his forms, when new and unusual cases came up. But he found that the time he'd spent creating the forms had been well-worth the effort.

When his Dive Team report started spewing out of his printer, Jack settled in with his notebook, picked up his phone, and pressed the pass code for his voice mail. Clackamas County had come up with nothing on his vic. Sharmila had called back, giddy with the news that she had a possible hit for him. His last voicemail had come from Claire.

73

Jack leaned back in his chair and listened to her message. Then, he pressed a few buttons and listened to it a second time. "Jack, it's Claire. I know we haven't spoken in a long time, but, well, the truth is, I'd like to talk with you. I tried to catch you a while back when I was at Ron's office. He'd told me you were working with him on graveyard shift. That's why I was there, actually. I was hoping, well, I kinda thought maybe you'd seen me, but when I turned around, you were heading out like a bat out of hell. You probably didn't even know I was there. But, well, anyway, can we meet? For coffee? I'd like to talk with you. Please."

Jack glanced down at the caller ID, wondering if he should copy down her new cell phone number, or if he should erase the number and pretend he hadn't heard her message. Out of all the days that she'd call, today had to be the one. Jack rubbed the stubble on his face, then ran his hand through his hair. Emotions ran like roller coasters through his belly. Screw it. He was too tired to resist. He reached over and pressed the numbers on his phone, committing her number to memory along the way.

The roller coasters ran another track through his belly while the phone rang. When she didn't answer, he fumbled his way through a short message, wondering if he'd have the courage to return her call when and if she got around to calling back, leaving him another message. He took a swig of water, and returned Sharmila's call.

She answered on the first ring. "Oh Jack! I had a feeling it would be you."

"Sharmila, what have you got for me?"

"Well, you know, you called at just the right time today. I briefly took a look at the few reports that came in over the weekend, but nothing seemed to even come close to your Jane Doe."

Jack grunted.

"But you know, the funniest thing just happened. I just had a couple come in and turn in a missing person's report for someone who looks like she might be a good match for you."

Jack sat bolt upright in his chair, and grabbed his pen to start taking notes. "Really? Hit me with it."

Sharmila laughed, her Indian accent bubbling through the phone. "I knew you'd be happy."

"Sharmila, you always make me happy!"

"Well you know, Jack," she chastised, "only God can bring you true happiness. I cannot bring you happiness. You have to go and seek out God, and seek out happiness every day if you wish for God's blessings to rain down upon you."

"God's blessings."

"Yes, Jack. Our faith is truly the only thing that sustains us, you know."

Jack grinned, bowing his head to her admonitions. "Sharmila, you are a wise woman."

"Well of course I am, Jack. But I tell you, I must get back to your missing woman. You see, the young couple who came in this morning, well, they're missing a young woman named Katie Martin. Now let me look at my notes, so I can get this all right for you."

Jack gripped his pen so hard that his fingers began to turn white. His heart rate slowed, his blood pressure calming almost immediately as the world around him grew quiet.

"Yes, here it is. You see? She is Miss Katie Martin, aged 38. She weighs about 135 pounds, has long blonde hair, brown eyes. Last seen, Friday evening at work. The woman who filled out the form was her roommate. She says, yes, it's right here, she says that Katie's boss called this morning and left a message on the machine at home, wondering if she was at home sick. Katie never calls in sick, so he was concerned. Katie's boyfriend says that he was in Seattle this weekend with his buddies to see a game, and that he didn't even expect to see her until tonight. He was just as shocked as Katie's roommate that she wasn't at work."

Jack nodded his head, jotting notes down in his book. "Did they check her cell phone? Look for her purse?"

"Yes, yes, that's all written here. Her purse is missing. Looks like they called all of Katie's friends, and only one of them heard from her on Friday. Seems no one has heard from her since then."

"Sharmila, you're an angel! Can you please email me a copy of the report so I can contact them?"

"Well now, I have to tell you Jack, I have already sent a copy of this report to you, and it should be in your inbox as we speak. But I have to tell you, I must go now. My paperwork is piling up, and I must see what I can do to try to match up some of these other missing people."

Jack pulled up his email, and smiled when he saw the one waiting for him from her. "Absolutely, Sharmila. Thanks again, you're an angel."

"Well now, I don't know about that, Jack, but I will take credit for this one. I do believe I've found you your match. You have a wonderful day now, Jack."

"I will, you too!"

Jack hung up the phone and beamed as he read the report. Everything seemed to fit so nicely. Sharmila was right. They'd found their match.

Chapter 9

THE CAR ROCKED when he slammed the door. "Well, Diamond, what do you think of the boyfriend as our best suspect?" Nick pulled his notebook out of his suit jacket pocket and buckled his seatbelt, looking over at Jack.

Nick Buchanan had been with the Sheriff's Office for fourteen years. He'd spent the better part of his youth playing football and dreaming about a professional career playing for the Chicago Bears. Everything went according to plan for the most part. The OSU Beavers offered him a full ride to play outside linebacker and he thrived in Corvallis. He loved the team's camaraderie and the whole atmosphere of being a part of something bigger than himself. Absolutely nothing in the world could beat the amazing experience of working so hard in front of a crowd of thirty-three thousand screaming fans in Parker Stadium who wanted nothing more than to applaud his outstanding performance.

He spent hours in the weight room strengthening and training. After practice he focused on speed, getting his forty yard dash time down to just 4.3 seconds — just slightly slower than the receivers. By his junior year, he'd grown massive. At six feet, three inches tall and weighing in at roughly 240 pounds, Nick had become a force to be reckoned with. He studied the play books in his spare time, watching his opponents' games, constantly searching for flaws in their strategies. By the time November came around, he started pulling up monster numbers, earning a lot of good press buzz. His name started circulating for the Butkus Award. The NFL scouts began to sniff around, hinting at pro ball offers and signage bonuses. Nick hid the offers from his defensive coach, desperate to keep the news from reaching his head coach until he'd made his decision.

The only regret he had to this day was in not heeding his favorite professor's wise advice. One afternoon after class, Nick had confessed his multitude of pro football offers to Scott Bailey, his communication professor. Scott urged Nick to stay at OSU for one last year to complete his Bachelor's degree and to earn one more year of great stats for the Beavs before heading to the pros. Scott believed — and strongly urged Nick to agree — that Nick should have at least a B.A. to fall back on should Nick's career not be as successful as his dreams. He should have listened.

Instead, he took them up on their offers, trading in his Beavers jersey for the Bears, quitting college with only one year to go. Three years later, with two seconds left on the clock, the Bears up by two, Nick created the memory of a lifetime. In a spectacular blindside hit, Nick sacked the quarterback on their Hail Mary long bomb pass, winning the game for his team, and sending them to the playoffs. In a massive adrenaline rush, he jumped up to celebrate the game winning tackle just as someone else was jumping down. Not until the players started to dissipate did they realize something had gone terribly, horribly wrong. In a single play, Nick had blown both his ACL and his professional career dreams. Game over.

Nick pocketed his earnings, giving some money to his baby sister to pay for college, and some money to his folks to dole out to their favorite charities. Then he headed back home to the Pacific Northwest, earning his criminal justice degree from Portland State University, and getting hired on at the Sheriff's Office shortly thereafter.

Easing the car away from the curb and out into traffic, Jack headed back to the office where he could type up his notes from their interview with his victim's roommate and boyfriend. "I don't know, Nick. Seems like he's genuinely upset that we've positively identified her. And I think, perhaps a bit guilty about something? But not about killing her."

"Yeah, but guilty about what?" Nick kept jotting notes down in his book, making sure to capture Jack's ideas as well as his own.

"Probably about not being here this weekend. Guilt about drinking too much with his buddies up in Seattle at the game. Guilt about shutting off his phone and not answering her texts. Guilt about not being here to protect her. I don't know, Nick. He seems pretty shaken up about her death."

"Good. At least we're both on the same page there. He's not our bad guy."

Jack nodded his agreement, and turned left at the traffic light.

"And the roommate?"

"Yeah, she's good to rule out as well. She's pretty messed up about the whole thing. Especially when we asked her about the tattoo."

"Dude. Seriously. Matching tattoos from 'Twilight'? Good grief. Want me to call in to the M.E. to confirm that the chess piece tattoo is the same size as the missing skin on our vic?"

"No, I'll do it. I have to ask her about the tox screen results anyway."

Nick laughed. "Yeah right, as if you'll be getting the tox screen results back any time soon."

"Hey, it's good to know the medical examiner."

Nick laughed again. "I bet! So, what's your next plan of attack?"

Jack pulled the car into the lot. "Well, I've got to pull her cell phone records and her credit card receipts and see what that turns up. Could you go over my notes from my interview with the firefighters and the drunk guy who found the body? Make sure I didn't miss anything?"

"You got it. Let me know if you need anything else."

"Thanks, Nick!"

The next few days flew by in a blur as the mystery of the victim's last few hours began to unravel themselves. Katie Martin, Jack's victim, had been seen last at a bar in downtown Portland, not far from where her body had been dumped over the sea wall. The bartender didn't recognize her or remember her from her picture, but he made up for it by allowing Jack and Nick to make a copy of the bar's digitally stored video surveillance data. That's when things started getting interesting again.

Jack spent hours reviewing the surveillance data from that night at the bar. Katie spent quite a bit of time texting on her phone, but seemed to get frustrated with her phone after a while, and threw it into the bottom of her purse. Several guys bought Katie drinks over the period of a few hours. But two of them made a point not to have their faces caught by the cameras. They clearly knew where the cameras were located. Both were just shy of 6 feet tall. Both wore dark, long sleeved Columbia Fleece jackets. The kind you could get at any number of stores here in Portland. Both wore ball caps. Again, nothing distinctive. In fact, the two were somewhat indistinctive. Jack couldn't even tell which one of the two actually led her out the door.

The time stamp on the video data indicated that they'd left the bar at 1:26 a.m. Plenty of time to walk her over to the bridge, slip on a condom, have sex with her, walk her over to the sea wall, carve out her tattoo, and dump her body into the river. That still gave the drunk guy about an hour or so, give or take, to take a leak on the wall, and glance over, seeing her body floating in the Willamette. It was pure bad luck that her body caught on something under the Ankeny Dock. Had she simply slipped into the water, she could have floated downstream and been out toward the Columbia, or even out toward the ocean, in no time at all.

When the phone rang, Jack leaned back against his chair and rubbed his hand over his stubble. He reached down, grabbed the receiver and braced himself for the latest news from the Medical Examiner.

"Jack? It's Liz. I've got good news for you on two fronts."

"Groovy! Whatcha got?"

"First off, my forensic dentist has confirmed the identity of your victim."

"So it's Katie then?"

"I'm afraid so."

Jack sighed. On the one hand, getting a confirmation was great closure for the victim's loved ones. On the other hand, knowing your loved ones were dead — well, that was never easy. Jack took a deep breath and cleared his throat, grateful that Monday had given him a moment to process. "And the second piece of good news?"

"I've got your tox screen results back."

"Already? Monday, you're amazing!"

"Of course I am. Listen, she tested positive for Rufies."

"You're kidding."

"Nope. Too bad for your bad guy. If he'd only waited another couple hours before killing her, they'd already be out of her system."

"What?"

83

"Rohypnol goes through your system really quickly. That's why it's perfect as a date rape drug. Most folks who ingest it metabolize it almost immediately as it enters the blood stream. Give the girl a Rufie, take her upstairs and rape her, she wakes up a few hours later with very little memory of what happened, and all traces of the drug are metabolized through her system by the morning."

"Huh. I guess I didn't know it worked that fast."

"Yeah. Your bad guy may be smart enough to pick Rohypnol, but he was stupid to kill her so soon after giving it to her."

"Yeah, or perhaps he had to kill her sooner than he wanted. Perhaps the drunk guy snuck up on them a bit sooner than he had planned." Jack ran his fingers through his hair. "So, hey. I have a question about the excision mark where the guy had cut off her skin in the shape of a diamond."

Jack heard typing in the background as Monday looked up information on her computer. "According to my notes, the skin was cut off post-mortem."

"Any chance that it could have been a tattoo that was removed? About three inches long?"

"Absolutely. Why, did your victim have a tattoo on her breast?"

"Yeah. In the shape of a chess piece."

A long pause on the other end of the telephone made Jack smile. "Well, to each her own."

"Indeed. Hey, thanks, Monday. I owe you one."

"Jack, you owe me so many we can't even count."

Jack laughed and disconnected their call.

Nick rolled his chair over into Jack's cubicle just as Jack was hanging up the phone. "So, Rufies, eh?"

"Yeah."

"Guess you'd better get a call into Betty Hamilton down at Oregon State Patrol."

"Betty Hamilton?"

"Yep. She's in charge of the Sex Offender Registry down there. She can hook you up with all the Sex Offenders who like cutting, using Rufies, and who use condoms; S.O.s who are somewhere in the Portland area. Can't be a very long list."

"Right. I'll get on that."

Nick smiled and slugged Jack in the arm and headed back to his cube.

The Sex Offender Registry pulled up two prime suspects. Both S.O.s used Rufies, both liked using condoms with their victims, and both liked knives. Although neither of them had any record of cutting off pieces of skin. But it's not like these fellas didn't slowly devolve over the years of sexually abusing victims.

They started with the older, nastier of the two and headed out into the field.

"So how long has this guy been off parole?" Nick stepped over a questionable looking, foul smelling puddle against the wall, and kept his palm on the butt of his gun as they made their way down the suspect's hallway.

"Just about two months. This is it, right here." Jack took a deep breath and looked at Nick. Nick nodded his head, and Jack pounded on the door.

"Patrick Ellis? Open up. Sheriff's Office!"

The door flew open, and Jack took an instinctive step back.

"What the fuck do you want?" The grizzled man, in his late 50's snarled at the two detectives. The man's glare gave Jack's heart a jolt of adrenaline. A lighting flashback zipped across Jack's memory of his father, towering over him, baseball bat in one hand, cigarette sucked down to the very bitter end in the other. Son of a bitch scared the crap out of Jack.

Jack felt his face flush, and he steeled his nerve automatically. "Mr. Ellis? We just want to talk to you."

The man sucked on his cigarette, and blew the smoke directly into Jack's face. "Yeah? What about?"

"We'd just like to talk with you about something that happened last Friday night."

The man looked from one detective to the other, and sucked down another lungful of smoke.

"Am I under arrest?"

"No."

"Got a warrant?"

"Well no, but —"

"Go fuck yourselves. I'm not talking to you. You can talk to my lawyer if you have any other questions." The entire wall shook as the man slammed the door in their faces.

Jack's heart pounded as he turned to face Nick. "That went well."

"He's not our guy."

Jack's eyebrows furrowed together. He wasn't so sure. He spent the next few seconds mentally cleaning up the guy, giving him a shave, putting him in a dark long sleeved jacket, washing his hair — trying to picture the guy as his bad guy. It took no visualization at all to imagine the bastard as *a* bad guy. He just wasn't sure the guy was *his* bad guy. His heart clenched at the thought of the poor women who had been forced to endure the wrath of his anger. But Nick was right. He wasn't their guy. "He's too short. And too damned cocky."

Nick pressed a hand against Jack's arm, holding him back. "Don't underestimate the cocky, Jack. The cocky is usually what gets them caught in the end. But the cocky can also be quickly turned into over-confidence, which can easily be interpreted as a positive feature, if he's trolling for vics in a bar."

Jack nodded his head. "So why don't you think he's our guy?"

"Too short for one thing. But too damned addicted to cigarettes for another. Our bad guy didn't smoke. Or at least not as much as this one does." He nodded back to the building as they drove away. "From the smell of him, this guy wouldn't be more than fifty feet away from his cigarettes."

Jack nodded, his mind reviewing the bar's surveillance clips in his head. Nick was right — not once had he seen the bad guy smoke. Of course, all bars were smoke free these days in Portland. "And,"

Nick added, "that asshole likes to strong-arm his vics. He's a bully. He'd definitely want to overpower his victims. Assert his control over them by strong-arming them."

"Yeah, but the knife…"

"Don't get hung up on the knife, Jack. This asshole? He's used a knife in the past, but that was only after he beat the crap out of his victims. Our vic didn't have any physical abuse marks on her at all, except for the minor rape bruising and the cut on her chest. And that was post-mortem. No signs of a struggle. The Rufies would definitely make her more cooperative. This asshole? He doesn't seem to want, or need, cooperation from his victims."

Jack nodded again. He unbuckled his seatbelt as Nick pulled their car into a parking spot next to a meter. Jack reached into the glove box and pulled out a Police placard so that the Meter Reader patrol wouldn't give them a ticket while they were inside grilling their Sex Offender. They headed inside together.

The smell greeted them before they'd even crossed the threshold. Decades of urine and cigarettes created a palpable stench difficult to traverse through. The flop house this S.O. lived in was a single resident hotel room located in the seedy part of downtown Portland. "Watch your step, Jack," Nick warned. "On a good day, you'll only see cockroaches."

Jack grimaced.

"Ugh. I can't even fathom having to live here."

Jack plodded up the stairs, and let out an involuntary groan when a man opened the common bathroom on the floor above. He didn't even want to imagine what kind of condition it must be in if the hallways and stairwells reeked this bad. His thoughts immediately turned to Han Solo gutting a Tauntaun, saying, "And I thought you smelled bad," [gasp] "on the outside!" Jack stifled a chuckle and headed down the hall.

Nick knocked on the door this time. "Gerald Frank? Open up, Sheriff's Office!"

Something metal clanged against the floor, and the door opened up an inch or so.

"Can I see some ID?"

Jack leaned against the wall in the hallway, his gun at the ready. Nick flashed his badge and his credentials, and Gerald held the door open for them.

The room was small. Barely enough space for a single bed, a small dresser, and a small bookshelf in the corner with an even smaller television perched precariously atop it. Jack fought the urge to scratch the imaginary (he hoped) fleas off him. His head started itching immediately, just like they did whenever someone mentioned head lice at the office. His fingers clenched, his head tingled. He just wanted to start scratching immediately.

He hated interviewing people in their homes. He'd grown soft in his 36 years. He liked the comforts of the simple necessities of life. Things like clean running water. Daily use of soap. Breathable air.

But interviewing suspects in their comfort zone led your bad guys to believe that they weren't really in trouble. You could often lock them into a story. And you didn't need to read them their rights, because they're not under arrest. And better yet, you could get a good look around at their stuff, because you don't need a warrant if they invite you in to their homes. Then, when they slip up, and you could find a way to disprove their stories, well now, that's just almost as good as a confession.

Nick eased his way into the interview while Jack continued to look around. Gerald was younger than their other S.O. In his late 20s, early 30s, this guy could definitely pass for a little more clean-cut than their other guy. His modus operandi indicated that he was known to use a condom and threaten his victims with a knife. But he was definitely more likely to charm his victims, rather than strong-arm them. This guy definitely fit better with their bad guy model than the other S.O.

Nick kept the interview short, and before Jack had really even started focusing in on what kinds of things Nick had asked Gerald, they were headed out the door and down the stairs.

Jack took in several deep breaths as soon as they burst out the front door and into the fresh air. Nick had evidently been holding his breath too. Jack wondered how he could have managed to neglect to appreciate clean air as much as he had. The building's odor had latched onto their clothes and soon filled up the inside of the car. Jack's nose scrunched up in repulsion. He rolled down the

90

window, letting in the fresh air and the sounds of downtown traffic. He was definitely going to burn his clothes as soon as he got home.

"So what'd you think of this one?"

"Well, he definitely seems to fit the bill a bit better than our last Sex Offender."

"Absolutely. And his alibi is crap."

"Are you sure?"

Nick laughed, "Yeah, he's lying about something. We've got to get some evidence on this dude so we can get a warrant and search his place. I think he's a good fit for our guy."

"Did you see something that I missed?"

"No, but it fits. The last time he raped a girl, he used a knife on her."

"Yeah, but not to cut her, just to threaten her."

"The dude's a wimp. He can't resist his urges or his addictions. He'll just keep escalating until he cuts someone. And it seems to me, our vic might just be that someone."

"How long did he say he was off parole?"

"Three months."

"Huh. And now he's found Jesus, and is all healed, and couldn't possibly have hurt another girl last Friday night."

Nick laughed. "So he says."

Chapter 10

GERALD FRANK'S ALIBI had indeed turned out to be sketchy, at best. His credit, having been destroyed by his ex-wife's retaliation for his infidelities, had left Gerald with the annoying necessity to pay cash for all his purchases. Cash left no record of Gerald's supposed trip to the grocery store the night in question. A grocery store, convenient enough, which had no video surveillance cameras, nor any known witnesses, who could verify Gerald's claims as to his presence there around the time of the murder.

Gerald's lack of credit also made proving he was watching a movie during the time of the murder difficult. Gerald's recent job loss, raping the boss's wife will do that, also left him with very little cash — certainly not enough cash to buy a laptop or a computer. And his lack of credit prevented Gerald from being able to buy one on credit. So unfortunately, Gerald wasn't at home streaming a movie or t.v. show online, which could have at least verified that someone using his computer in his residence was streaming an online movie at the time of the murder. Furthermore, without credit, Gerald couldn't rent a movie via Redbox, which could have at least partially verified his alibi. Alas, Gerald's lack of credit forced him to rent movies at the local library. Which, he had in fact done. Three days before the murder. Unfortunately, his poor timing, and his lack of credit, did nothing to verify his location during the actual time of the murder.

On top of it all, Gerald's lack of money, and credit, also prevented him from owning a cell phone. Therefore, Gerald couldn't even claim he was talking to his mommy on the telephone at the time in question. No telephone, no telephone records.

And finally, Gerald's unpleasant choice in residences left him living in a building filled with shady folks unwilling to verify Gerald's presence the night in question. Folks who, even if they found themselves willing to testify on Gerald's behalf, had such poor credibility themselves, their character references and their testimony would hold very little weight in his defense. Poor Gerald. Time to bring him in for questioning.

The pit stains under Gerald's arms expanded with each moment he waited, not so patiently, in the Multnomah County Sheriff's Office's interrogation room. Jack watched Gerald's discomfort from behind the two-way mirror. His heart pounded at the thought that he might have Katie's killer sitting there, right there, in the room in front of him. Even sitting down, Jack could see that Gerald fit the rough description of the last man seen with Katie Martin. His criminal record spoke volumes of his sexual proclivities. And his ex-wife's acidic views only led Jack to believe — no, to truly hope he'd caught the right guy.

Nick walked in with a swagger, smacking his notebook against his hand. "You ready for this, Diamond? Looks like our guy's got something to hide!"

Jack chuckled. "Absolutely. Let's get 'er done."

Nick smacked Jack on the back with his notebook and headed into the interrogation room.

"Mr. Frank, I'm Detective Buchanan. This is Detective Diamond."

Gerald nodded, his pit stains growing.

"Mr. Frank, we asked you to join us here today to go over your statement regarding your activities last Friday night. You're not under arrest. We just want to ask you a few questions."

"Okay." Again, Gerald's pit stains began to lengthen with each tick of the room's clock.

"Let's start at the beginning shall we? You said that you were at the grocery store, and then you rented a movie, is that right?"

Gerald cleared his throat, nodding his head.

An hour later, Nick and Jack had gone through Gerald's entire statement piece by piece, line by line. Clearly, something still didn't add up. Gerald grew more and more agitated as the interrogation progressed, and the room began to reek of his body odor, Gerald's deodorant having lost the battle long ago.

"Why is it, Gerald, that there doesn't seem to be a single person who can verify your whereabouts that evening?"

"I don't know! I don't know!" Gerald ran his hands through his hair, worry beginning to trickle over into fear.

"Hey now, there's no need to freak out here, Gerald. We're actually on your side."

"You are?"

"Of course! We just want to figure out what seems to be missing here. We want to believe you!"

"You do?"

"Of course." Nick turned to Jack who nodded almost imperceptibly and took over.

"So, Gerald, we just have a couple of small problems here. First of all, we have a victim who fits the description of the kind of girl you used to like to, uh, pick up. And some of the things that happened to her just happen to be things that you like doing to girls."

Gerald blanched.

"I can understand how things go, Gerald. You spent a long time on parole. You had to deny all of your impulses, keep yourself clean. That takes a lot of willpower. And I understand how sometimes, well, sometimes your willpower slips up just a little bit. Who knows, maybe it was her fault. Maybe you were sitting at the bar, drinking a nice refreshing beer. And maybe you see her, sitting there, all hot and bothered and just itching for someone to come along. Someone who can take care of her needs."

A subtle change started to work its way around Gerald's demeanor. Little things, almost unnoticeable, began to settle around his body. Nick froze, his eyes soaking in every movement, every bead of sweat breaking out on Gerald's forehead.

"You know she was there for one reason. And maybe, maybe you were just the perfect guy to take care of that reason. Maybe things just went a little too far. Maybe things got carried away."

Nick watched Gerald's eyes glaze over as Jack continued to press on.

"Who knows, Gerald. Maybe she asked you to choke her out or something. Sometimes these things can go a little kinky. And if that's the case, we just need to know. Then it's not really your fault. That's understandable. We can work with that."

Jack suppressed the urge to shudder. He hated intimating that the victim could possibly be responsible for the crimes that were inflicted upon her. Interrogations like this were tougher than he thought they'd be. And in the few short months that he'd been working at the Detective's Unit, he still felt like he needed a shower every time he had to try to get the bad guy to trust him, to get the bad guy to think Jack was on his side. Jack hated leading them into thinking he understood, that he empathized with their feelings and urges. The whole thing made him feel dirty inside. But the battle raging inside of him was easily defeated when he thought of the justice he was providing for the victims when he walked a bad guy straight into a confession.

For a moment, Jack flashed back to the Sheriff's conversation up on the roof of the Multnomah

Building. For the first time, Jack truly felt the wisdom of the Sheriff's wise words.

"So, Gerald, have you ever gone into that bar? Have you ever seen this woman?" He slapped a large 8x10 photo of Katie onto the table and slid it in front of Gerald.

Gerald blinked as if in a trance.

"She's your type, isn't she?"

Gerald swallowed. His eyes flicked up to the picture, and Nick tensed, searching Gerald's eyes for that moment of recognition. Something definitely flickered in Gerald's eyes. Nick smiled in smug satisfaction.

After working him over for about two hours, Gerald finally broke down. "You guys just won't ever believe me! I swear! I know, I know I've done some bad things in the past." He wiped the sweat off his upper lip with the cuff of his sleeve, and then wiped the corner of his eye. "But honest to God, I didn't do what you say I did! You just won't ever believe me!"

"Come on, now, Gerald, let's go through this one more time."

"No, I swear, it wasn't me. I, I..." Gerald looked up at Jack and searched his eyes. "I want a lawyer."

The silence that followed crackled in the air. Gerald's arm pits dumped another dose of sweat onto his shirt, and another wave of foul stench permeated the room. Jack bit his tongue to keep from smiling. Yep, he's the one.

Nick rose and smacked his notebook against the table. "All right, Gerald. We can stop now. You go talk to a lawyer, and give us a call when you know who that is. We'll talk again soon."

The interview had lasted just over two hours, give or take, and Jack grinned at his good fortune to have found the right guy so soon after Katie's death. He hated not being able to get an outright confession, and hated it even more that they couldn't arrest the chuckle-head right then and there. But at least they had enough for a search warrant on his apartment.

Jack flirted with the receptionist on the way back to his cubicle and booted up his computer to write up the search warrant for Gerald's apartment. Hopefully they'd be able to find the knife he'd used to cut out Katie's tattoo, as well as a bloody, dark, long-sleeved Columbia jacket like the one seen in the surveillance data from the bar.

Jack's warrant practically wrote itself, and Jack smiled when the phone rang just as the affidavit for the search warrant was sent off to the D.A.'s office. He hoped the D.A. would approve his affidavit this afternoon so he could get the judge on the phone before the end of business today to get the warrant signed.

"Detective Diamond."

"Jack, it's Claire." Her sigh of relief at having reached him sent a shiver down Jack's back. "I'm so glad I reached you."

Jack's heart flip flopped. "I'm glad you reached me too." He cleared his throat and tried again. "What's up? You sounded rather urgent on the phone the other day." Jack stifled the smug grin that threatened to take over his face. He was pleased with how nonchalant he sounded. As if talking to her again for the first time in twelve years wasn't something he'd thought about so many times.

"Yes, well, um, it is rather urgent. But I'd rather not talk about it over the phone. Could we meet somewhere? Maybe at Clive's? Across the street from your office?"

"Absolutely. When?" Jack started tapping his pen on top of the pad of paper sitting on his desk. His heart began pounding, racing faster and faster as each second ticked by. Then, just as suddenly, his heart seemed to slow down completely, as the world around him began to fade out. He lost all sense of time as the short silence filled the space.

"I hate to ask, but are you free now? I really need to talk with you."

An adrenaline dump ran down to the pit of Jack's stomach and back up again as his protector's instincts kicked in. His voice quieted to an almost whisper. "Are you okay? Is everything all right?"

"Jack, please, can we not talk about this on the phone? I'll meet you over there in, what, fifteen minutes? Will that give you enough time?"

Jack blinked. "I'm on my way." His heart simply ceased to beat any longer. He was on his way to meet her. To see her. Again. For the first time in twelve years. For the first time in forever.

"Thanks, Jack." She sounded relieved.

A lump formed in the back of his throat. He'd do anything for her. Simply anything at all. And now, after all this time, she'd asked him for something. The thought pleased him. Warmed him to his very toes. "Always. You know that."

Jack slipped the phone back onto its rocker, checked to make sure the email went through showing that his warrant had made it through to the D.A.'s office without harm, and grabbed his jacket off the back of his chair.

No more than twelve minutes passed before he found himself sitting at one of the back booths, his hands wrapped around an iced tea, his nerves in a bundle of tension. When the door opened and she strode in, automatically untying the pretty blue scarf from around her neck and removing her jacket, a jolt of awareness flooded the pit of his stomach. Even after all this time, after all these years, she could still stir feelings within him in ten seconds flat.

She pulled her blond hair out from beneath her purse strap, scanning the restaurant for any sign of him. Her smile sent another surge of adrenaline into his belly, and he waved a hand in welcome to greet her. She slipped into the booth in a quiet rush, and a waft of her perfume teased his nostrils. He closed his eyes and remembered, his heart clenching uncomfortably in his chest, and greeted her eyes with a smile.

"Thank you, Jack." She reached over and squeezed his hand. In a flash, she'd taken her hand back, nervously readjusting herself and her belongings in the seat beside her as he stared at his empty hand, missing hers already.

The efficient waitress prevented further conversation for the next minute or so while Claire ordered a diet soda, and the waitress bustled to the counter and back refilling Jack's iced tea and delivering the soda in a few swift moves. Even from across the room she could tell that they needed privacy. The waitress gave Jack her prettiest smile and rejoined the other waitress, the two of them daring to steal glimpses every now and again, envious of the pretty blonde woman who had managed to nab the attention of the incredible hunk at booth nine.

"Claire, you are even more lovely today than the last time I saw you."

Her blush betrayed her pleasure in his compliment. "Jack." She brushed her silky blond hair behind her ear and wrapped her hands around her glass, bracing herself for the onslaught she was about to fling upon him.

It had been twelve years since he'd seen her. Twelve years since he'd held her in his arms, running his fingers across her back, listening to her talk about her dreams of specializing in plastic surgery so she could travel the world, fixing birth defects. Twelve years since she walked out of his life, promising to come back. A million years since he heard through a friend of a friend who'd read it on Facebook or something that she'd married Ron Wilcox. Jack grimaced. Ron Wilcox got to hold her in his arms, brush her hair, kiss her goodnight.

"Claire," Jack ducked his head down to try to reach her eyes, "whatever it is, you can tell me. We can work through this."

She sighed, and a small tear trickled down across her cheek. She brushed it off absentmindedly. Jack marveled for the millionth time at her loveliness. Her clear complexion, completely devoid of make up, glowed with a natural beauty that only healthy living and regular exercise could impart.

She took a shaky breath. "It's about Ron."

"Okay."

"He's having an affair."

"Okay."

Her eyes dashed up toward his, then just as quickly looked away. "And he's drinking too much."

"Okay."

Claire bit her lip, trying to stem off the rush of tears that had been threatening to spill out. She took a shaky sip of her soda and then raised her eyes up to Jack's once again.

Jack reached out his hand and pressed it against hers. "So how can I help?"

Claire looked away again, as if she was ashamed of her gut instincts.

Jack cocked a grin. "Want me to break his kneecaps for you? I can send Guido and Johnny out back."

Claire chuckled and wiped another tear off her cheek. She took a shaky breath and then met Jack's eyes and kept his gaze.

"So what do I do?"

"What do you want to do?"

"Don't do that, Jack. Can't you just tell me what to do?"

He nodded. "All right. So, first, I think I'd get some proof."

"I have proof." Again, she glanced away, her cheeks reddening.

"What kind of proof do you have? Pictures? Did you walk in on them?"

"I, uh," she cleared her throat, "found a box of condoms."

"Condoms?"

"Mmhmm. We don't, well, um, we don't use them."

"Ah."

Again, she looked away, embarrassed.

"Claire, you don't need proof of infidelity in Oregon to file for a divorce. You just need a good attorney. Do you want me to help you find a good attorney?"

"I'm not looking for a divorce, Jack."

Jack's eyebrows furrowed together as a large rock of dismay landed smack dab into the pit of his stomach. "Okay." He tried not to allow the disappointment sound in his voice. "So what is it you do want?"

"I want to know who."

"Why do you want to know who? What's the point?"

Claire whipped her head up and glared at him. Her eyes shone with a cold fury he hadn't had the displeasure of ever experiencing before. Jack jerked back instinctively. "Because it's insulting!" Claire grit her teeth. "I'm just so fucking disappointed. I mean, for Pete's sake, I'm a surgeon. I'm good looking. I make a decent living. What the hell?!? What more is he looking for? I mean, seriously?!? Really?!?" Claire took a deep breath. "Who is this woman?"

Claire pressed her fingers against her forehead and let out a deep sigh. "I'm sorry I lost my temper."

Jack let the silence surround them. He waited for her to look at him, but she avoided his gaze.

Her voice grew quieter, more resigned. "I guess it shouldn't really matter. It's not like we were really together any more." She ran her fingers through her hair and sighed again. "It's just so damned insulting." She took a sip of her soda and let her gaze wander around the restaurant. "I just want to know who she is."

Jack appraised Claire with a new found respect. The coldness in her eyes was new. The hurt, fresh. He wished he could go back in time, do things differently, erase the pain etched permanently across her face. But there was no rewind button in real life. No do-overs. If there had been, he would have used them up long before he'd even met Claire. He wanted to stand up, pull her against his chest, wrap his arms around her, and kiss her until her toes curled and her mind wiped clean of all the bad memories. He wanted to taste her lips and smell her sweet breath against his face, to listen to her quietly whisper his name as they made love in the dark quiet hours of the night. But she was no longer his to comfort this way. And the jerk whose job it was had found someone else with whom to share that privileged intimacy. Jack swallowed the bitter bile in his mouth and offered up the only thing he had to give. "Want me to help you find a good private investigator?"

Claire nodded, relief flooding her face.

Jack searched her face one last time, hoping to read something different. When he found only the love of a friend staring back at him, he nodded his head. "I'll call you tomorrow with a couple of names."

"Thanks, Jack." She reached her hand out once again and squeezed his. Then she gathered her things and slipped out of the booth. "I'll talk with you soon, then?"

"Absolutely." Jack reached into his pocket for his wallet, throwing a few bills on the table to cover the check. By the time he'd turned around to slip on his jacket, the restaurant's doors were already closed behind her, leaving the restaurant, and Jack's heart, empty.

Chapter 11

APPLE SMOKED BACON from Trader Joe's, Jack thought, truly made all the difference in a tasty egg frittata. Jack savored another bite as he worked on a crossword puzzle. Back in the day, he'd sit down to breakfast with the crossword puzzle from the Oregonian. Mrs. Patinkin, his next door neighbor, would save the crosswords for him, leaving the paper on Jack's porch every night. She'd spend her mornings clipping all the coupons, completing the daily word jumble and the sudoku, reading the comics, pouring over the obits for any friends she may not have yet heard about, and then save the crosswords for Jack. Neither of them had really bothered with the rest of the paper; most of the time the entire stack headed straight for the recycling bin. Nowadays, Jack simply read his news online, and bought his crossword puzzle books at the Dollar Store or Target.

Even though newspapers had all but gone extinct, Jack continued to repay the favor by taking out Mrs. Patinkin's garbage and recycling bins to the curb every Monday night, and helping out with her seasonal chores; like cleaning the wet leaves out of her gutters and hanging up her Christmas lights. He even went to far as to rototill her garden every spring. His mother brought him up right. His father, on the other hand, well, perhaps that was why his mother spent so much time teaching Jack and his brother.

When his phone chirped, Jack groaned. Cold egg frittata just didn't taste the same. He knew, before he even took the call from Max, that the magic he'd created in his kitchen was about to go to waste. What a shame.

"What do we have this morning, Max?"

"Some early morning hikers found a body in the pool beneath Horsetail Falls this morning. Figured you'd want to go primary to determine whether she's a jumper or if she was pushed."

Jack glanced down at his half eaten breakfast and sighed. "Copy that. I'll be on my way in ten minutes. Is the scene secured?"

"Yep. We've got a Deputy holding on to the two hikers, and a U.S. Forest Service Ranger keeping folks away. Not too many people out yet this early in the morning."

Jack glanced up at the clock. "No, but there will be soon. All right. I'm on my way."

"See you in a bit."

"Oh, and Max?"

"Yeah?"

"Can you have Pete bring in the dive van this morning? I'd like you to be the back up diver, have him run lines. It's your turn to bag a body, isn't it?"

Max grinned, pleased that he remembered. "Sounds great. I'll get hold of Pete, Mason and Hank, and we'll meet you out there."

"Copy that. Is Shea not coming?" Jack shoveled as much of the rest of the eggs into his mouth as would fit, only to open his mouth a second later to let out some of the steam before the whole thing seared the inside of his mouth.

"Shea's got a thing with her boys today. She can't miss it."

Jack smirked at the playful use of the word "boys." None of Shea's sons were under six foot four. And youngish though they may still be, they were hardly boys any longer.

"Groovy. See you out there." He quickly rinsed off his dishes, placed them in the sink, shoved the rest of the eggs into the fridge and glanced around. His phone and keys were all ready for him in the dish on the shelf next to his front door. His jacket hung on the hook beneath. All he needed to do on his way out was call Nick and ask him to run the search warrant on Gerald Frank's apartment this morning without him. He hated to miss it, but Dive Team call outs always took precedence.

Only three cars littered the parking lot outside Horsetail Falls this early in the morning, one being the green Sheriff's Office patrol car. Jack ran through his work emails on his phone to take care of a few minor things while waiting for Pete to arrive with the Dive Team's van. Nothing urgent, other than the search warrant, needed to be handled. He was pleased to see Pete pull up just a few minutes later.

They gathered their gear from the dive van, and headed across the road to where the Deputy and two hikers stood anxiously awaiting instructions. Jack dumped his gear, pulled his notebook out of his back pocket, and turned his back to the waterfalls, keeping his eyes away from the waterfalls and the pool beneath. He wanted to avoid making his own impressions of the scene until after he'd heard the couple's version of the story. He sized up the couple, and ruled them out as a likely set of candidates for murder. They both seemed to be in their late 60's, early 70's, dressed head to toe in Columbia Sportswear. The white hair that poked out of their hats curled a bit at the ends with the moisture from the waterfalls nearby. They instinctively reached for each other's hands when Jack began to approach, and Jack felt his face flush a bit, touched by their intimacy even at their ages.

"Hi there. I'm Detective Diamond. I understand you saw something in the water while hiking this morning?"

The two hikers looked at each other, and then back at Jack. The man spoke first. "Yes, sir. We were headed up to Triple Falls this morning. We got up to the top of Horsetail Falls and were looking down at the water."

"It's so clear this time of year." The woman added her part of the narration seamlessly to her husband's. They clearly had been finishing each other's sentences for years.

"And we saw what looked like a..."

"Well, it looked like a body." They both nodded.

"All that white skin, and what looked like a leg, flowing with the water. Kinda going with the current rushing down from on top."

"Don't know how we couldda missed it from down below."

"Well, we didn't really stop and take a look at the pool before heading up the trail."

"Anyway, we took a picture with our camera and tried to see it up close." The woman held out her camera to show Jack. He took the camera, but didn't bother to look just yet.

"And what we saw was enough to worry us."

"So we went back down the trail to the back of the waterfalls over there to get closer to the pool and took a good look."

"Frightened us to death!"

"So we called 911, and this nice young man came in no time at all."

Jack took a look at the picture on the camera. Sure enough, it looked liked a stark white leg floating out from underneath the rush of all the water.

The Deputy confirmed the hikers' stories and added, "so that's when I called y'all in."

Jack gave the Deputy a quick once over. The kid couldn't have been more than 22 years old, fresh out of college, still eager to save the world. Jack patted him on the shoulder. "Good thinking, Deputy. Now, can you please get these folks' contact information and take their statements for your report, and then make sure that you keep everyone else out of the area, and off the trail back there behind the falls? We're going to be up here for a while."

"Yes, sir, Detective."

The Deputy took the two hikers off to the side and began to take the rest of their statements. The Forest Service Ranger began rolling out yellow tape to close off the area around the falls, as well as the nearby trail while the investigation continued.

Jack met up with Max and Pete at the wall in front of the pool surrounding the front of the waterfalls, and waved to Hank and Mason as they pulled up in another county rig. They gathered their gear and walked around the rim of the pool toward the back of the falls. Jack gave the pool a good once-over before donning his gear. He could see what looked like the leg floating up beneath the power of the falls themselves. The rest of the body appeared to be submerged beneath the torrent of water.

"I think you should take the video camera with you for the first go round. Document the body since we've got such good visibility." Pete pulled out the small hand held mount, shaped almost like a pistol, and gathered up the video equipment so they could get real-time video on the surface, enabling them to watch what Jack was seeing under the water.

Jack nodded in agreement. He donned his gear, pulled on his full face mask and tested out his mics. Max suited up as well, then helped set up the video monitor to watch Jack's surveillance. Mason and

Hank brought their gear to the site and settled in to work.

Jack checked his tether and hooked it into his harness. As he slipped into the pool, he could feel the cold water slip inside his neoprene gloves. Damn, it was cold. Biting cold. He hoped that the water wouldn't slip inside his neck seal. Nothing made you feel more alive than melted snow slipping down the nape of your neck.

Jack dropped down away from the body so that he could swim toward it, allowing the video camera to get a good view. "Are you getting all this?"

Pete clicked on his mic, "Looks good so far." He, Max, and Hank watched in waiting, tensing up as Jack began to approach where the body was sure to be floating. Mason checked his video feed, verifying that everything was getting recorded straight to the hard drive. He wanted to make sure everything was up to snuff, because the video documentation would be used as evidence, documenting the crime scene before they even touched the body.

"All right, here she is. Are you getting this okay?"

"Roger that. Everything looks good so far."

An eerie silence washed over Jack as he began to approach the body. She was lying face down under the water, the upper part of her body being held down from the turbulence of the waterfall flowing from up above. He could only get a good view from the mid torso down her legs to her feet. She was wearing a short skirt, but the water had pushed it up.

"Jack, can you go back over her waist again? Can you tell if the water pushed up her skirt? Or if it was up before she hit the water?"

Jack panned the area again. "No way to tell." He swam down the length of her legs a bit. "But she's not wearing any underwear." Jack's heart clenched. Things were going south. In all likelihood, this was not a suicide.

Jack took a moment to look around. He looked up and a strange feeling washed over him, as he realized he was sitting on the bottom of a pool looking up into the rushing, roiling water pouring down on top of him. It was pretty awesome to see the water turbulence above him. It wasn't really strong enough to knock him around. A small trout flitted beside him and he smiled. Several more swam past. How did they get in here? Were they carried downstream? Did they fall from the waterfalls?

But then he realized he had a dead body to turn his attention back to.

Jack pushed himself back toward the agitated water, swimming closer to the body. He tried to get the camera to get a view of the top half of her, but the rushing water from the falls prevented his ability to see anything. He pushed the camera and his hand into the raging water, away from the rest of his body, keeping his head turned away out of the roil to avoid getting knocked around. It reminded him of sticking his hand down a hole, feeling around for critters. He had no idea what his video camera was recording. He tried to pan the camera around her body, wondering if the body was even showing up on the view screen.

"Are you getting any of this? Is she showing up on screen okay?"

"Jack, stop. Go back. Did you see that?"

"See what? I can't see anything with all these bubbles. You'll have to walk me back through what you want me to point the camera at — my hand is in the turbulence, but my head's out, so I can't see what I'm shooting at."

"Okay, so go slowly."

"Copy that. Where do you want me to go from here?"

"Okay, so go left just a little bit."

"Like this?"

"No, no, you're other left. My left. Your right. Go right just a little bit."

"Like this?"

"Okay, now point up just a smidge."

"Is that enough?"

"A little more. Okay. Right there. Hang on, let me make sure we get a good view of this. What the hell is that?!?"

Jack's hand started to shake a little as the fear of the unknown started to snake down his neck. "What are you guys seeing?"

"We're not sure. But we got a good view of it up here, whatever it is. You'll need to take a really good long look down there for evidence."

"Already on it." Jack finished videoing the body and began surveilling the bottom of the pool. He found a pair of sunglasses and a ratty baseball cap, but nothing much else. He swam over to the edge of the pool and passed the camera back to the Dive Team on the surface.

"Do you think we should bag her up here? Or down below?"

Max looked at Pete and then back down to Jack. "I think Pete, Hank and I can all say it looks like we'd better bag her underwater." Jack nodded. So they agreed then. Her death looked suspicious to them too.

"What was it you saw on the video?"

"Not sure yet. We'll take a better look when we get her up and out of the water." Jack nodded his head and put his face mask back on.

Max slid into the water beside Jack, carrying the body bag with her. The bag was almost solid on the bottom, made out of a very fine mesh heavy plastic tent material, allowing water to flow out, but keeping small pieces of evidence trapped inside with the body.

Max swam down next to the body and lay the bag out on the bottom of the pool. Jack swam to the other end and opened up the bag, prepping it for the body. Jack reached up to her shoulders while Max took her feet. They tried to move her as little as possible, keeping her body face down. He didn't want to stir things up too much, because that would just kick up silt at the bottom of the pool. They didn't want to lose any evidence, either.

They got her into the bag, zipped it up, and then they each grabbed hold of one end and lifted it up off the bottom. They couldn't really swim, since the body weighed them down.

"Okay, on the count of three, let's power inflate up to the surface, then swim the body over to the edge."

"Okay. On three. Three, two, one, up."

The three of them floated up toward the surface in a pile of bubbles. Jack and Max maneuvered the body up and Pete, Mason and Hank helped to pull her up and out of the water.

Max stayed at the edge of the pool, her face under water, watching for trouble. Jack dove back down, taking one last look around for anything that might be able to be used as identification: her purse, cell phone, weapons, anything that didn't belong. The great visibility made it a quick and easy search. But Jack still felt a bit disappointed at not having found anything. He bagged the sunglasses and the ball cap, but he wasn't convinced they had anything to do with her death. They looked like they'd been under there a while.

By the time Max and Jack were out of their dive gear, Pete and the U.S. Forest Ranger had her body out on the sidewalk at street level. Jack looked up and swore under his breath. The media had started to arrive, and the Public Information Officer (P.I.O.) was no where to be seen. The young Deputy had done a nice job of cordoning off the area, but he hadn't learned enough to keep the media away from the Dive Team and the other investigators.

116

Jack finished drying off his hair just as the M.E. arrived. Monday greeted them all, and unzipped the body bag, getting straight down to business. She took a good look around, searching for visible signs of trauma. She looked at the woman's hands, and noted the scraping of her knuckles.

"That's not uncommon for a body that's been knocked around in turbulent water," Jack pointed out. "You'll probably find some scraping on her knees, and again on her forehead — points where the water pushed her against the bottom."

Monday nodded and continued on with her examination. "Did you find her underwear?"

"Not in the water."

Jack turned to the Deputy. "Hey there. Can you please get someone else up here to help out with a search? I want you to search the parking lot and the trail itself for women's underwear, maybe condoms, cigarette butts, and anything else that may have been left behind."

The Deputy straightened up and smiled, eager to help out on a death investigation. He quickly turned away from Jack and Monday and began to speak rapidly into his mic.

"Oh, and Deputy? Can you please have someone search up above on the trail up there? See if she left a suicide note." The Deputy nodded, and began talking into his mic again.

Mason looked around the parking lot. The only cars parked in the lot were those belonging to the two hikers who found the body, the M.E.'s office, the

Sheriff's Office, the Dive Team, and the media. "She didn't come here on her own."

"Unless she parked at another trailhead and hiked over." Jack absentmindedly spoke in a matter-of-fact manner, keeping his focus on the body in front of him. But his statement made Mason blush. The thought hadn't occurred to him that the victim may have hiked over.

"I didn't see any other cars parked along the way here." Defensive, Mason's voice sounded a bit petulant.

"Me, neither." Hank patted Mason on the back, smoothing over any tension that might have bubbled up in the quick interaction. Hank excelled at keeping the group calm, keeping moods even. Except, perhaps, when it came to interactions between himself and Max. He smiled to himself. He deliberately kept those interactions as turbulent as he could. He chuckled, and set back to work.

Pete looked around and nodded. "Looks less and less likely to be a suicide."

Monday looked up at Jack and nodded. "Let's flip her over."

Jack looked up at the woman's face, trying to see if he could recognize her. He jumped when Pete exclaimed, "What is that?!? That's the thing we saw on the video that we couldn't get a good look at."

Jack's eyes moved down her body, searching for the cause of the fear in their voices. Monday slipped her gloved finger under the edge of the woman's white tank top and moved it gently aside.

The view made Jack's blood run cold. A piece of skin, about three inches long and two inches wide had been carved out of the woman's chest.

The Deputy walked over and whistled. "Hey look, it's a diamond for Diamond!"

Jack's eyes flew up just as the reporter's startled face caught the remark. Jack knew in that split second exactly what that hour's tweet and what the media headlines would read. Jack tore his eyes away from the reporter's and met Monday's stare. Her grave concern was etched upon her face. Clearly, they both agreed. Portland had a serial killer on the loose.

Chapter 12

THE NEXT SEVERAL hours flew by in a flurry of activity. Several Deputies from the day shift patrol came by and secured the area, allowing Pete, Max and Jack to gather the Dive Team gear and head back to the boat house. Mason and Hank followed behind. They hadn't found a suicide note or the woman's underwear or car. The Detectives Unit had bagged a couple of miscellaneous items for evidence, but Jack didn't hold his breath for anything relevant.

After a brief conversation with Monday, Jack discovered that the Horsetail Falls victim was a close enough match to the Ankeny Street Dock victim that the two could have been sisters. Same body type, same color hair and eyes, roughly the same weight. Even the carvings proved to be nearly identical in size and shape. One major difference between the two victims seemed to be the cause of death. While the Ankeny Street Dock victim had been strangled to death, the Horsetail Falls victim had been stabbed in the heart. The stab wound had been roughly disguised by the post mortem diamond-shaped carving out of her chest.

Monday planned to run further tests to determine if the same type of weapon was used on the wounds, but her cursory examination showed that they were, in all likelihood, a good match. She put in an expedited order on the blood work to check for Rufies. And she confirmed Jack's fears; this victim had also had recent rough sexual activity, again with a condom.

Jack rubbed his hand against his forehead as he hung up the phone. The paperwork in front of him seemed to be growing by the minute. By the looks of things, he would get no closer to finishing the paperwork on the Ankeny Street Dock victim with a second victim so close on her heels.

He glanced over at his computer, knowing that he should write up the Dive Team report as soon as possible after his dive to keep everything fresh in his head. But Jack's fingers itched to wrap themselves around Gerald Frank's neck, wishing that he'd put the damned Sex Offender under arrest yesterday afternoon, before Gerald had been granted the opportunity to strangle, rape, murder, and then mutilate another innocent woman. A wave of bile crept up Jack's throat, and he swigged a gulp of water down, trying to wash the vile taste away. He closed his eyes for a moment, and an image of the woman's body flashed before his eyes before he could stop it. He watched as her long hair floating behind her, her face pushed roughly under the turbulent water. Her head turned, and her eyes opened. Jack jumped out of his chair, his chair flying across the cube.

"Jack, you okay?" Nick raced over to Jack's cube, and took in the man's grey pallor. His hand slipped down to his cell phone, his fingers itching to call the paramedics.

"Claire. It could have been Claire."

Nick's hackles stood up. "Who could have been Claire?" He waved over another detective from the unit, getting ready to call in the troops. Jack never freaked out.

Jack closed his eyes and began to sway. Nick dropped his phone and shoved the rolling chair behind Jack's legs, just as Jack sank into it. Jack pressed his hand against his eyes and rubbed them. "The vic. Today's Dive Team recovery. She was the spitting image of Claire."

Nick turned to the other detective and shooed her away. She rolled her eyes and headed back to her cube, reconnecting her headset back to her ear as she went.

Nick knelt down next to Jack and spoke softly. "Your vic today?"

Jack looked down at Nick. "Yeah. She *and* the first victim. The Ankeny Street Dock vic. They both could be Claire's sisters, they look so much alike."

"Jesus."

Jack nodded his head.

"Are you sure it's not her?"

"I'm sure. The resemblance is close. But not *that* close."

"Well that's good news at least." Nick's heart had stopped racing, now that some of Jack's color had returned. He no longer felt the urge to call for an ambulance.

"So what the hell happened just then? Did you have a bad dream? Or what? You scared the crap outta me!"

"I don't know, Nick. Maybe I'm losing it." Jack rubbed his face with both his hands and then sat back in his chair, looking up at the ceiling. A dozen very sharp pencils hung like stalactites from the ceiling in a random pattern. Nick had won last week's pencil flicking competition hand's down. Jack hadn't even come close.

Jack took a deep breath and looked back at Nick. "Maybe I'm just imagining things."

Nick shook his head. "Nope." Nick took a good, thorough look at Jack, pleased to see some color returning to his face. "You don't imagine anything. I trust your instincts. You should trust them too." Nick stood up, his knees popping as he rose. He thumped Jack on the arm. "Maybe you should give her a call. Make sure everything's okay."

"Yeah. Maybe."

Nick headed back to his cube, but kept his chair pulled back from his desk so he could keep an eye on Jack for the next little while. He hated to admit it, having a great deal more experience, and a few more years on the force, but Jack's instincts were somewhat legendary. Nick had learned quickly to listen to Jack's instincts and to act on them whenever possible. He turned half his attention back to his latest report, but kept his eyes and ears on Jack. Then, with a quick change of heart, Nick picked up the phone and called Chris, wanting — no needing — a little domestic connection, a small reminder that everything was fine on the home front. Whenever things got rocky at work, he tended to touch base at home. Well, if he was honest about it, if and when things ever got rocky at home, he tended to touch base at work. Not that things ever got rocky at home. At least not very often. He smiled when Chris answered the phone. He turned his chair and lowered his voice, allowing himself a moment of privacy.

Jack scooched his chair toward his desk and felt his eyes close. Claire's face flashed in front of him. He ran through his favorite memories: her smile as he told her he loved her; her eyes just as she was about to climax; her hair as it blew in the wind while out on a walk. Her face, blueish grey, frozen forever under the water as he scooped her dead body out from the river. Jack clenched his fists through his hair and forced the nightmare premonition away. He ran his fingers through the piles of paper in front of him, searching for the Private Investigator's telephone number that he'd promised to give her. It took some doing, but he finally found what he'd been looking for, and picked up the phone, dialing her number from memory.

"Claire, it's Jack."

"Jack! It's so great to hear from you." She sounded breathless, as if she'd just come in from a run. Vibrantly alive, healthy, well.

A wave of relief washed over him and he hung onto her last words, wishing she would keep talking, just so he could hear her voice again. But it was his turn to talk. He glanced down at the number in his hand and cleared his throat.

"Did I catch you at a bad time? Are you just heading into surgery?"

She laughed. "No, I'm on a break at the moment. Just got out of a good one. Facial repair on a three-year-old — attacked by his uncle's pit bull. You're barely gonna see a scar."

Jack grinned. A warmth of pride spread across his chest. He loved how much she truly was able to change children's lives for the better. Removing scars, correcting birth defects, erasing bad luck and bad genes with her magic surgical fingers. His heart did a little pitty-pat, and he smiled. Then, remembering where he was, he cleared his throat.

"So I've got that number for you."

"Number? What number is that?" He heard clinking in the background. Dishes? perhaps? Washing dishes? Putting them away? He heard a liquid being poured, and he smiled. Ah. Coffee. Time for her caffeine fix.

He cleared his throat again. "The number for the Private Investigator you wanted."

A dish clattered through the phone. She'd put her coffee cup down. Hard. "Oh. That."

Jack's hopes dashed. She didn't want a private investigator any more. She had no more intentions of leaving her husband. She said she hadn't wanted to, but he'd hoped.

"So, I take it you don't need it any more?" Jack tried not to sound too pathetic, but he wasn't sure he was quite as successful as he'd hoped.

"Well, um, no."

Jack's hopes dashed away, dashed away, dashed away all. He watched them fly off into the sunset with Santa and his reindeer. "Alrighty then."

"No, it's not like that. It's just, well, um, Shelly gave me the name of hers."

Jack's hopes began to flitter about again. He squelched them. Like gnats. He had to stop getting his hopes up over a woman who was firmly committed to another man. Seriously. Stop. Even if she was having him investigated. A hope flittered. He squished it too. But not too hard. "Who is Shelly?"

"Shelly's my best friend."

"Ah. And, if you don't mind my asking, how did Shelly come up with a name of a P.I.?"

"Well, she's, um, kinda dating one."

Jack smiled. "Ah."

"So, thanks all the same, but I think I'm good."

Yes, she is good. Good at so many things. Good and kind. Good and smart. Good and lovely and wonderful. Jack squeezed his eyes shut and tried to focus. "Alrighty then, so you won't be needing my investigator guy?"

"No. But thanks. Really, Jack. Thanks. I appreciate your doing this for me."

She really did sound grateful. Jack let that wonderful, positive feeling wash over him, just for a second. And then he remembered. Again. She was married. To his asshole of an ex-boss. And the feeling just as quickly rushed away. "Any time, Claire. You let me know if you need anything else."

He felt her smile on the other end of the phone before he heard it in her voice. "Thank you Jack. It's nice knowing I can count on you." Her voice had grown quiet, and he heard the pain leak through once again.

He swallowed the urge to throttle her husband. "Claire, you can always, always count on me. For anything. You know that."

Her voice had shrunk to a whisper. "I know that Jack. And thank you."

"Any time."

He held onto the phone, long after the silence of the ended call had reached his ears. He replayed his memories, allowing them to wash through his mind like a cool breeze. He hated Ron Wilcox. He hated it even more that Ron had been given the opportunity to marry Claire. To be Claire's husband. To make love to her every night. To hold her hand at the movies. To make her coffee after her run. To break her heart. Jack swore.

His eyes landed on Gerald Frank's mug shot. Jack's fury with Ron Wilcox slid right on over to Gerald Frank. Transferred easier than a biscuit sliding off a cookie sheet. He wanted to strangle that sonofabitch. His eyes flitted over to the picture of Katie Martin, the Ankeny Street Dock victim and then over to the victim at Horsetails Falls. Their grey pallor, their sunken, cold, unseeing eyes. The bruises on their inner thighs. The torn skin on their private parts. The skin carved and stolen from their breasts. What Gerald Frank did to those girls was hideous. And Jack was going to make it his life's goal to make sure that sonofabitch paid for his crimes. And paid for them again and again and again.

"Nick?"

Nick rolled his desk chair into the mouth of his cube and leaned out. "Yeah?"

"Let's go arrest that sick sonofabitch Gerald Frank before he rapes, carves up, and kills someone else."

Jack had made it half way down the hall before Nick could blink. In a flash, he ran up and grabbed his arm, wheeling him around. "We've got a problem, Jack."

Jack's fury had amped up to riot level. If he'd had a pitchfork and a pack of villagers, they could have hunted down the dragons and had them slain before dinner. "Hmm? What's that?"

"Gerald Frank's not our guy."

Chapter 13

"I beg your pardon?" Jack's eyebrows reached the ceiling. Nick instinctively took a step back.

"Jack, I just got off the phone with Portland Police Bureau. They've got our guy."

"Good. That'll save me the trouble of thumpin' him before we get him in cuffs."

"No, Jack, you're not listening."

"No! *You* are not listening. This sick and twisted bastard raped, mutilated, and killed two women, Nick. Two women. He's a serial killer. We are not letting him get away with this. And we are not going to let him get to any more women." He couldn't help it. His mind flitted back to Claire. Claire's breezy voice talking to him on the phone. Claire thanking him for his help.

"Jack, I need you to listen to me. He's not our guy."

"I hear you. He's not our guy. He's P.P.B.'s guy. Fine. Whatever. Let them take the collar on this one. But he's going down for this. I want him gone. Forever. Let the sick and twisted chuckleheads in jail get their dirty hands on him. Give him a taste of his own medicine while he's in custody."

"Jack! He's not P.P.B.'s guy either."

"Wait, what?" Jack's confusion began to echo around him. Nick pulled him by the arm and dragged him into the conference room where their argument wouldn't be heard, and then repeated by, the surrounding detectives in the unit.

"Sit down, Jack. This isn't going to be easy for you."

"What's not going to be easy?"

"Gerald Frank is not our guy. He..."

"Nick, we've been through this…"

"Jack, shut the hell up and listen to me. Gerald Frank didn't do this. He didn't get your vic this morning, and he didn't get the vic up at Ankeny Street Dock, either. He's not our guy."

Silence bounced off the walls and filled their ears.

Jack let the silence fill him. Nick braced himself against the conference table, watching Jack's face, and waiting for it all to sink in.

After a moment, Nick opened his mouth to speak, but Jack put up a hand to silence him.

A full, solid minute passed before Jack raised his eyes to Nick's. "So what do you have?"

Nick let out a sigh of relief. He was afraid that Jack's personal attachment to this case would no longer allow him to see reason. "Chucklehead's got an alibi."

"A good one?"

"The best. Stupid ass got himself drunk right after we left him. He went down to the local bar, got himself liquored up good and drunk. Then he made a pass at one of the dancers, and tried to take her home with him. Bouncer thumped him up good, and they got him locked up in detox. He was there all night. Didn't get discharged until after you'd scooped your body out of the waterfalls. He couldn't have done her."

"But maybe he could have gotten her..."

"Jack, Gerald Frank's not our guy. You've got yourself a serial murder here, and Gerald Frank just alibied out with a solid on your second vic. His first alibi's shaky, but it'll stand when the M.E. gets up and testifies that the two vics were mutilated with the same knife, raped using the same type of condom, and strangled in the same way. No way these two aren't connected. You got yourself a serial killer, and you've just lost your only suspect."

Jack felt the air sag out of him, and he rested his face against the palm of his hand. "So where do we go from here?"

Nick hated the fact that Jack's voice sounded so resigned. But he hated it more what he was about to say. No easy way out of this one. "Jack, you've got to get yourself a team to help you out."

Jack nodded his head, and pulled himself up out of the chair.

"I'll call the lieutenant. You go snag a copy of the picture of the Horsetail Falls vic and get it over to the Public Information Officer. The PIO will need a copy to give to the media so we can identify our latest vic. The sooner we get her identified, the sooner we can start finding out where the connections are between our two victims, and the sooner we can start tracking down the real killer."

The two headed back to their cubes, and the nitty gritty work began.

Four days later, they were no closer in their investigation. No leads had come forward in the media's posting of the girl's picture on the news and on the internet. No further information had arrived yet from the M.E.'s office. Monday's office was slammed with a group of accident victims from up on Mt. Hood where a little old man and his dog veered into the oncoming lane and crashed into an SUV full of teenagers. Not even the dog survived. Monday hadn't been able to get the tox screen results back from the Horsetail Falls vic, and Jack tried not to pester her with his frustration.

Jack wrote up his Dive Team report on the Horsetail Falls recovery, and passed it along to his Sergeant for review. His team met daily to discuss the ongoing investigation into his serial killer. The Horsetail Falls victim remained unidentified, even through their connections with Missing Persons and the media. One of the team members had contacted the knife guy at the FBI to help them identify the kind of knife used on the victim to carve out the tattoo on Katie Martin and on their second victim. No results had been returned on that lead yet either. Jack had just started reviewing the video surveillance data from the night Katie Martin was murdered to see if he could find any connection to the two women when his cell phone chirped.

Jack groaned. Pete's name had popped up on the caller ID. Nick looked up. "What's the matter?"

"It's the Dive Team."

"Oh God. Another one?"

"I guess we'll find out." Jack picked up the phone and answered. "Pete?"

"Jack — we've got another dive call out. Looks like a dumped stolen vehicle in the Willamette. Can you come on out and run leads on this one?"

Jack's relief spoke volumes. "Absolutely. I'll call you back when I get to the car, and you can give me the location."

"Copy that. Call me when you're ready."

Jack looked at Nick and smiled. "Well, at least our serial killer isn't out hungry today!"

Nick laughed. Jack grinned, grabbed his jacket, and headed out the door.

Less than five hours later, Jack's serial killer proved him wrong.

Chapter 14

THE BODY OF the serial killer's third victim was fresh. Very fresh. Jack donned his dive gear for the second time in six hours, a weariness settling over his bones. He hadn't been fast enough. He hadn't been smart enough to catch the damned bad guy before he'd had a chance to grab another victim.

He felt Pete's eyes looking down on him, but Jack avoided looking at him. He didn't want to face the failure he felt. Everyone on the mission had been quiet since the call had come out. No one wanted to talk about it. No one wanted to face the dead woman, floating in Laurelhurst Pond amongst the reeds and the grasses and the ducks.

The media had arrived before Jack had finished suiting up, and the P.I.O. was doing her best to keep their attention off the crime scene. Jack looked up, just as she was flashing a picture of the Horsetail Falls victim to the reporters, hoping someone would be able to help them identify victim number two. She'd inadvertently caused a feeding frenzy, not realizing that the media hadn't yet figured out that they had a serial killer on their hands. The camera's flashes reminded him of red carpet events before the Oscars. His scuba recovery would be the latest media headliner. God forbid the victim also have a piece of skin mutilated off her breast too. Yet one more diamond for Diamond. He slipped his face mask over his neck seal, wanting the privacy more than the protection. Laurelhurst Pond wasn't deep enough to warrant the use of the full facial mask, but he'd need it to protect himself from the duck and goose droppings that made up the bottom two feet of muck and filth he'd have to search through for the victim's purse and cell phone.

Portland Police had cordoned off the area, and were doing a nice job of keeping most of the onlookers at least somewhat away. He could see people standing at their windows in the houses surrounding the park, trying to see what was going on. Jack turned his body away from the crowds and took the video camera from Pete. He plodded through the murky sludge toward the victim's body, and began to video the evidence. Again, he found the victim's body face down. She, too, had been wearing a skirt. Her long blonde hair tangled itself in the pond's reeds. He shooed away a curious duck, and got as much video evidence as he could before slipping under the water's surface and recording what he saw beneath.

"Pete, did you get this?"

"The diamond-shaped carving?"

"Yeah."

"Yes. It's showing up well on screen. Is she also nude? We can't tell from our angle."

Jack slid over a few feet for a better angle. "Can't tell. I can't see while she's here in the water. Let me go muck about for a bit in the sludge, see if I can turn up anything. Can you get the body bag ready?"

"Copy that, Jack."

Jack turned his camera down to the muck in front of him. Half of the silt had already begun to swirl around him. Too much duck poop, not enough visibility. He held the camera out in front of him, pointing it down toward the sludge, and allowed his other hand to sift through. Once again, he said a silent prayer of gratitude to the folks who had paid for his full body protection scuba gear. About three minutes later, Pete crackled through Jack's ear. "Jack! Stop. Do you see that? About what, three feet to your right? Do you see that white thing? What is that?"

Jack turned his head and moved his body to the right, trying to catch a glimpse of what Pete had seen in the camera. He panned the area, but the silt swirling around made it nearly impossible to see anything. "I don't see anything, Pete. Are you sure you saw something?"

"Wait! There it is again. It's right in front of you now. Pan in front of you and straight down. Right there! You've got it! What is that?"

Jack's heart started pounding. Something white was definitely sticking up out of the muck. "Probably just some kid's toy boat or something." Jack knew it wasn't true, but he couldn't help but try not to get too excited.

Jack calmed his body down, slowed his breathing, and slipped his hand into the filth. He felt something. Something definitely solid. He pulled it up and out of the muck, and allowed the silt to settle a bit, while he pointed the camera and its attached flashlight toward his find. Slowly the silt sifted away, and he gasped. "It's a purse. A purse. Pete, are you getting this?!?"

Pete's grin stretched a mile wide. "Absolutely, Jack. We've got it. Bring it on up to the water's edge, but keep it under the water if you can. I don't want the media to get a picture of this. We'll slip it into the body bag, and bring it up with her."

"Copy that. Come on in, the water's fine."

Pete laughed, and stepped into the muddy waters. His distaste for the body recovery slipped his mind as he walked toward Jack. They'd found their first real piece of evidence in the serial killer's case, and he couldn't have been more pleased than if he'd found it himself.

Chapter 15

"JACK, YOUR BODIES are beginning to pile up like Fibonacci numbers."

"Not helping, Monday. Particularly because you're making me feel like a dimwitted numbskull for not even knowing what on Earth you're talking about."

"Fibonacci numbers? The Fibonacci series? Hello? Do you not remember *anything* from your math classes at Duke?"

"I remember that I called you 'Wee Willy' for a week when you lost that bet."

Monday cleared her throat, ignoring the comment. Jack could feel the heat of her blush through his iPhone and smiled. "Fibonacci numbers," she lectured, "are numbers beginning with zero that when you add the last two digits together, they make up the next number. So the series begins zero, then one, one, two, three, five, eight, and so on."

Vague memories of an over-enthusiastic math instructor at an ill-timed eight a.m. Calculus class began to float toward the surface of his memories. "Ah, *those* Fibonacci numbers. Why didn't you say so? Well then, that would explain the vast number of my ever increasing pile of dead bodies." Monday's chuckle warmed his heart and helped ease his own embarrassment.

"Thought I'd pass along some not-surprising grim news. The Laurelhurst Pond woman appears to be the next victim of your serial killer."

"No real surprise there. Let me guess, ruffies, rape, and a diamond-shaped piece of skin missing from her breast?"

"Right on all three counts! You win the bonus prize of the day!"

Jack shuffled the ever-expanding pile of papers in front of him and sighed. "Then why does it feel like I just lost?"

"For the record, she was also strangled to death, like your first victim. Not stabbed, like your second victim."

Jack nodded his head while he took notes, then realized that Monday couldn't see his response. He cleared his throat. "Interesting. And disturbing."

Monday could hear his discouragement through the phone. "Keep up the good work, Jack. You'll get the bastard." The connection started crackling. Monday's bluetooth headset never responded well when she covered it up to talk to someone else when she was on the phone. Her voice came back even more cheerful than before. "Happy news! We've got a hit on your Laurelhurst Pond victim! AFIS pulled up a positive ID. Your vic evidently got tagged for a DUI when she was 19. I'll have Ned send over the details."

"Ned Ryerson?"

"No, Ned Quon. My deputy ME."

Jack chuckled. "Seriously? You don't remember the movie, 'Groundhog Day?' As in, 'Phil? Ned! Ned Ryerson!'"

The silence that followed answered Jack's question. He refused to back down. "I'm seriously going to call him Ryerson from now on."

"I wouldn't recommend it if you want him to answer." Monday's curt retort only made Jack more determined. "I'll let you know when I have anything new to report." She hung up before he had a chance to reply.

Jack hung up his phone and rubbed his face. He leaned back in his chair and stretched his arms over his head, feeling his spine pop and crack.

"You need to make a list, Jack." Nick popped his head out of his cube and into the walkway separating their workspaces.

"I know, I know, I know. And check it twice."

"Don't get that song stuck in my head, Diamond."

"How is it you always know what I'm thinking?"

"Who trained you, Diamond? I'm the man! Now get to work on that list." Nick disappeared into the recesses of his cube, and Jack pulled out a fresh pad of paper.

After a good half hour of uninterrupted work, Jack had fleshed out his to do list, keeping his priorities focused, and plugging in a few key reminders of what needed to be accomplished next. He called an impromptu meeting of the task force, and ran the list by his team. Taking the opportunity to guzzle a bottle of water and eat an apple, Jack felt significantly more refreshed after the meeting. The team had revised the list further, adding a few things that Jack had missed, and then they split the tasks between them to keep the ball rolling.

Using the information he'd received from Ned "Ryerson" Quon, Jack had just finished writing up an affidavit for a search warrant for credit records, cell phone records, and access to the Facebook page for Marie Caruso, his Laurelhurst Pond victim, when the phone rang.

"Jack it's Claire."

The panic in her voice sent a chill down his spine. He lowered his voice to a near whisper. "Are you okay? Is everything all right?"

"Jack I know who the Horsetail Falls girl is."

"What?! How?! We didn't find any ID on her, and we ran a fingerprint check and got zip. How do you know who she is?"

"Jack please. Hurry. Meet me at the same place we did before. I'm leaving now. I'll show you. Please hurry!!"

Claire hung up before he had a chance to respond.

Jack grabbed his jacket and headed for the elevators, not bothering to notice his co-workers' curious glances as he strode toward the door.

The restaurant was nearly empty when Jack slipped into the back booth. Claire nervously swiped the sweat off her soda glass in thin, straight lines waiting for the waitress to deliver Jack's iced tea.

Feeling the tension between her two customers, the waitress quickly poured his tea then made herself scarce in the kitchen.

Jack allowed the silence to envelope them, waiting patiently for Claire to gather her courage and fill him in. He hadn't seen her once in twelve years, and now he found himself sitting across from her for the second time in just a short span. His heart ca-thumped at the giddy thought. But then he glanced up and saw her face, and his protective instincts kicked in automatically. He stretched his arm out across the table and covered her hand with his. She rubbed her thumb against his hand and took a deep, shaky breath before daring to look him in the eyes.

"I got these yesterday." Claire reached over and retrieved a large manilla envelope and slid it across the table. "The P.I. dropped them off." She took another shaky breath. "It took me three glasses of scotch to get up the nerve to even open the blasted thing. I just sat there on the couch, staring at the envelope. I had the news on in the background. I like to, um, keep the news on when Ron's working. You know, just in case."

Jack nodded. He'd heard that a lot of wives and husbands of police officers kept an eye on the news while their spouses were working shifts, just to make sure their loved ones were okay. His beloved grandmother, GranNini kept a close eye on the online news programs watching out for him. She called him after every dive mission she'd seen on television just to make sure he hadn't been injured during his dives. If only she knew how often he'd been in much more serious danger, she'd have never left his side. He made a mental note to call her later that evening. Maybe bring her over a pie or some cookies or something. GranNini had a fierce sweet tooth.

"I don't know, Jack. Maybe it was the scotch. Maybe it was that obnoxious bimbo who does the weather. But something just snapped and I grabbed the envelope and slid out the photos. And there she was. The blonde bitch who's been sleeping with my husband."

She looked up at him then, staring into his eyes, so glad he was there, so grateful for his friendship. She felt herself relax for the first time since she'd glanced at the photos. "It was like a baseball bat socked me in the stomach."

Jack jerked.

"Jesus, Jack! I'm so sorry. I didn't think. I wasn't even thinking."

The color had all but run off Jack's face. His grey pallor did not improve, even after he took several long gulps of his iced tea. He glanced over at the waitress who dashed over with a pitcher and refilled his glass. Again, her eyes darted between the two of them, and she hurried back to the counter, not wanting to disturb them.

Claire's voice came out a croak. "I'm so, so sorry, Jack. It was careless of me."

He cleared his throat. Closing his eyes, he willed the image of his brother's baseball bat lying in the pool of sticky blood on the orange linoleum floor to wash away. He could hear his mother's voice pleading with his father to stop. The sound of the baseball bat bashing in her skull, making that horrible "thuck" sound as his father pulled it out of her face, blood and hair and ick oozing down the side as he swung up and then bashed it down once again, "thud!" into his brother's shoulder. Jack winced, rubbing his hand across his face. He took a deep, shaky breath, and willed himself to think of something else. Anything else. After a moment, the memories passed, and the sounds from the restaurant started making their way back into his consciousness.

"Don't even worry about it." He took another sip of his tea and forced his breathing to slow down, slowing down his heart. He focused his eyes back on Claire, beautiful Claire, and felt his heart clench and then slowly ease back into its normal rhythm. He sighed. It was over. He could move on. "So, the P.I. sent you a few pictures?"

Kicking herself for her thoughtless slip of the tongue, Claire squeezed Jack's hand, grateful that the color had started returning to his face.

"Jack, I really am sorry."

"It's fine. Really." He allowed the corner of his lip to curl up, just a little. Even if it wasn't quite a full smile, it seemed to help.

Claire rubbed her thumb across his fingers. She allowed him another moment to collect himself, giving her a chance just to feel how good it was to hold his hand once again.

"Jack, I swear, it was kismet. I had just pulled out the pictures, I was staring at this poor girl's face, and that's when they interrupted the news with the information on the Horsetail Falls drowning victim. I turned up the volume when I heard the soundbite."

"Oh no, let me guess, 'Diamonds for Diamond?'"

"Yeah! That was kind of funny. In a sick and twisted kinda way."

Jack groaned.

"Anyway, so the newscaster started talking about the poor girl at Horsetail Falls, and then they popped up with a picture of her on the screen. And there she was! The same girl! She's the same girl as the one in the pictures I had just pulled out of that envelope from the private investigator. It's the same girl, Jack. I swear!"

Jack's heart flip flopped and fluttered as he watched her slide the photo over toward his side of the table. His heart skipped a beat entirely when he watched the dead girl he pulled out of Horsetail Falls come alive again in the photo in front of him. A diamond for Diamond indeed.

Chapter 16

SCOOPING UP THE mounds of paperwork off his desk and dropping them into the chair in the corner of his cubicle, Jack slipped out the photos from the PI's envelope and set them out in front of him. Claire hadn't wanted to bother looking at the other photos or the rest of the information the P.I. had provided. The picture had been too much of a shock. First, confirming that her husband had, indeed, slept with someone else, but then finding out that the same woman had drowned was just too much.

At the restaurant, she'd given Jack the envelope for safe keeping, and they'd hugged goodbye. Jack tried not to linger in the hug. He let the smell of her coconut shampoo comfort him. He found it so hard not to miss her in times like this; feeling her warm hands pressing against his back; squeezing her body close to his. And then he held on just a moment too long. Claire stifled a sigh, and pulled away, kissing his cheek and promising to stay in touch. Disappointment washed over him, and he quickly ducked his head to the ground, trying not to let her see how much it hurt to watch her go.

After she'd pulled out of the parking lot, Jack took the envelope and dashed back to the office. He wanted to go through everything the P.I. had given her with a fine tooth comb equally hoping for, and praying not, that the contents of the envelope would confirm his gnawing fear.

The P.I. had included a lot of photos. Over zealous perhaps? Wanting to make sure he would get paid his commission? Seeing the Horsetail Falls victim alive and laughing left a knot in Jack's stomach. He found it jarring and surreal to examine photos of someone so vibrantly alive just a few short days ago. Jack went through the photos one at a time, ignoring the woman for the most part; instead he carefully scrutinized the backgrounds of each picture, looking for other people in the photographs. But the private investigator had been pretty careful with his photography. Most of the pictures focused on her face, with the background and the other people in them blurry.

His disappointment washed over him, and he turned the pile of pictures over and went through them one more time, this time focusing on her jewelry and other accessories, wondering if, perhaps, his serial killer had started collecting earrings or handbags of his victims as souvenirs. Would he one day be going through the serial killer's lair finding this woman's favorite hoop earrings? Her iPhone with its purple platypus phone case?

It wasn't until he flipped through to the fourth picture that he realized that she had let her second ear piercings close up. In the first three pictures, she had double sets of earrings. In both the fourth and fifth pictures, she clearly only had one piercing. And then in the sixth picture, she had ear cuffs, and three piercings. Screwing his eyebrows together, Jack went back and looked at the date stamps on the pictures. That couldn't be right! The pictures were in chronological order. What on Earth?!?

The third time through the pictures, Jack's world fell apart.

"Nick? Get over here now!"

Recognizing that unmistakeable sound in Jack's voice, Nick said a quick "Gotta go" to Chris, ended his call, and dashed to Jack's cube. Heads popped up in the cubes around them, and then settled back down when they were greeted with silence.

Jack gave Nick a pointed look.

"What's up?"

Jack showed him the top picture.

"Who's that?"

"That's a picture of my Horsetail Falls victim."

"Okaaaaay."

"I got it from Claire."

Nick blinked. "Okay, so why does Claire have a picture of your Horsetail Falls vic?"

Jack gave Nick the pointed look once more.

Nick leaned over, scooped up the stacks of photos. "Are there more?"

Jack pointed to the envelope. Nick grabbed that too and then marched Jack down the hall, leaving a wake of curious co-workers peeping over the tops of their cubicles, once more trying to figure out what was going on. Nick led Jack into the conference room, then shut the door a little too hard behind them.

"Start at the beginning."

"So I had a drink with Claire."

"Well, shit. That complicates things." He paused long enough to see the look of misery on Jack's face. "Did you two start things up again?"

"No. No! It's not like that."

"But you'd like it to be."

"Yes. No. No! It's…complicated. She's married."

"To that rat bastard."

"And that's where it gets complicated."

Nick's face lit up like he'd just won the lottery. "The rat bastard's involved in this?"

Jack's face contorted with a combination of glee and grief.

Nick, a master at nonverbal communication, read everything that he needed to see. "Ah. That does complicate things. So how does that rat bastard fit into all of this?" He pointed to the pile of pictures.

"I'm not sure yet. But clearly I am not being very unbiased. I'd like you to walk through this with me. Make sure that I'm not seeing things I *want* to see, versus things I need to be seeing. Things that are really there."

Nick looked slightly confused. "Okaaaaay. So. Start at the beginning."

"Claire called me the other day, said she thought Ron had been having an affair."

"That rat bastard!"

"Yeah. Right. So I offered to set her up with a P.I., but when I called to give her the name of one, she'd already gotten the name of a P.I. from her best friend."

"'K."

"So evidently she was drinking up some courage to see the photos of her husband's new go-to gal, and Channel 8's news of the Horsetail Falls vic came on."

"'K."

"She slit open the envelope, slid out the pictures, saw the photo of the woman who her husband is sleeping with, looked up, and watched the same woman's face show up on the news as the drowning victim at Horsetail Falls."

"Jesus."

"No shit. So then she calls me up, brings me the envelope, and says she doesn't want to know any more."

"She gonna leave him?"

A stab of pain jarred Jack's face. He shook his head.

"Rat bastard."

Jack raised his eyes and gave Nick that look for the third time that day.

"Dude, what?!"

"You're focusing on Claire. You're missing the point I'm trying to make here."

"Shouldn't *you* be focusing on Claire? And getting her away from that rat bastard?"

"Yes, of course. Of course. But you're missing the most important piece here. According to Claire's PI, Ron was having an affair with my Horsetail Falls victim."

Nick sat down. "Well, shit." He picked up the photo and then put it down again, everything clicking into place. "Was he the last one to see her alive?"

Jack lifted his eyebrows and shrugged his shoulders. "That's why I need you to walk me through this. Check this out. Here's where things get scary."

Then wordlessly, Jack flipped the cards out one at a time like he was dealing a game of solitaire. Sixteen photos in all. Sixteen different outfits. Sixteen different sets of accessories. Four different piles. Four different women.

"Jesus, Jack. They could be sisters. Are they sisters? They related?"

"No idea. But listen, Nick. There are four different women, Nick! Claire's P.I. gave her sixteen photos of four separate women that her husband has been sleeping with. Four women, Nick. Four."

Nick's senses all went into overdrive. Unpleasant theories began to percolate in the back of his mind and his skin began to tingle. "So if this is your Horsetail Falls vic," he pointed to the first picture on the table, then picked up the photo of the next woman. "Then who is this?"

Jack took a deep breath and looked Nick in the eyes. The lengthy pause made Nick think that perhaps some of his unpleasant theories may, in fact, be true. "Who is this, Jack?"

Jack swallowed the nausea that began to build inside. He took a shaky breath and braced himself. "Are you ready for this?"

Nick's heart quickened. A wave of fear washed over him, just like it did when the beeping started in that <u>Alien</u> movie, knowing that one of those creepy crab-like things was about to click click click across the floor. No, Nick definitely no longer thought he was ready for this.

"That is a picture of my Ankeny Street Dock victim. Her name was Katie Martin."

The walls of the conference room started to close in on Nick. All at once he knew exactly how Newt and Ripley felt when they found themselves trapped in that glass enclosed room, locked inside with that vicious, single-minded alien.

When he opened his mouth to ask about the next photo, nothing came out at first. He cleared his throat and tried again. "This one?"

"Kelly Stewart. Horsetail Falls."

Nick hesitated, then pointed to the next photo.

"Marie Caruso. Laurelhurst Pond."

He could practically hear the click click click of that damned crab alien crossing the glossy floor, getting ready to impregnate Newt and Ripley.

Wordlessly, Nick pointed to the last photo, his eyebrows quirked up.

Jack sat down and lowered his voice. "That's where this gets even more scary."

"More scary than what you're already implying here?!"

Jack nodded. "Her name is Heather Allen. She's the girl that was up on Larch Mountain. The one I told you about."

Nick blinked, trying to remember. The Larch Mountain incident. And then the whole story came back to him in a rush. "The crazy chick who thought someone was chasing her? The one you ran over with your car?"

"I didn't run her over. Just kinda ran into her a little bit. And, by the way, she's not pressing charges. But yeah. She's the one. And she wasn't crazy. Stupid, yes. Crazy, no. K-9 unit got a couple hits on someone up there. We were just too late to get him."

"Did he rape her?"

"No. But he tried to. Dislocated her elbow. Smacked her upside the head. She pepper sprayed the sonofabitch."

Nick smiled. "Good for her!"

Jack cocked a grin, picturing Heather spraying a whole can of pepper spray into her assailant's face. But then his smile turned south as the grimness of the whole situation settled in around him.

The reality of Jack's insinuations kicked in, and Nick straightened up. "Ron Wilcox may be a rat bastard, but are you honestly suggesting what I think you're suggesting?!"

"As much as I hate him, I hope not. But what else does it look like?"

"Dude, you need to get the task force on this. Have them help you work through this whole thing."

"No! Are you nuts?!? Do you not see the problem here? Three of those women ended up dead. One was assaulted. And according to the PI, Ron Wilcox dated all of them." Jack took a deep, and shaky breath. "Sergeant Ron Wilcox is now our primary suspect."

"You honestly believe that not only did he date those four women, not only was he the last person to see them alive, but that he *killed* them? That he's a serial killer who raped and choked three women to death and tried to kill a fourth?!?"

Jack nodded his head slowly.

"You have got to get the task force involved. They have got to help you with this, man. You are no longer unbiased about this! You've got to get some help. Got to get the task force moving on this!"

"Are you crazy?! If Ron Wilcox is even remotely connected to any of this, we need to keep the task force away from this. I seriously do not need IA crawling up my ass to find out why I'm looking into the husband of my ex-girlfriend."

"Okay, so leave Ron's name out of this. Get the task force to help you go through the credit card receipts. Try to make a connection between the women." Nick chewed on his lip, tilting his head onto one shoulder as if to view the problem from the side, and then tilted his head onto the other shoulder to gain a new perspective. "Well, I mean, other than the fact that they look so much alike."

Jack cleared his throat. "It's more than just that, Nick."

"What?"

"All four of them look like Claire."

"Jesus." Nick pulled one of the photos closer to his face and looked her over. "No kidding." He sat down, the heaviness of the situation weighing on his heart. "You're right, Diamond. Damn if they do. All of them."

Jack nodded his head. "When I first approached the Ankeny Street dock victim when I was under water, well, for a second there when I dove closer and got my first glimpse, I could have sworn she was Claire. Maybe not quite so much now that you see her in the photos and all, but underwater?"

"What a sick ass bastard." Nick leafed through the photos once more, again noting the resemblance to the four women. He shook his head and stood up. Clamping his hand on Jack's shoulder, he squeezed tightly, giving his friend his support. "Listen, I'm sure the P.I. put dates and times on these pictures here." He flipped over a couple of pictures and confirmed his theory. "You've got to connect up these photos with Ron Wilcox if you're going to be able to put the rat bastard away for the rest of his miserable life. And you've got to get photos of the women with Ron together. You've got to get credit card receipts proving that they were at the same restaurant at the same time. You've got to get video surveillance from the bars to see if they've got any footage of Ron with any of those women. You've got to check his phone records to see if he called or texted any of them. You have to make the connection, man, or this bastard is going to walk. Keep it all hush-hush for now. But before you do anything else, you've got to get Larry and Manny on board."

Jack nodded his head once more. He was overdue to update his detective sergeant and lieutenant on the task force's progress anyway.

"They'll let you know if they want to get the Chief Deputy and the Sheriff involved."

Again, Jack nodded his head.

"Listen. After you get the go ahead from Larry and Manny, I'll write up a sealed affidavit and search warrant for Ron's credit card receipts, cell phone records and bank statements. See if we can make a connection." He took a deep breath. "I don't know, Jack. Maybe this is all moot. Maybe the rat bastard's got an alibi." He glanced down at the photos on the table and cleared his throat. "Four alibis." Then he pointed to the large manila envelope that had contained the photographs. "What's in there?"

"I don't know. I haven't looked."

Nick rolled his eyes and pulled a few sheets of paper out of the envelope. One was a bill for services rendered. Nick whistled at the fee, grateful that he wasn't the one footing the bill. The other was a detailed time, date, and location sheet indicating when each picture was taken, and how soon after each woman had met up with the target, a.k.a., Ron Wilcox. Nick whistled again. "That lovely bastard has done all your legwork for you, man! Check this out!"

A strange look crossed Jack's face as he read through the PI's report.

"He even got the name of your fourth victim!" Nick pointed down at all four names. "After you notify her next of kin, you can run her credit report along with the rest. Match it up with the information that's so neatly outlined right here." Nick punched the paper on the last three words to emphasize his point.

Nick squeezed Jack's shoulder one last time.

"Listen, Jack. Take a breath. Go meet up with Larry and Manny. Get that all squared away. Then call Claire. Tell her to go and stay with her mom, or her sister, or her best friend for a few days. Get her away from him. Give her something to do to. Keep her busy. Get her mind off things. But don't you dare let it on that you're looking into her husband as the suspect on these vics."

He pulled Jack close and lowered his voice. "And Diamond, tell her that she should seriously get herself tested. *Why*, again, is she not leaving him?!?"

Jack shook his head, still staring at the paper in his hands.

"And don't forget to call and set up a meet and greet with this PI. Maybe he has more information than he gave to Claire. See if he has any more photos, particularly any photos of the women *with* the rat bastard. Snag me when it's all set up. I'll go with you." He smiled, looking forward to that conversation. "Then call," he looked at the list and found the name he was looking for, "Heather Allen. Make sure Sgt. Wilcox hasn't diddled around with her again. Perhaps suggest she go visit her mother for a few weeks until this all dies down."

Jack nodded his head again.

"And then get the task force on this ASAP. I want to get this rat bastard cleaned, dressed, and in the pot before anyone else ends up drugged, raped, carved up and dumped in a puddle of water."

Chapter 17

"WHAT YOU'RE IMPLYING could ruin a man's career. You had better make damned certain you have proof to back up these assertions." Larry's face had turned an ugly shade of reddish purple. Jack's eyes dashed around the room looking for the nearest automated external defibrillator. He did not want his detective sergeant to have a heart attack while he and Nick were giving him bad news. Bad enough that they were investigating one of the Sheriff's Office sergeants as a possible suspect in three murders and one attempted murder. No need to add a heart attack to the mix.

Manny cleared his throat and drew the room's attention toward himself. His presence had a calming effect on everyone. He nodded at the large manila envelope in front of Jack, took a long look at Larry, and then eased his gaze over toward Jack and Nick. "Why don't you show us what you've got, and we'll go from there." Manuel "Manny" Rodriguez, Jack's lieutenant, had a way with defusing upsetting situations. He'd made his way up the chain of command at the Sheriff's Office quickly and efficiently, being equally gifted in understanding the broader implications of difficult and complicated situations, and in coming up with creative solutions to those difficult situations. During meetings, he stayed quiet, focusing his attention equally on the participants' nonverbal behaviors as well as on what each person was trying to say. His calm and quiet demeanor came across as disinterested at first. But those people who'd had the privilege of working with Manny throughout the years quickly learned to realize that Manny was a force to be reckoned with.

Jack respected Manny deeply. Over the past few weeks, he frequently sought out Manny's advice, and bounced his ideas past Manny when he needed a clear head to help him see through the muddle and muck.

Larry's face turned an even deeper shade of purple. Manny let his gaze rest on Larry's face until Larry found himself breathing more slowly, and calming down.

"Claire Wilcox, Ron's wife, approached me a few days ago, saying she believed Ron was having an affair."

"Why would Claire approach *you*?"

Jack disregarded the scornful derision in Larry's voice, and tried not to feel Larry's death stare burn a hole in his blazer. "Claire is an old friend of mine."

Nick cleared his throat.

Jack rocked his head back and forth and added, "We have a history together."

Nick glared at him.

"It's a little…complicated."

Nick nodded his head, and Jack continued. "I offered to give her the name of a PI, but she had already gotten the name of a P.I. from a friend of hers." He took a deep breath, and glanced up at Manny. His face remained noncommittal, so Nick went on. "The P.I. gave her this envelope," he slid the envelope toward Manny, avoiding Larry's gaze, "and told her that Ron was indeed having an affair."

Larry opened his mouth, but Manny shot him a look, and Larry closed his mouth again. "Go on."

"Inside the envelope were these."

Jack laid out the four piles of pictures of the four different women. "He also included a list of dates, times, and locations where he claims to have seen Ron with each of these four women." Jack slid the list over to Manny, and took a shaky breath. "It looks like Ron was sleeping with all of them."

Manny looked over the list of dates and times while Larry, whose face had deepened to a dark merlot, glanced at the pictures. Jack waited a full minute while they reviewed the evidence before sharing the last bit of information.

"Each of these four women looks very much like the other three. And," he paused for effect, "each has a very close physical resemblance to Claire."

Manny looked up from the pictures, and then back down again. Both he and Larry looked through the pictures again. The looks on their faces showed they couldn't argue with Jack's assessment.

"And here's the bigger problem. This woman right here," he sorted through the pictures and pulled out four of the same woman, "she's my Horsetail Falls victim."

Nick pulled the pile of photos toward himself, and then sorted through the photos. He re-arranged them in four separate piles, then slid them toward Jack.

"This woman is my Ankeny Street Dock victim."

"This is my Horsetail Falls victim."

"This woman is my Laurelhurst Pond victim."

"And this woman is the one whom I ran into up on Larch Mountain."

Larry's face drained of all color. Manny sat back in his chair. Jack allowed the information to sink in before he went on.

"I know I've been updating you along with the task force on my serial killer, but let me just recap. Three of these women were drugged with ruffies. Three of them were raped. Three of them had diamond-shaped pieces of skin excised from their breasts. And three of them ended up murdered, face down, in a pool of water somewhere here in Multnomah County. All in places where Sgt. Wilcox had access to and intimate knowledge of." He took a deep breath. "And, according to this PI, Sgt. Wilcox had slept with all four of these women." He nodded to the photos in front of him.

"As for my fourth victim," he pointed to his Larch Mountain victim, "she ended up with a dislocated elbow and lacerations, as well as being terrorized, threatened, and chased until she ran, literally, into my patrol car."

Manny nodded his head, and peered at the pictures once more. Larry remained stoic.

"And, on the night she ran into my car up on Larch Mountain?" he looked up at Manny and Larry, wanting to make sure they heard, and understood the implications of, his next few words, "Sgt. Ron Wilcox had called in sick that night, and wasn't working patrol."

Nick jerked his face up toward Jack's. He hadn't known this last tidbit of information. He glanced toward Jack's audience to read their responses. Manny wiped his face with his hand, and Larry looked away.

This time, Nick spoke up. "I'd like permission to obtain an affidavit for a sealed search warrant to begin a formal investigation into Sgt. Ron Wilcox, to rule him out as a possible suspect in the murders of these three women, and the assault of this woman."

Manny nodded his head. Larry shoved back his chair and started reading the bulletin board behind him.

"I'll inform the Chief Deputy and the Sheriff, so you and Jack can continue onward with the investigation." Then Manny stood up and pushed his chair back. "Let me know what the P.I. says after you've had a chance to interview him. Get his take on all of this." He pointed the the photos in front of him. "And fellas, I'm sure I don't need to remind you both to keep all of this information completely confidential — and I mean absolutely hush-hush, until you have more information for us to deal with." And with that, Manny swept out of the room. Larry glared at Jack and Nick, his face turning red once more. Then he stormed out of the room, slamming the door behind him.

Chapter 18

"I FOUND SOMEONE to notify your Horsetail Falls vic's next of kin as to her untimely death."

Jack quirked a smile. There wasn't much to smile at these days. "Really? Who'd ya get?"

"Some poor patrol newbie who didn't know better than to agree to volunteer to help me out before finding out what he had to do."

Jack's smile grew. "He won't make that mistake twice."

Nick smiled back. "I sent the county chaplain with him. No sense in making him go out there alone. Giving notice sucks."

Jack nodded his head. Having to notify the next of kin that their loved one had died truly was the worst part about his job. He avoided the experience as often as he could. Particularly when the loved ones who had died were little kids. "Thanks, man."

"You got it." Nick glanced at his notes, tapped his notebook, then looked back up at Jack. "So why didn't you tell me that Ron wasn't working that night?"

"I completely forgot about it until we were laying it all out for Larry and Manny in there."

"Honestly?"

"Completely slipped my mind. I only remembered when I thought back to getting the paperwork done that evening, and how grateful I was that Ron wasn't working. He would have made my life so much harder that night, mucking up the paperwork and wanting to put his nose into the investigation." He bit the inside of his cheek, gnawing at a new idea forming in the back of his mind. "Has anyone checked…"

"…to see if he was working on the nights each of these women were killed?"

Jack looked up to see Nick smiling. "I'll take a look and see what comes up. Right after I write up that affidavit for you." Nick glanced around at the ever expanding piles of paperwork on Jack's desk and frowned. "So what's next on your list of things to do?"

Jack glanced down at the papers in front of him and sighed. "The task force is still working on the credit card receipts, Facebook pages, and cell phone records for all four vics. Still trying to come up with connections."

He pulled out he PI's report. "This report will make things easier to narrow down the search."

"So will having Ron's affidavit come back so we can make any connections there."

Jack nodded his head.

"And, I still have to call the P.I. to set up an interview, and call my Larch Mountain vic, tell her to skip town for a while."

"Have you called Claire yet? Filled her in?"

Jack glanced back at his messy desk, then shook his head.

"You'd better get that over quick. Like ripping off a bandaid."

Jack nodded his head.

Nick turned and headed toward his cubicle. "I'll get the latest from the task force and then have them narrow down their searches, using the dates from the PI's report."

Jack nodded his head and picked up the phone. Nick called over his shoulder, "Just like ripping off a bandaid, Jack."

Chapter 19

"I'M NOT GOING to like what you have to say, am I?"

An awkward silence filled the airspace.

"All right. So give it to me straight."

Jack wished for the fourteenth time that he had gone to Claire's house to deliver the news in person, rather than chickening out and calling her on the phone. He couldn't reach over and grab her hand when he was on the phone. He couldn't brush the tears off her face. He couldn't read her nonverbals, wondering what she was thinking. He couldn't pull her toward him, allowing her to bury her face in his chest, to cry all over his sweater. He couldn't hand her a tissue, and another, and another, as the tears flowed down her face. He couldn't rub her back with his hands, feeling her sobs, and squeezing her tighter, allowing his body to protect her and comfort her from the pain as much as he could.

He most certainly wasn't going to Skype or Facetime her the news. It was bad enough having to receive bad news — one didn't need the additional humiliation of having someone else see you fall apart, not having the privacy to grieve in peace, and not having the added bonus of having their physical presence there to provide the much needed comfort.

No, if he wasn't going to be able to be there to comfort her in person, he wasn't going to eliminate her privacy.

"So the contents of the envelope confirmed your fears. According to the PI, Ron was having an affair."

"Oh God."

"It gets worse, Claire. I'm going to rip it off like a bandaid, ok?"

"How could it be worse? He was having an affair." Her voice cracked on the last word, sounding like a newly pubescent boy complaining.

"Claire, the P.I. gave you pictures, dates, locations, and times of not just one woman. There were four women in that packet."

"Four?!?"

"Yes."

He allowed himself a moment during the silence that followed to wish he could tell her the rest. That it looked like not only was Ron sleeping with these four women, but that he may have killed them as well. He hated not telling her. He hated that, once Claire eventually found out the truth, discovering that he had known the worst for a long time and not told her, Claire might never forgive him for not sharing that information with her. Jack had to live with that. He'd had to live with a lot of hatred in his life. Hiding things had helped him live with that hatred for many, many years. Besides, telling people didn't always help. He'd watched in horror as his own mother had found that out.

But as much as he wanted to share that information with Claire, he had his priorities. He had to gather all the evidence he could in order to prove her husband guilty of those three murders, as well as for the assault of a fourth woman, then to put Ron away for the rest of his life. And he had to do that without telling Claire. He couldn't risk her letting Ron know. He couldn't risk Ron's running and getting away with the crimes, or his committing suicide to get away from being punished. Not that suicide itself wasn't a form of punishment. The families of Ron's victims certainly wouldn't get justice if he committed suicide. Claire most certainly wouldn't be happy if he killed himself. The only people who would gain from Ron's suicide were those future women whom Ron would have hurt had he lived. Having Ron live permanently behind bars would solve the same problem without leaving anyone else dead. No one else should have to die. No one should ever have to die.

Jack's memory flashed on the picture of his mother's face, her lips whispering to him in the moments before her death. Her pleas to have him call the police to help his brother. Her pleas to make sure the ambulance took him first. The memories stirred an old, achy sadness into his heart; and he reaffirmed his vow to find the killer of those four women, whether it be Ron or some other sonofabitch. Jack's job was to serve and protect. He'd had this passion since that fateful day so many years ago when he'd called the police to come help his mother and his brother. He'd been too small to protect them, too little to stand up to his father like his brother had done. Well, tried to do. But he'd been big enough to grab the phone, dial the number, and hide in the pantry, hide from his father. Call and get help for his mother and his brother. Vow that when he grew up, when he was big enough and strong enough, he would protect people from bullies like his father. He would be a police officer and help people in need, just like those police officers did when they came to his house and pounded on the front door. Just like those police officers did when they bounded in, and his father finally, finally stopped beating his brother with the baseball bat. Just like those police officers did when they screamed at him to drop the bat, and the bat dropped to the floor with a thud, rolled across the orange linoleum, and settled into a pool of his mother's sticky blood. Just like those police officers did when his father picked up the shotgun they hadn't seen lying there. Just like those police officers did when they aimed their guns at his father, screaming at him to put down the shotgun, put it down, put it down, put it down when his father pointed the shotgun to his mother's already mangled head, mangled from the beatings from his brother's baseball bat, mangled and malformed from smashing it against her head again and again and again. Just like those police officers did when they screamed at him to put down the shotgun, but he cocked the shotgun instead, and they screamed at him to stop, and he laughed, a maniacal sick and twisted laugh and they shot him to death.

But not before he blew her beautiful face into nothingness.

Jack had taken that vow many years before he'd been sworn in as a deputy, and he had abided by that vow every single day of his career. But he had never had the chance to protect those three women who had died. And now Jack was not going to let another opportunity go by.

"Claire, you need to go stay with Shelly for a few days. Your best friend will take care of you while you sort things out."

"Jack, I can't just up and walk away. I have patients. Surgeries that can't — or shouldn't be postponed."

"Claire, your patients can wait. You need to get away for a little while."

She sighed. "You're probably right. It's just that right now just isn't a good time."

"It's never a good time, Claire."

She sighed again. "I guess I could have Lauren take over for me for a couple of days."

Jack allowed the silence to stretch out while Claire scrolled through her work schedule. "DeAngelo is going to have a conniption trying to reschedule all these."

"Claire, DeAngelo can handle it. You need some time off. When was the last time you took a couple days off?"

"It hasn't been *that* long. I was in South Africa a couple months ago with a few tough cleft palate cases. And I was in Ecuador with that sweet set of sisters who were born without ears..."

"Claire, I mean vacation time. Taking time off to just enjoy life for a bit."

"That is what I enjoy doing during my time off, Jack. There are so many kids, all over the world! If I just had a few more days off a year, I could..."

"Claire. I get it. I do. I truly do. Those kids are lucky to have you." He could almost hear her smiling through the phone. "Now, why don't you and Shelly head to the coast for a few days. Take a couple bottles of wine. Stay at GranNini's place. Put your feet up. Walk on the beach. Just take a few days to get out of town and forget about Ron for a little while."

He heard her sigh again.

"You're right. Maybe I could use a couple of down days. Are you sure GranNini wouldn't mind?"

Jack grinned. GranNini was his ace in the hole. Always had been, always will be. Claire always had a soft spot for GranNini. The feeling was quite mutual. GranNini excelled at making other people feel better with her endless chatter, her bottomless cookie jar, her squishy hugs, her shoulder to cry upon, and her warm, inviting home. GranNini collected strays, like some people collected snow globes. She welcomed them in, listened to their problems and doled out advice, all the while feeding them heaps and gobs of food and baked goodies. Every weekend she made brunch for whomever wanted, or needed, just a little extra lovin' for the day. Summers she spent in the garden or at the coast. Autumns she spent traveling the world. Thanksgiving through Christmas was a sight to behold at GranNini's house with all the people coming and going, and the mounds and mounds of cookies, candies, and tasty treats she whipped up every year. She spent tireless hours baking and cooking in the kitchen; always striving, and failing, to curb her insatiable sweet tooth. When she wasn't whipping up something in the kitchen, one could always find her either tending her vegetables and her flower garden, or typing on the computer, writing the beloved "GranNini and Me" children's stories.

Jack grinned. "No! Never! GranNini loves you, Claire." He choked up a bit, thinking of the months GranNini had spent comforting him when he finally realized that Claire had left him for good. His voice was quieter when he found it again. "She's always loved you."

Claire sniffled on the other end of the telephone call.

"Claire, honey? Did you hear me?"

"Yes." She cleared her throat. "Yes, that's probably a good idea."

"Do you need Shelly to come over and help you pack?"

"No, I can take care of that."

"It's just for a couple of days, Claire. And it's probably a good idea that you not tell Ron where you're going."

"What? Why?"

Jack hesitated and opted for the quick lie. He'd pay for it later, but he was already fairly deep into it by now. "Frankly, GranNini doesn't like Ron." He forced a sigh to make his lie seem to hold more truth.

"Just leave him a note that you're going to take a little break. That you just need some time to think and regroup. Just tell him you need some time off. Or lie and tell him that Shelly asked you to come over, that she needs you for something. Do you think he'll understand that?"

"Oh, I don't know, Jack." She sighed. "Maybe I should just get this over with. Confront him. Face this together. Get some counseling."

Jack's stomach clenched. "Claire, do this for me. Just this once. Can you please just go? Not tell him where, just take Shelly and head to the coast. For a couple of days. Figure out what you want to do. When all this has blown over, then you can talk with him and make a more well-informed decision."

He could hear Claire's brain processing this information, and he hoped she would consider and take his advice.

When she agreed, Jack sighed audibly. "Okay, good! Now, one last thing Claire — "

"Okay, what?" The wary tone of her voice made him second guess his next move.

"Claire, I think you should get tested for sexually transmitted infections."

The silence was abrupt. Jack lifted his phone from his ear — but she had ended the call. His heart clenched.

Perhaps he'd gone too far.

He wished he hadn't had to keep the full truth from her. He hated lying to her, of all people. But he didn't find it as difficult as it probably should have been to keep the information hidden that he suspected her husband of multiple murders. He had always wanted to keep the harsh truth of reality from her. She tended to take everything to heart, feeling each and every pain of everyone around her. It's what made her such a great surgeon. That's why it had taken him so long to confide his past to her. Every now and again when he looked at her, he could see his own pain reflected in the way she looked at him. He didn't need, nor want, that kind of reminder. He found it easier just to keep the information to himself. She had agreed to stay with Shelly, her best friend, for a few days. Perhaps she'd get a few days' respite before all the rest of her husband's misdeeds hit the fan.

Feeling down and frustrated by the negative aspects of his job as a Detective, he picked up the phone once again to handle the last bit of unpleasantness for the day. He liked the idea of having all the unpleasantness dealt with at once, leaving the rest of the day with the hope and possibility of being more uplifting. He dialed the number for Heather Allen, the woman he had almost run over on Larch Mountain, to give her the much-needed suggestion to skip town for a while. She didn't answer his call, so he left her a voice mail, and punched in the numbers for her work phone.

"I'm sorry Detective, is it? But Heather hasn't bothered to show up for work in the last couple of days."

Jack's stomach lurched. His intuition radar began to beep a warning. "Have you heard from her? Did she call in sick?"

"Well, she isn't here, so she's either sick, or out playing hooky again. But no, we haven't heard from her. At least *I* haven't. And she knows she's supposed to call *me* when she's going to be absent from work. It is my job, after all. She obviously couldn't be bothered to let us know what her plans are." She sighed audibly over the phone. "Can you please hold? I have another call."

Jack waited impatiently for the woman to finish their conversation. The elevator music played a saxophone solo version of Elton John's <u>Tiny Dancer</u>. Why couldn't they just play the original version of the song? Why did they have to butcher and mangle it? Jack shook his head in disgust.

The receptionist clicked back on, and started in on the conversation as if she'd never clicked off. "So anyway, like I was saying, she's not here. And if you ask me, she's getting pretty darned close to using up all of her personal time off. She took a couple days off a few weeks ago, you know, when she *fell* and *dislocated her elbow*."

Jack could swear he heard her put those few words in quotation marks. Her sarcastic tone of voice irked him. Clearly she did not believe Heather's elbow had actually been dislocated.

"I mean, who knows. She could have faked the whole thing. Putting make up on her arm and wincing every time she wiggled her fingers, pretending to take all that time off for physical therapy appointments when she was actually at home goofing off or something."

"Uh, her elbow was definitely dislocated. I was there right after it happened."

"Huh. Well. I don't know about that. But I do know that the boss is going to be pissed that she hasn't even bothered to call in sick. I mean, you know, she could get in trouble for that kind of stuff. I can only cover for her for so long." Then the receptionist whispered into the phone, her voice filled with undisguised glee, "She might even get fired!" The receptionist squeaked a little "Oh!" as if she'd just gotten caught with her hands in the cookie jar. "Hang on, I've got to get this." Before Jack could reply, she'd already clicked off the line to answer someone else's call.

Jack hung up the phone, not bothering to wait for the receptionist to get back on the line. His thoughts turned dark. He grabbed his jacket off the back of his chair, tapped Nick on the shoulder and motioned for him to follow. Nick ended his call, grabbed his own jacket and quick stepped it to catch up with Jack at the elevators.

"Where're we going?"

"Heather, my Larch Mountain vic?, isn't answering her phone."

Nick nodded slowly.

"And she hasn't shown up to work in the last couple of days."

Dread went for a stroll through the pit of Nick's stomach.

The two of them listened to the idle chatter of the elevator, grunting noncommittal responses, and willing the elevator to quit stopping on each and every floor on the way down. Nick smirked at the ogles that followed Jack wherever he went, always amazed at how oblivious he was to the whole thing. Either that, or how well he handled it without letting it show on his face.

They made it half way up the front steps to Heather's house-turned-apartment before the stench confirmed their worst fears. The detective shows on television at least got this part right. Nothing else in the world smelled like a dead human body.

Chapter 20

JACK KNOCKED UNNECESSARILY, and they waited impatiently for no one to answer. Nick pounded on the door, getting ready to bust the door in, and then just for good measure, he turned the knob. A look of surprise crossed his face when the door opened.

It didn't take them long to find her. They simply followed the stench. Her killer had left her swimming in the bathtub face down. Her elbow, perched over the edge of the tub, had been obviously re-dislocated at some point close to her death. Poor thing.

After a cursory run-through of her apartment, they headed outside. Nick called it in. Jack turned and sat down on the front stoop, picking up his cell phone to dial Monday's number. They didn't have to wait long before Ned Quon arrived.

"Hey look, it's Ryerson." Jack smiled as Ned closed the van's door and headed up the stairs.

"My name's not Ryerson, Jack."

Nick grinned, knowing Jack well enough to know that Jack would never let go now. Poor Ned was going to be stuck with the nickname forever. It wouldn't be long, he guessed, before the entire M.E.'s office was going to be calling Ned "Ryerson." He chuckled.

"So, what do we have?" Ned looked between Jack and Nick, his curiosity helping him move past the whole nickname fiasco.

"Don't know yet. We haven't looked." Jack winked at Nick behind Ned's back, his voice coming out all too nonchalant for the situation.

"So whydja call me down here so soon?" Ned seemed rather annoyed. He pushed his way past Nick, took three steps up the staircase and promptly took one step back down. "Ah. Someone's been dead in there for a bit."

Jack and Nick chuckled. Nick was astounded at Ned's naiveté. As if they'd ever let a medical examiner's technician into a crime scene without securing it up first.

"And that's why you're here." Jack looked at Nick, and then back to Ned. "Ryerson, we're dealing with a homicide here."

Ned nodded, and went back to his van, picked up his extra bag, and then headed back up the stairs. He put on his booties and gloved up, his camera handy. "Ready when you are. The rest of my team will be here in a bit." He glanced down the street as if half expecting to see them pulling up behind him.

Jack let Ned follow his nose up to Heather's bathroom. After the cursory examination and photos, Jack and Nick helped Ned remove her from the tub and placed her on the body bag on the bathroom tile floor. A diamond had been carved out of her chest — just like the others, and the marks on her neck gave them at least a cursory cause of death as strangulation. She matched the other murders.

Nick looked down at the gaping wound in her chest where the killer had carved out the obligatory diamond-shaped piece of skin and sing-songed, "Hey look! It's another diamond for Diamond!"

Jack punched Nick's arm.

Over the next hour or so, Jack and Nick supervised the team of criminalists and technicians who had invaded Heather's house, watching them dust fingerprint powder over every visible surface throughout her house. They acted like a locust invasion, searching everywhere for the one connection between the poor, dead woman upstairs and the yet-to-be-named serial killer. When his cell phone rang, Jack had been wrist-deep in the papers on Heather's desk, hunting for her cell phone. He saw Claire's face on his iPhone's caller-id, and almost put the call through to voice mail. He didn't have time for her right now. He was, after all, currently searching the home of her husband's lover, looking for evidence to put her husband away for the rest of his miserable life. How could he talk to her now?!

But loyalty won, and he pressed "answer."

"Jack. Come. Come now."

"Claire, honey, I'm in the middle of someth-"

"Jack. She's dead, Jack. Dead. She's floating. In the pool, Jack. And there's blood. Jack. She's floating. With her face under the water. She's dead. She's dead. She's dead." With each declaration, her voice had dropped to a mere whisper, and Jack had to plug his other ear just to hear her voice on the phone.

Jack snapped his fingers at Nick. No sound came out of his gloved fingers, but the quick movement was enough to wave Nick over.

"Claire? Where are you? Who's dead?"

Hearing the alarm in Jack's voice, Nick saddled up next to Jack and put his ear near Jack's iPhone so they could both listen.

"Shelly! She's dead! She's dead, Jack. She's dead."

"Claire honey, you're in shock. I want you to go sit down. Can you do that for me? Go find a place to sit down."

He could hear her sniffling, trying to squelch the torrent of tears that had begun to stream down her face.

"Claire, where does Shelly live?"

She sniffled, then took a shaky breath. "She's up on NW Vista." She took another deep breath. "The high rise. On the corner. Vista and um, Park Place." She dropped her voice to a near whisper. "Can you please hurry?"

Jack reassured her that he'd be there as soon as he could. Nick had already pulled out his work phone and was calling for back up.

"Ryerson? Where are you?"

Ned looked up, despite himself. He hollered down the stairs. "I'm just finishing up with her up here, Jack." He lowered his voice and talked to no one but himself. "And it's Quon, not Ryerson."

Jack took the stairs two at a time and found Ned zipping up the body bag. "Ryerson, I need you to bring your case," he nodded to the bag next to Ned, "and come with me." He looked around one last time, wondering what he was going to be missing by leaving the crime scene before he'd had the satisfaction of making sure he'd gone over every inch of the place. "And bring your team."

Ned raised his eyebrows. "You got another one?"

The three techs in the room all turned to stare at Jack. He nodded. The techs all turned to each other, impressed, and then went back to work.

Ned got up and spoke to the team he wanted to take with him, then asked two of his criminalists to transport the dead woman back to the ME's office. He stripped off his right glove and pulled his phone out of his pocket. "I'd better tell Liz."

Jack took one last look around and then honed in on Ned. "Tell Monday to call me when she's done talking with you. I've got to tell her I've got more Fibonacci numbers for her."

"Who's Monday?"

Jack smiled. "Your boss. The M.E. The big kahuna. Liz. Dr. Willner. Wee Willy. I call her Monday." Jack turned and headed back downstairs.

Ned frowned at the empty doorway and said, again to no one in particular, "I bet she doesn't like to be called Monday any more than I like being called Ryerson."

Jack's voice floated up the stairs and into the dead woman's bedroom. "Oh, and Ryerson? Don't take too long. I want to get the crime scene secured and assessed pronto!"

Chapter 21

NICK TOOK ONE look at the upturned body of the serial killer's last victim and blanched. "I've got to go, Diamond."

Jack looked up from his notebook, curious. "Why?" Jack looked around at the techs and criminalists who were just now starting to arrive and place their gear around Shelly's pool. "We need you!"

Nick stepped closer to Jack and stage whispered into his ear. "I have got to go and start checking out those credit card receipts on our suspect. Then I've got to log into Telestaff and check the staff records on the patrol log to see which of those evenings he called in sick." He took one last look at Shelly's carved chest and battered legs, and gave Jack a long and hard look. "I can't let him do this again, Jack. He's getting out of control. They're happening faster and faster, and he's being more brutal with each one."

Jack's eyes flitted over to the bruises between Shelly's legs, and then back up to Nick. He nodded his head. "Call me as soon as you get *anything*."

Jack watched Nick's long strides as he headed out the door and watched with surprise when

Monday stepped through the very door Nick had just vacated.

He strode over and met her half way.

"Hey there, Monday." He smiled down at her pretty face. "Finally catch a break in your busy day?"

Monday squeezed Jack's arm. Her smile didn't quite meet her eyes. "Been a rough one." She let her eyes wander to the corpse. "Wow. Four bodies already, huh?"

"She's the fifth, Monday."

"What?!"

"Ryerson just sent the fourth off to your office not more than an hour ago."

"Don't call him that." She swatted him on the arm. He chuckled, and then realized where he was.

He gave a noncommittal "Hmmm," and looked over at the dead woman lying on the cold, wet cement floor.

"So how did I miss the fourth?"

"Ryerson took the case, said you were tied up with a bad one."

Monday glanced away, admiring the pretty garden through the glass windows. "Yeah." She winced. "Shaken baby. Three weeks old."

"Sonofabitch. Who did it? Stressed out mom? Or baby daddy?"

"I think they said it was the uncle. He was only babysitting for a couple of hours. Couldn't handle an eight pound baby crying, I guess."

"Sonofabitch."

"At least it wasn't worse."

"Worse than shaking a baby to death?!"

Monday slid her gaze over to Jack's and let it linger.

"Ah." He swallowed the thick lump that had formed in his throat. "Well that's at least a relief. At least the poor kid didn't have to worry about sexual assault at the ripe old age of three weeks old." His sarcasm echoed through the vaulted ceiling of the pool room.

"Like I said, at least it wasn't worse." She let her gaze land once more on the dead woman lying in front of the pool. "So tell me, before I get to work on number five there," she nodded to the body, "who was victim number four?" She pulled out her iPad and began to type in notes.

"Name was Heather Allen. She was an assault victim a while ago. I happened to, erm, run into her up on Larch Mountain as she was running away from the guy. She ended up with a dislocated elbow and some lacerations, but all in all she faired pretty well, considering. Guess the bad guy came back and finished the job."

Monday's face grew dark.

"We found her in her bathtub a couple hours ago. Looks like she died the same way as all the rest."

"Diamond cut out of her chest as well?"

"Unfortunately."

"Hmmm." She let the information sink in as she scanned the pool area. "I'll take good care of them, Jack."

"You always do, Mon."

Jack's eyes scanned the room until they found Claire. The chaplain had wrapped her up in a big blanket and was comforting her with soft, friendly assurances. He seemed to be leading her out of the room.

Monday scrutinized Jack. She'd seen that look on his face before, and worry lines began to form between her eyebrows.

Jack tore his gaze away and turned his attention back onto Monday. "What?!"

"You know what."

"Yeah," he sighed, "I know."

"She's married, Jack."

"I know."

Monday squeezed his arm. "You okay if I…"

"Absolutely. Hop to it."

Chapter 22

THE HOURS FLEW by as Jack, Monday, the criminalists and technicians scanned, searched, and took evidence from the pool area. Jack watched as they bagged and toted off Claire's best friend. Monday caught his eye and waved goodbye from across the room. Jack jogged over to meet her.

"Hey Mon, I was wondering if you could do a favor for me."

Monday nodded to her transport team, giving them permission to load the body into the awaiting truck. She slid her iPad into her purse and looked up into his face. "Anything, Jack. You know that."

"Could you please give Claire a scrip for something to help her relax? Something that might make her sleep for a little while? Let her rest for a bit? She's been through a lot today."

"Absolutely. She could probably benefit from a mild sedative. She dug around in her giant purse, more fondly known by her staff as "the great big bag of everything," searching for her prescription pad. "Is she currently taking any medications?"

Jack shook his head. "I have no idea. You'll have to ask her."

Monday studied her friend's face for a long moment. She put the pad and pen back into her purse. Then she scanned the pool area. "Where is she?"

Jack looked around, surprised he hadn't noticed her leave. "I don't know. The lobby maybe?"

Monday nodded. She squeezed Jack's hand. "I'll see if I can find her upstairs before I head out. If I don't find her, I'll text you, and we'll work something out."

"Thanks, Mon. I owe you one."

She smiled, and headed out the door, not wanting the transport team to have to wait too long for her to join them, accompanying the body back to the ME's office for the autopsy.

Jack made a final run through, making sure he hadn't missed anything significant. He answered a few of the technician's questions, and got updates from a few others. Most everyone had already begun to pack up, preparing to begin anew upstairs. He could tell the new team members from the ones who'd been around for a while. The newbies bounced slightly on their toes, talking excitedly to one another. The ones that had been around for a while all seemed to act a bit sluggish. It was going to be a long day. Jack smiled. What an old salt he'd become, already rueing the hours of tedious work he knew were coming. With one last look around, Jack made his way out of the pool area and back to the apartment lobby. Jack headed over to the chaplain and Claire, wanting to get her settled in before heading upstairs with the rest of the team to Shelly's apartment.

He knelt down beside her and reached for her hand. It was surprisingly cool to the touch. His own felt clumsy and oafish holding her thin, dainty fingers. He pressed his house key into her palm. She looked at him, her gaze vacant and unseeing.

"What's this?"

"It's a key to my place. Why don't you head there, get yourself some rest. Take a nap. Grab something to eat from the fridge. There's some leftover lasagna in there I made the other day."

Claire grimaced at the thought of food.

"Honestly, it's pretty good, even if I do say so myself!"

Claire looked up and patted his hand. "Oh, I know, Jack. You're a good cook. Honestly. GranNini taught you well." She smiled softly, then looked back down at her hands, rotating the key back and forth between her fingers. "I just can't imagine eating at a time like this."

Jack nodded his head. Claire always lost her appetite at the slightest offense. He never truly understood this habit of hers. He never lost his appetite. He could eat a sloppy joe while watching an autopsy and still have room for seconds. But he understood her grief and all that entailed.

"Well if you change your mind, there's other stuff in there too. Piece of fruit, some cucumbers. There's a loaf of banana bread on the counter I baked yesterday. Whatever. It's yours."

Claire nodded her head.

"I'll just have one of the deputies run you over to my place. You go straight to the back, and crawl on into bed. You'll feel better after you get some sleep." He lifted his hand and let the palm of his hand rest on her oh so soft cheek. Then all too soon, he slipped his hand back into his pocket.

Claire nodded her head once more, still staring at the key between her fingers.

"Did Monday stop by on her way out?"

"Who?"

"Dr. Willner?"

The puzzled look on her face straightened into pleasure. "Oh! The nice doctor, tiny little thing? The one who gave me this?"

Jack glanced down at the small, square piece of paper she unfolded from her pocket.

He recognized the scrip and smiled. "Yes, that's the one." He glanced over to the lobby doors and eyed two deputies, quietly chatting with one another. "Claire, I'll get one of the deputies to take you to a pharmacy to fill that prescription, and then have them take you home."

She nodded her head, and then squeezed Jack's hand in gratitude.

Jack stood up and pressed his hand to the chaplain's shoulder. "Thank you."

The older man smiled and reached up to shake Jack's hand. "Just doin' my job."

Jack shook his hand and headed over to one of the Portland Police officers who had been standing guard in the apartment lobby. The officer started to raise his eyebrow out of curiosity and innuendo at Jack's request to transport Claire, but, after getting elbowed in the ribs by his wiser and more worldly partner, he straightened his shoulders and wiped his face clean of all emotion. Jack cleared his throat and gave the officer his address, quite aware of the officer's slight. He explained that he'd given Claire a key, took one last look at the beautiful woman grieving over the whole mess, turned back to thank the officer and his partner, and then headed upstairs to Shelly's apartment.

Chapter 23

JACK SPENT THE better part of an hour searching for Shelly's cell phone, purse and computer. After coming up with nothing, he began poking through her kitchen drawers, bedside table, and the end tables next to her living room couch looking for Shelly's boyfriend's telephone number. Her boyfriend was obviously not Shelly's next of kin, so Jack wouldn't be able to tell him about Shelly's death until they had notified her next of kin — unless, of course, he showed up at the apartment, demanding to know what the police were doing there tossing the place. However, Jack could contact him as Claire's private investigator, to determine if he had more information or some sort of physical evidence connecting each of the victims to Sergeant Ron Wilcox. Jack chastised himself for not contacting the P.I. sooner. The P.I. had been on his list of people to contact since he'd walked out of the conference room earlier that morning. But he had called Claire, then Heather, then found himself firmly ensconced in two separate crime scenes in just a few short hours. There simply hadn't been enough time. The whole case was snowballing out of his control and Jack felt the stress of it all coming down, and coming down hard, upon his shoulders.

Jack took a look around at Shelly's apartment and suddenly felt claustrophobic. He rubbed his hands through his hair, and then strode over to the nearest officer.

"I've got to get out of here for a little bit. I'm going to head down to Zupan's, grab a sandwich or something. Can I get you something?"

The officer blushed her pleasure. "Um, yeah. A sandwich would be great!"

Distracted, Jack nodded his head, and made his way to the front door.

"Maybe a soda as well?" The officer's cheeks turned a slightly darker shade of pink, but Jack never even noticed. She wasn't even sure he'd heard her, as he seemed completely distracted and consumed by this case. Her stomach growled, and she peeked at her phone, wondering what time it was. She watched Jack take one last look at Shelly's living room before shutting the door behind him. No one noticed when she sighed her disappointment.

Jack opened the front door to Shelly's apartment complex and stepped into the grey. GranNini always called this kind of Oregon rain "mizzle," a true cross between a mist and a drizzle. Like walking through a cloud, the air seemed to seep out moisture, causing glasses and windshields to fog, hair to frizzle, and sidewalks and freeways to grow more slick. Jack never minded the Oregon rain. Even though it seemed to permeate the essence of Oregon nine months out of the year, leaving many Oregonians and misplaced Californians negatively affected by the lack of direct sunlight, Jack found the grey comforting. The mizzle left a clean, fresh smell in the air and turned everything in Oregon a lovely shade of green. He understood, logically, why some people found central Oregon more physically attractive, with the sunny weather and the dry desert scenes. He, too, enjoyed spelunking in the lava tubes in the hot, dry summers; climbing the face of Smith Rock; biking the myriad trails. He loved skiing up on Mt. Bachelor in the winters. But all things considered, Jack still preferred the damp grey skies of beautiful Portland. Honestly, in all his travels, he had never found a place more beautiful, or more appealing, than Portland and the whole Pacific Northwest.

Jack made his way downhill on Vista toward Burnside, his feet slipping and sliding on the mossy slick sidewalks. He purchased a variety of sandwiches, fruits, and drinks for the folks on duty, and lugged his haul back up to the lobby of Shelly's building, his thoughts working through the details of this complicated case. The flustered and stressed apartment manager hurried to assist Jack in setting up one of the empty apartments as a break room, of sorts, for the deputies and technicians, trying not too subtly to avoid scaring his current residents by an overwhelming presence of deputies and police officers in the apartment lobby. It was bad enough they'd taken over the entire floor of Shelly's apartment, the apartment lobby, as well as the pool area. Jack assured the manager that the officers would be gone before the evening was over, and the manager sighed his relief. Jack assigned another deputy to reinterview the apartment manager, both to uncover any new information that the manager had forgotten, or neglected, to mention during his initial interview immediately following the discovery of Shelly's body, but also to help answer the manager's questions. As Jack made his way out of the apartment, he overheard snippets of their conversation as the manager asked the deputy how soon the building would be returned to its normal state, whom the manager could contact regarding the vapid state of the pool area, and whether or not a special organization existed to clean and sanitize pools after one found a dead body floating in it.

Chapter 24

BY THE TIME Jack made it back to his office, the place had been abandoned. It never ceased to amaze him how fast the county workers that filled the place with noise, and life, and vitality during the day could scatter, the instant the clocks turned to five. He made his way up the elevators, surprised to actually miss the pathetic elevator music. His brain numb and overused from the long and tedious day, he mindlessly flashed his key card in front of the box to the right of the security door leading to the detectives offices, waited for the light to turn green and the door to unlock with a click, and let himself in.

The cubicles had been abandoned several hours before. The whole place felt eerily quiet. The faint hum of a distant vacuum cleaner couldn't compete with the echoing emptiness left by the lack of ringing telephones and the missing murmur of a dozen people all talking at once, solving crimes and making the world a better place. Jack made his way through the maze of cubes, and looked up, startled by the strange sliver of light eking out of the conference room. One of the slats from the louvered blinds had landed askew leaving a tiny opening, and through the small space, Jack could just make out the conference table covered in paperwork. Then Nick entered the window, pacing back from one of the tables to the other, his hands filled with more paper.

Jack altered his course and knocked on the conference room door.

"I'm busy. Go away."

"Nick, it's Jack." He tried the door, but couldn't get the knob to turn.

"Jack? Thank God you're back!"

With a ruffle of metal as the louvered blinds swished out of the way and back again, Nick unlocked the conference door, and let Jack in. The heat and stench of Nick's body odor were strong enough to make Jack want to take a step, or two, or more, back out into the hallway. But Nick glanced through the door, making sure no one else followed Jack, and then quickly locked them both back in.

"Quite a project you have going on here, Nick."

"Jack! Jack, listen! We've got ourselves a humdinger here."

The manic in Nick's voice worried Jack. He glanced around the room and spotted several empty disposable coffee cups. "Have you eaten anything since I saw you last?"

Nick looked around, distracted. "I don't think so. But listen, Jack, just listen, we've got to go through this. I do not like what I'm seeing here."

"Shall we go get you something to eat and we can talk about it there?"

"No, no, I can't leave all this! Someone could come across it, and then we'd be in a world of trouble!" Nick looked around again, as if he was afraid someone was going to steal his favorite toy.

Jack frowned. Nick had obviously found something significant. He worried that it could mean only one thing.

"Nick, just give it to me straight. Did he do it? Did Ron Wilcox kill those women?"

Nick stopped pacing around the table, placing the small sticky notes in piles, and looked up. He took a step back and then allowed his brain to slow down and stop. Really stop. He half sat, half collapsed into the chair against the conference room wall, and then took a deep breath. "Yeah. I actually think he mighta."

Jack sighed. He ran his hands through his hair and rubbed his face, taking a good, long look around at the conference room table and the myriad piles of paper stacked throughout. "So can you walk me through this quickly?"

Nick nodded his head, and then stood up, revitalized. "So here's where it all starts. These, he pointed to one stack, are Ron's credit card receipts."

Nick proceeded to explain, in detail, the connections between Ron and each of the four victims. The task force team had highlighted the credit card receipts from each of the victims using the PI's information to narrow down their searches. And even though none of the women had met up with Ron at the same bar or restaurant, the pattern had been the same with each woman. Forty-three minutes later, they had sorted and organized the information into three hole punched plastic, color-coded file folders, and placed all the file folders into a large three-ring binder. Exhausted, Jack grabbed the binder as Nick turned off the light and they headed toward the elevator doors.

"So when are you going to tell Larry and Manny that Ron's our guy?"

"I'll give Manny a call on the way to the restaurant. He, Larry and the Chief Deputy will all want to meet in person tonight to discuss this and to get our ducks in a row. We'll grab something to eat while they make their way here, then we can head back here to meet up with them."

"Do we really have enough to ask them to approve a search warrant for his house and car?"

Nick looked down at the files in his hand and then back up at Jack. "Yep. I think so. I'll get working on the new warrant as soon as we get their approval, and while we wait for Ron to come in."

"Do you think he'll come in quietly?"

"He has to. If he gets squirrelly, Manny will order him in. If it really looks like he's going sideways, he'll send a couple of detectives and a marked car to help assure his quiet and willing participation. But I don't think it'll come to that. Once he gets here, standard policy is to take his badge and gun, put him under admin leave, and have the detectives sit him down to question him." Nick pressed the down button on the elevator's panel. "Then we go from there."

Jack furrowed his eyebrows. "Do you really think he'll come in quietly?"

Nick took a deep breath and slowly nodded to the floor. "As long as he doesn't get tipped off that we're on to him." He looked up sharply, his eyes boring holes in Jack's pink cheeks. "Did you advise Claire not to…"

Jack nodded his head, avoiding Nick's eyes as he spoke to the elevator doors. "She won't say anything. She's in too much of a shock as it is." He cleared his throat. The elevator doors slid open and the two stepped in. "Besides, I had Monday slip her a little something so she could sleep."

Too wrapped up in their own worries, neither of them noticed Larry's head poking out of the bathroom door. Nor did they notice, after the elevator doors slid shut, as Larry pulled out his phone and pressed the numbers that would soon alter the course of the investigation in a way that no one would have predicted.

Chapter 25

JACK DROPPED HIS sandwich, half-eaten, onto his plate and shoved the plate away from him. Exhaustion crippled his appetite, the desire for sleep overpowered his hunger.

"Something wrong with your sandwich, hon?" The waitress' worried look snapped him out of his reverie.

He gave her a brief smile and shook his head. "Just not as hungry as I thought. Could you please bring us the check?"

She scooped up the plate in her spare hand, swinging the decaf coffee pot she wore as an accessory in the other, and eyed the two weary men at her favorite booth. "Sure, hon. Is there anything else I can get for you? Some coffee maybe?" She proffered her favorite pot, but he shook his head.

"Just the check."

"Sure thing."

As she sauntered off with his dirty dishes, Jack took a deep breath and closed his eyes. If he'd been at home, he would have been half way to dreamland by now. Rubbing his face, he cocked open an eye and took a good long look at Nick. He looked as exhausted as Jack felt.

"How much longer is it going to take them to get Ron back to the office?"

Nick pulled his phone out of his pocket and checked the time. "We're still a ways off yet. We're lucky we got Judge Bennett this late at night. She's always happy to sign warrants against police who think of themselves as above the law. That will speed things up. But, even with that in mind, it is just three o'clock in the morning. Even Judge Bennett takes a while to wake up and get her noggin going when it's still too far from oh-dark-thirty to be awake." He clicked off his phone and put it back in his pocket. "And you heard Manny. He's not sure how Ron's going to handle the news when we do get around to showing up at his place and convincing him to make his way on down here."

Jack nodded, then settled his head against the back of the booth once more.

"Diamond, you look like death warmed over."

"Gee thanks. If I didn't feel like death warmed over, I might have to punch you." He yawned, rubbing his eyes. "How much longer do you think it'll be before he gets here? I want to be the lead on Ron's interrogation."

Nick guffawed. "Absolutely not."

"Why not?" Jack winced at the whiny, petulant tone of his own voice.

"You're kidding, right?"

Jack raised his eyebrow and glared at Nick.

"Jack, you're too close to this. You're exhausted. Look at yourself for Christ's sake! You're a wreck!"

Jack rubbed his face and stifled another yawn, disappointed that his body had betrayed him.

"Seriously. Go home. Take a cat nap. I'll call you when Ron gets here so you can listen in on my interrogation. It'll be a few hours yet before things really get rollin'."

Jack didn't respond, and for a moment, Nick thought he'd actually fallen asleep.

"Jack?"

"All right, all right! I'm goin'!" Jack stood up and pulled some cash out of his wallet, dropping it on the table. "Call me as soon as Ron gets there. I'll be back before he can swear to his grandma's first cousin that he had nothin' to do with this."

Nick chuckled and waved the waitress back over as Jack made his way out of the restaurant.

Jack hadn't even made it five minutes down the road before his work phone chirped at him. He clicked the button on his bluetooth headset and answered, "All right, all right! I'm turning my rig around right now!"

"Jack?"

"Nick?"

"No, it's Pete."

"Pete?"

"Pete Spencer? From the Dive Team?"

"Oh! Pete!" Jack stifled a yawn. "What are you doing up so late, Pete?"

"We've got a dive call out, Jack."

Jack groaned. "Well, shit. Another woman?" He looked around, trying to figure out where he was. He'd been driving on autopilot and had temporarily lost his bearings. He turned on his blinker and moved to the right lane, preparing to exit the freeway.

"Nope, we've got a stolen dump in the Columbia."

Jack instantly relaxed and tried, then failed, to stifle another yawn. "Pete, I'm too stinkin' tired to deal with a dumped, stolen vehicle in the Columbia River. Can you and Max handle this one?" He slowed his car down as he made his way up the off ramp, heading — at long last — toward home.

"Well, um, we need you on this one, Jack."

"Dammit, Pete! Can't you *just this once* handle a stupid stolen dump? Call the damned tow truck, throw on your suit, wade into the Columbia, hook the sucker up, and watch it all come magically out of the water. Boom, you're done. It's not that complicated!" Jack's tires squealed as he turned the corner a bit too quickly.

The silence that followed created a bitter taste in Jack's mouth. He regretted his temper the instant he realized he'd lost it. He loathed losing his temper. Losing his temper reminded him all too much that he was a simple product of genetics. He was, whether or not he prayed every single day of his life he was not, his father's son.

"Pete, I'm..."

"I know, Jack."

Pete's quiet acceptance merely made Jack feel that much worse. "No, really, Pete. I'm sorry. I shouldn't have lost my temper like that. It was completely inappropriate and unprofessional. I apologize."

"Jack, it's fine."

"No, it's not fine. I'm just so bone-numbingly tired, Pete. This whole serial killer thing is getting to me, man. I've got five dead bodies, and everything is piling up around me. I just can't seem to hold it all together any more." Jack pulled over into a gas station, and parked the car in the lot next to the convenience store. He put the car in park and stifled the urge to sob.

Pete allowed the silence to surround them both, providing Jack a sense of comfort, and allowing himself a moment to rethink his approach.

"Jack, I know it's been tough. Everyone knows how hard you've been working on this. You, Nick, the task force, you've all been putting in so many hours, it's crazy."

Jack buried his face in his steering wheel.

"But Jack, I really think you need to come down here."

"Pete, I…"

"Jack. I wouldn't ask, really, I wouldn't, if it wasn't important." Pete swallowed the hard lump that grew ever larger with each time his mind's eye flashed back onto what he had seen under the water. "This isn't just any normal stolen dump, Jack." His heart began to beat impatiently against his chest as fear slowly snaked its way back up his chest. When he finally got the words out, his voice was little more than a whisper. He didn't want anyone to overhear him. "It's a patrol car, Jack. One of ours."

Jack's heart jerked. "What?!"

"Call came in just a little bit ago. The caller was putting in his boat at the Columbia office boat ramp. Said his boat hit something. He went out to take a look — see if he'd damaged his boat, hit a rock or something. Peered into the murky water and said he thought he saw what looked like the bumper of a car." Pete let the information sink in. "He didn't get a good look at it. Pissed him off, though. Now he has to put in at Chinook Landing."

"So how do you know it's one of ours?" Jack was already backing out of the parking lot and headed right onto 33rd up toward Marine Drive.

"Portland Police was first on scene. Officer went down to the boat ramp, flashed his mag light on the bumper, saw the word 'Sheriff' stared right back up at him. Freaked him out."

Jack swore under his breath. He wasn't going to be able to contain the scene if he had to deal with both Portland Police gossip and Multnomah County rumors.

"Shea was next to arrive. She went down there, saw the same thing. Told the Portland guy not to say anything. Called the rest of the Dive Team."

Jack relaxed an inch. "Good thinking. She okay?"

Pete nodded, turning his face back to Shea's, and watching her shaking hands grip her coffee mug too tightly. Then, realizing Jack couldn't see his nod, he spoke into the phone. "Yeah. We're okay."

Jack could hear the stress and anxiety in Pete's voice, but couldn't do much to alleviate the situation. "How did someone get a hold of one of our rigs?"

"That's a good question."

Jack reached down to pull up the information on his MDC, keeping his eyes on the road as much as possible while his fingers fumbled across the keyboard. "Has anything come up on the MDC?"

"Not as far as I know."

"Is the rest of the Dive Team there at the Columbia River office?"

"Not yet. They're on the way in. Shea has been on the phone coordinating everything. I offered to get you on the phone."

"'K." Jack started plotting out the dive in his head. A million questions ran through his mind, each one more important than the rest. "Did the caller see the car go in?"

"Don't think so, at least the dispatcher didn't say."

"Were the lights on?"

"The lights?"

"Yeah. Did you see the car's tail lights on when you were out there?"

"Um, no, I don't think so. Hang on." Pete muffled the phone up against his jacket and Jack could barely hear him asking Shea the same question. "Shea says she thought she saw a faint glow of the tail lights when she pulled up to the River Patrol office, but by the time she got down to the car they weren't on any more."

Pete muffled the phone once again, and then Shea's voice came through. "Jack? It's Shea. Yeah, the tail lights were out by the time I got down there. Looks like whoever stole the car, dumped the car at least an hour ago, and then took off by foot right after. I didn't see anyone lurking around the parking lot — I checked. And no one was in the parking lot when I arrived except the Portland officer. Bad guy either took off by foot, or had a buddy come pick him up. Here's Pete again."

Jack nodded his head, plotting out his plan for the upcoming dive. It never ceased to amaze him how quickly the adrenaline in his system could kick in, and erase all traces of his exhaustion. "Pete? I'll be there in about twelve minutes or so, depending on traffic. Can you please get my dive gear laid out if you get there before I do?"

"Will do, boss."

"Pete?"

"Yeah, boss?"

"I'd like you to take the lead on this one. I'll be your safety diver."

The brief silence that followed only convinced Jack further that he needed to have that long-overdue conversation with Pete about his involvement with the Dive Team sooner rather than later. Jack rubbed his face with his hand and peered out into the darkness. Just not tonight. He was too damn overworked and over tired to do it tonight.

"Oh, and Pete?"

"Yeah, boss?"

"I really am sorry I yelled at you."

Pete allowed the apology to sink in. He truly loved working for the Sheriff's Office Dive Team, and admired working with Jack. Only rarely had he ever witnessed Jack losing his temper, and never had he been on the stinging end of Jack's barbed tongue. Pete wanted to take a few moments to replay the conversation in his head, trying to figure out what he'd said that had triggered Jack's ire. He never wanted to make that same mistake again. Just as he began to go over his side of the conversation, he jolted, realizing he had left the silence linger for too long. He cleared his throat. "No problem. See you in a bit."

Chapter 26

JACK COULD BARELY make out the green patrol car's bumper, so eerily out of place under pitch black water. His mag light caught the reflective stickers of the bright golden SHERIFF letters on the right end of the bumper. His hopes that the rumors that the dumped, stolen car might not be that of a Sheriff's Office patrol car disappeared into the murky waters, like the rest of the car. He pointed his light toward the license plate, but couldn't make out the numbers. Nor could he make out the letters and numbers on the left side of the bumper. No chance, then, of identifying whose car it was until Pete got into the water and could read the numbers up close.

Max opened the River Patrol office door and met him at the top of the stairs, a banana in her hand. Jack trotted up the stairs and took the proffered fruit with a tired smile, holding the door open for her and following her inside. His team knew him so well. He liked to eat a snack before diving, especially before diving at night when his senses needed to be working doubly hard.

The place seemed eerily empty without the River Patrol staff monitoring the dispatch channels and the local river traffic radio channels. They'd left reminders of their presence throughout the office.

Coffee mugs and water bottles sat at nearly every station. Orange River Patrol jackets and black PFDs slung to the back of every squeaky rolling chair. The smell of diesel fuel and stale air clung to the smeared windows. Duct tape created a mosaic pattern on the carpet, serving to hold the larger pieces of the tattered carpet together. Extension cords were duct taped to the floor in long strips, to prevent people from tripping. The office was in serious need of upgrading. Unfortunately for River Patrol, the Hansen Building which housed the patrol units — condemned several years ago for asbestos and black mold — was higher on the list for improvements. Rumors circulated that the budget would soon find its way toward the Hansen Building, and then trickle on down to the River Patrol offices. But one never knew how long it might take for those plans and all that money to make its way into practical application.

"Who all has been notified?"

"River Patrol and Portland Police were called at the same time we were."

"None of the River Patrol is here yet?" Jack peeled the banana and peered out the windows, trying to get a look at the car from up above.

"Not yet. But Portland's here."

"Yeah, I saw the Portland Police officer gawking as I pulled in. Any witnesses see the car go in?"

"Not as far as we know."

"We have got to keep this whole thing quiet, Max." He examined her face thoroughly, wanting to make sure she knew the seriousness of the situation. Jack nodded, convinced that she, at least, could remain completely professional, even in the most dire of all circumstances. Max always took her job seriously.

"Where's the rest of the team?"

"Out in the dive van, pulling it around, getting gear together."

Jack pointed to the bathroom with the remains of his banana. "I've got to head in there for a minute. Can you head outside? See if you can get the Portland officer to close down the boat ramp?"

Max bit her lip, embarrassed that she hadn't already thought of that. "Sure thing." She bounded out of the office, chastising herself for her simple error. By the time she'd made it out of the River Patrol office and down the cement steps, two more Portland Police cars had shown up, lights flashing. She strode confidently over to the nearest car. "Which one of you is in charge here?"

Eyeing the spitfire in her eyes, the Portland Police officer bit the smirk off at the corner of his mouth and pointed to the car next to his. He watched in admiration, noting her tight little ass marching itself around his patrol car and over to his sergeant's car.

"Ma'am, are you in charge of these other officers here?"

The Portland Police sergeant stepped out of her car and eyed the woman in front of her, raising her eyebrows. "We got a call there was a dumped stolen car at the boat ramp." She shined her search light down toward the water's edge. The car wasn't visible from this angle. "Are the rumors true? About it being a Sheriff's Office patrol car?"

Max straightened her already rigid posture, and took command of the situation. "Ma'am, I need to take you in my confidence here. Yes, we have a dumped stolen car right there at the end of the boat ramp. But ma'am," Max swallowed, trying not to allow the myriad thoughts that scrambled through her brain interfere with her professionalism. "I am going to need you to keep this completely off the air for now." Max nodded toward the water. "I'm afraid we have ourselves a delicate situation here. The car is, in fact, one of ours."

"A patrol car??"

"Yes, Ma'am. Most of our people haven't arrived yet, but they're on their way. In no time at all, we're going to be short staffed, and we could really use your help." Max watched the sergeant's face as the color drained from her face, instantly understanding the negative implications of having someone steal a county patrol car and dump it in the river. Sympathy at their troubles and relief that the car wasn't one of hers played on the woman's face.

"Could you and your officers here," Max pointed to the two patrol cars flanking her on either side, "please shut down the boat ramp and only let in essential Multnomah County personnel?"

Sympathy won over, and the sergeant nodded. "Absolutely."

"Oh, and Sergeant? I hate to ask, but could you please also have them start redirecting the traffic on Marine Drive? Those fishermen are not going to be happy when we tell them we've closed down the boat ramp. They're going to have to put in at Chinook Landing."

The sergeant nodded her head, noting the two trucks with boats that had made their way into the parking lot while they had started talking.

"I'm sure I don't need to tell you that this all needs to stay completely quiet. No one can know about this until we get it all sorted out."

Chewing the inside of her cheek, the Portland sergeant silently wished the deputy good luck with that whole concept. She was quite certain that the scuttle butt was probably already making its way around the Portland Police Bureau, if not the Sheriff's Office as well.

"Oh! I just thought of something else... once this parking lot starts filling up with lights and sirens, I'm sure the media will eventually find its way here. Could you please direct them elsewhere?"

"Easy enough." She nodded over to the restaurant next door. "They can take over the Sextant's lot." She looked up, admiring the stars above them. "At least you won't have to worry about the media's helicopters."

"No helicopters? Why not?"

The sergeant nodded up the hill, across Marine Drive toward the field. "Portland International

Airport has this whole place permanently closed to air traffic."

Max bit her lip, once more chastising herself for not knowing the obvious. Portland International Airport was located directly across the street from the Columbia River Boat Ramp's parking lot.

The sergeant put out her hand, and Max shook it. "If you need anything else, you just let us know."

"Thanks."

As Max headed toward the Dive Team's van, she could hear the Portland Police cars already making their way over to the entry way to the Columbia River Boat Ramp's parking lot entrance, preparing to shut things down. She looked over her shoulder, pleased to see one of the cars heading toward the two parked trucks and boats. Then she smiled when she saw two county cars heading into the lot.

She postponed her trip to the dive van, and waited for the cars to park. Like synchronized swimmers, the cars drove in side by side, the drivers' doors slammed simultaneously. Jack jogged down the steps and waited with her.

"Thanks for coming so fast." Jack shook hands with Miles and Ju-Tau as they made their way toward the commotion. Miles Trusnik and Ju-Tau Chin formed the solid base of the river patrol team. Both had worked for the Sheriff for a handful of years, and both enjoyed the quiet solitude that working on the river patrol offered. They'd formed an easy partnership on the river, taking turns — one being the skipper on the boat, the other being the deck hand.

Summers on the river could prove to be tricky, with extra long hours, drunken boaters to contend with, performing boat safety examinations — making sure all boaters stayed up to code with their registration papers, personal flotation devices, lights, whistles and so forth; assisting stranded boaters and jet skiers, homeland security checks, dealing with water traffic during suicide bridge-jumper season, endless reports to write, and the political drama of the various boating clubs throughout the Portland metropolitan area. But winters on the river stayed pretty quiet, and even in the spring not much happened until the Spring Chinook fishing run started up. They were only three days into the run, and already Miles and Ju-Tau found themselves excited about the prospect of something fun and interesting to do on the river, other than watching fishers sit in their boats in the middle of the Columbia River all day, even if it meant they'd only be watching from a boat on the river as someone else had the fun part of pulling a car out of the water.

"No problemo. So what's up? You got another dumped stolen?" Miles let his gaze wander over to the boat ramp. His car's headlights lit up the scene, but the sunken car wasn't visible from up where they were standing.

"You'll need to call your sergeant and lieutenant. Get them down here."

Miles and Ju-Tau exchanged a look. Jack's tone of voice raised the hairs on the back of Miles' neck.

"Got something hinky going on?" Ju-Tau's no-nonsense attitude kept things simple and to the point.

"Looks like it's one of ours."

"Well, crap!" Miles blanched. Ju-Tau furrowed his brows, gazing down toward the water.

"I'll get on the line." Ju-Tau jogged up the stairs and headed straight for the telephones. Miles put his hands in his jacket pocket and hunched his shoulders over.

Max bit her lip and looked toward the dive van, watching Pete slip into his dive gear, wondering who was going to get to be his safety diver. She couldn't remember if it was her turn yet. Probably not. Frowning, she turned her attention back to Jack and Miles.

"I'm going to need you and Ju-Tau to take out a boat, keep river traffic away from the boat ramp while Pete's diving."

Miles nodded his head. "What about the Coast Guard?"

Jack swore under his breath again. "Have they contacted you already?"

"No, but I've only been listening to the scuttlebutt on our radio, not the river channels. I'm sure it's just a matter of time." He let his eyes wander back toward the water's edge.

They both jumped when Shea Julian joined their conversation. "Sorry. Didn't mean to startle you. Jack? We're ready for you."

"Thanks, Shea. I'll be there in a couple of minutes."

As the oldest member of the Multnomah County Dive Team, Shea had years of personal experience watching the nonverbal behaviors of the men in her life, and could almost instinctually understand when she should stick around and when she should walk away. As a professional stay-at-home mom for most of her adult life, Shea had raised three incredible young men. All three of her sons stood well over six feet tall with blond, curly hair like their father's. And all three of them had fought and scuffled and disagreed as siblings do. Shea stood along beside them and watched, breaking up fights when necessary, allowing some fights to go on when necessary. She never let anything get carried away too far. Over the last twenty two years, she'd coddled them, scolded them, taught them their manners and how to cook, and drilled them into great shape for adulthood. She couldn't have been prouder of her boys.

Not more than three months after her baby had graduated with honors from Lake Oswego High School, with a National Merit Scholarship and a full ride to USC, she'd turned to her husband and announced that she was applying to be a Multnomah County Deputy Sheriff. She had spent long enough at home doing the same things she could get paid for out on the road. The hiring committee had raised their eyebrows when they viewed her application, surprised by her age. But Shea's confidence, fierce determination, her surprising physical agility and strength, her years of experience handling her boys, and her outstanding go-to attitude had won them over. It helped that she took down a six foot, four inch three hundred pound drunken scroat single-handedly her first night on the job. No one doubted her after that. Now, Shea's age became an advantage to her lack of experience on the job. Her authoritative attitude and quick-thinking decision making skills made her an asset to the patrol unit and to the Dive Team. Jack trusted her instinctively, and always took her advice seriously. The feeling was mutual.

Shea took one good long look at Jack, then headed back toward the dive van and her awaiting team. Jack turned his head, and took another look at the dive site.

"I see you've shut down the boat ramp already." Miles nodded to the Portland Police officers who were directing traffic on Marine Drive. "Pissed off the fellers who were trying to make a jump on getting a prime spot in the hog line, I suppose."

"The hog line?"

"The folks who are fishing for the Spring chinook run," he nodded to the trucks and boats turning around and heading away from the entrance to their parking lot, "all tie up their boats together in the middle of the channel and all fish as one big unit. Call it the hog line. The earlier you put in, the better the spot you get in the hog line."

Jack quirked his eyebrow. "I've never been much of a fisherman." In truth, Jack had never fished before. No one had ever been around to teach him how. He'd often thought of heading up to Alaska, try to learn how to fish on the Kenai. Maybe one day he'd get up there.

"I suppose I'd better get on ifish.com. See what the news is on their feed and on their tweets. See how quickly news gets around about all this. Then we'll get out on Boat One, give you some cover from the river side." Again his eyes made their way down to the water's edge and to the fears that lurked below.

"Thanks, Miles. Can you make sure that Ju-Tau's gotten your River Patrol sergeant and lieutenant on the way?"

"No problemo. We're still waiting for the patrol shift sergeant and lieutenant to get down here too. They'll want to be here when we find out whose car got stolen, and when. Someone's ass is going to get ripped a new one." Miles grimaced at the thought. But then, as his eyes found their way toward the car once more, an eerie fear began to creep up the back of his neck. "Jack, are we sure this is…"

"Let's not go talking all scary talk now. Let's get Pete in the water, have him find out whose car it is, and then we'll go from there."

Chapter 27

AT FOUR O'CLOCK on a weekday morning, nothing much of interest or excitement found its way to keeping the Multnomah County Sheriff's Office patrol unit busy. Businesses stayed shut for a few more hours. Families slept. The sleepy part of the shift, many on duty patrol deputies either used the bewitching hour to drive through the abandoned streets up on Larch Mountain, or through the nearly empty freeways of I 205 or east I-84. The bars had long since closed, the drunks had all made it somewhere safe to pass out. The early birders had not yet arisen.

Sometimes the deputies found themselves in the Wood Village office, finishing up leftover paperwork from the busier part of the shift. Other times they made their way back to the Hansen Building to fill up their gas tank, or to check out what news might have arisen since they had rolled out of the gated lot when their shift started hours before. It wasn't unusual for deputies to have to fight off the sleepies from sheer boredom when the county was all tucked in for the night.

As the deputies made their rounds through the county, driving through the nearly empty streets, occasionally they found each other. Starved for a quick fix of gossip or a surge of adrenaline, they would gather together in empty parking lots, and park their cars "door to door," with one car parked next to the other with the two drivers' doors only inches apart. The deputies would then spend the next little while comparing stories from the evening's activities, filling in details left off the air from their traffic stops and call outs, thoroughly enjoying the companionable one-upmanship. Music, turned down low, wafted through their windows along with the air conditioning, ever cooling down the deputies who tended to overheat, even in the cooler nights of spring, in their bullet proof vests and their thirty pounds of gear they carried with them around their duty belts. They left their motors running, the engines idling quietly, as if even their cars aspired for future adventure. Their conversations stopped abruptly with the periodic interruptions of the dispatcher, sending fellow compatriots on new and exciting adventures. Both deputies would turn their heads toward their pack sets, listening to the dispatcher's instructions, adrenaline rushing with the hope that they, too, would get called out on something exciting, then dumping in disappointment when they discovered the call was not for them. Then they'd pick up their conversations in mid-sentence, as if they had never been interrupted.

Idle times allowed rumors to fester into facts.

When Jack's call came through to Sergeant Steve Thatcher, he was half way through a colorful regaling of his evening's only source of entertainment — a drunken brawl at the Hole in One, a local favorite strip club, adjacent to a golf course. He'd parked his car door to door with Deputy LaMarcus Berg, always a source of a good story, and had been thrilled with the prospect of — for once this week — being able to have what he hoped to be the best story of the night.

He turned down the music on his radio, and put his cell phone on speaker. "Diamond. What can I do for you this evening?" He smirked at Deputy Berg, instinctually knowing he was about to catch a doozy of a good bit of gossip he could use later on. LaMarcus turned down his radio and leaned his body toward his open window, trying to overhear as much of the conversation as he could without looking like he was eavesdropping.

"Sergeant, we've got a situation brewing down here. Can you get to a place where you can talk for a minute in private?"

A rush of adrenaline surged through his gut. And not the good kind.

Steve looked over at LaMarcus and nodded goodbye. "Hang on a sec." Dropping the phone into his lap, he put his car into drive and eased the car to another part of the lot. He rolled his window up, turned the cell phone off speaker, and spoke into his phone. "What's going on?"

"Sir? We've got a situation down here. Dive Team is just about to put in at the Columbia River boat ramp. We've got a dumped stolen car here, and, well, sir, I'm afraid it's one of ours."

"One of ours?!?"

226

"Yes, sir." Jack took a deep breath and pressed on. "I'd like you to contact your shift lieutenant, but I think you're both going to want to get down here."

"I'm on my way." Steve ended the call and rapidly apprised his shift lieutenant as to the situation. Their brief discussion gave Steve more than enough to do for the rest of his shift, and he moved his car back toward LaMarcus's.

"What's up, Sarge?" LaMarcus looked at his sergeant's face and immediately knew something terrible had happened.

"We've got a stolen patrol car."

"Hooooooooo-ly crap." The two shared a look. LaMarcus blinked a few times, letting the gravity sink in. "Whose?" A foul mixture of adrenaline and fear churned in LaMarcus's stomach, and he did not like the feeling.

"Don't know yet. That's what I'd like you to find out. I need you to head back to the Hansen Building, get into the logistics room and grab the roster off the hook. Then I need you to go through the log, check it against all the cars in the lot, find out who's on duty, and figure out which of the cars in the lot is missing. We've got to find out who this car belongs to and how in God's green Earth they managed to allow someone to steal the sonofabitch."

"You got it."

"Oh, and Berg, when you're done with the list, call me ASAP. If it's not one off the lot, it might be one of the take home cars. Go through the list of deputies and command staff with marked take-home cars and see if you can find out who's missing their rig. Then I can go and rip him a new..."

Steve's phone rang. "Sergeant Thatcher."

LaMarcus heard a few muffled words on the other end, but couldn't make out their conversation. Steve waved at LaMarcus, and took off, lights flashing, sirens wailing, code three through the parking lot and down the street.

LaMarcus rolled up his window, flipped on his own lights, and followed suit.

Chapter 28

PETE TESTED OUT his communication gear, making sure that Shea could hear everything clearly. Max took over her search line, and Jack sat at the water's edge, watching Pete's every move as Pete's safety diver. Pete waded into the water, and turned on the light strapped to his left arm. He allowed himself to slip under the water and made his way straight for the car's license plate number. He pointed his light at the plate and carefully read the numbers off to Shea. Then, pointing his light at the car's unique identification number, he read those numbers back to Shea as well. That finished, he examined the back bumper in great detail, looking for signs of damage, and then slowly started making his way down the driver's side of the car.

"Did you get that?" Jack looked up at David Kent, the lieutenant in charge of patrol, and Steve Thatcher, the patrol sergeant, to make sure they'd both taken down the numbers correctly. Lieutenant Kent, looming over the scene at six feet seven inches, made a commanding presence. His jet black skin created such a contrast to his white eyes, his gaze seemed even more piercing and intimidating than usual in the dark night sky. His starched uniform still showed the crisp, sharp pleat lines despite being near the end of a long, difficult shift. In comparison, Steve looked positively rumpled. His crinkled uniform sleeves barely buttoned in the front, stretching with difficulty over his very large belly and his bullet proof vest. A stain, probably from dinner, but perhaps leftover from lunch, left an oily smear down the front of his green uniform shirt. His greying hair needed a trim. Steve noticed Jack's once-over and glanced down. He brushed off invisible crumbs, and tucked his shirt into the back of his pants, silently chastising himself for not having shaved before the beginning of shift. Why did it always seem like whenever he forgot to shave, something big came up? And why was it that Jack Diamond could look so damned good at four o'clock in the morning? And why, he wondered for the fourteenth time, did he care?

Annoyed with himself, Steve pressed his phone to his ear, passing along the car's identification numbers to Deputy Berg on the other end of the call. David nodded his head to Jack, his dark face lined with worry.

Jack focused his attention back to Pete, who was quietly reciting his perceptions of the car's condition to Shea. Although he couldn't hear what Pete was saying, Jack could follow Pete's progress along the side of the car simply by following his bubbles under the water. He sighed, realizing that Pete still hadn't made it past the rear tires or the back seat of the car. At this rate, the dive was going to take forever.

Steve pulled his phone away from his ear and looked up at David. "None of our patrol cars are missing from the Hansen Building lot."

Jack whipped his head around in time to watch David's ebony black face turn three shades lighter. "So what does that leave us with? The take home cars?"

"Deputy Berg is running the numbers that Pete just gave us against our list. We've narrowed down the missing car to four deputies with take home cars. One's on vacation, and we haven't yet been able to get hold of the other three."

David's anger sliced through the air, his deep voice booming in the dark. "Get our guys out there pounding down the doors of those four deputies who you can't get in touch with. Maybe they don't deserve those take home cars if they can't be bothered to answer their cell phones! You tell my deputies to keep searching until we know which stupid, idiotic, careless sonofabitch allowed some penny-ante asswipe to steal his rig, go joy riding through my county, and dump that rig into the *God damned drink!*"

Spittle sprayed through the air like mist. Steve pressed a few buttons on his cell phone, turned his face to the side, and got Deputy Berg back on the line. As subtly and as casually as he could, he wiped the spittle off his face. Out of the corner of his eye, he caught Jack's gaze once again. Blushing his embarrassment, he turned his body away from them both and took a few steps to the side, wanting a moment of privacy to regain his composure.

"Jack?"

Shea's shaky voice made Jack's heart stop.

"Jack, you'd better listen to this!"

Jack glanced down into the water, noting the rapid number of bubbles that had quickly begun to surface. His diver was in trouble.

Jack grabbed the headphones from Shea's shaking hands, and pressed them up to his ear. "Pete? It's Jack. Slow your breathing down buddy. Slow it down. You're okay. Can you slow things down, Pete?"

"Oh my God! Oh my God! Oh my God!"

"Pete?! Get hold of yourself. Tell me what you're seeing, Pete. Take a deep breath. That's it. A nice deep breath and tell me what you're seeing."

But just then, in a moment of horrifying clarity, Jack understood the problem. "Pete? It's okay, I'm going to walk you through this." He took a deep breath and lowered his voice. "I take it the driver is still in the front seat of the car?"

The patrol sergeant and lieutenant standing with Jack both jolted. It hadn't occurred to either of them that the guy who stole the car might still be in the car. Under water.

Unable to hear Pete's side of the conversation, every person standing at the water's edge relied solely on Jack's nonverbal reactions and his comments to Pete to try to follow what was happening under water.

As one, everyone's eyes zeroed in on Jack. Jack stayed focused on Pete's bubbles, trying to make sure he didn't hyperventilate. If things turned south from here, he'd have to dump the com unit and dip into the river, scooping his troubled diver out and getting him back on shore. Jack tried not to second guess himself for putting Pete in the water on this dive. He knew how much Pete abhorred dead bodies, how seeing them underwater gave him nightmares. He had limited Pete's exposure, trying to rotate the diving schedule so that Pete could dive on evidence recovery missions and dumped stolen cars — dive calls where bodies under water were unlikely. But he couldn't keep putting it off. And sometimes a body showed up where it wasn't supposed to be. Like tonight. With Pete's current reaction, Jack could no longer legitimately continue to keep Pete on the Dive Team. As soon as Pete was out of the water and calmed down, he'd have to give him the bad news. Might as well get all the bad news and bad experiences out at the same time. Maybe he'd ask the chaplain to come and help him out. He took a deep breath, and willed Pete to do the same.

"Pete?"

"Yeah, man, he's floating! He's totally floating."

All eyes honed in on Jack as he closed his eyes and nodded his head.

"Is he buckled in? Pete? Is it just his arms floating? Or is his whole body floating about in the car?"

"His arms, man. They're totally floating out in front of him."

"Okay. You're doing great, Pete." Jack took a deep breath and steadied himself. "Now Pete, I need

233

you to look around, okay? Is there a big air bubble inside the car?"

"An air bubble?"

"Yes. Is there an air bubble?"

"No, uh, I don't see one."

"Are any of the windows open in the car?"

"Yeah. The driver's window is open a little. I can't see very well on the other side. Hang on, I think the passenger side window is down too."

"Okay. Are there any tiny bubbles coming out of the driver's mouth?"

"No man, his arms are totally floating out in front of him. He's dead, man. His eyes are all open and weird and dead, man."

"Pete, I understand that. I'm going to take care of this, okay? I just need you to do two more things for me, Pete. Just two more things and we'll get you out of there."

"I gotta get out, Jack. This is creepin' me the hell out!"

"I know, Pete, but take a deep breath. You're doing great, Pete. You're doing great. Just two more things. Is he wearing a uniform, Pete? Or is he in civvies?"

Again, all eyes honed in on Jack. Not being able to hear Pete's side of the conversation grew increasingly more frustrating as the officers dared hope that the driver remained the bad guy.

"He's one of us, Jack!! He's wearing a uniform!!"

A wave of grief washed over Shea, David, and Steve when Jack simply shook his head. Stunned, Steve bent over, putting his hands on his knees, trying not to vomit. Shea's face turned even paler. David looked away.

"Breathe, Pete. Take a deep breath. Okay, now Pete, can you tell who it is?"

They all collectively took in a breath.

"No, man, his face is turned away. I can't see him at all."

"That's okay, Pete. That's okay."

Together, they all let out their breath in one loud whoosh.

"Can you run your flashlight over the front of his jacket? Over the front of his uniform shirt?"

"You want me to look at his shirt?"

"Pete, I want you to look for his name tag. Can you see his name tag?"

A phone chirped in the eerie pocket of silence that anxiously awaited Pete's reply. Steve turned his body to the side, plugged his ear, and cupped the phone next to his face. "This is Steve."

"His body is all slumped over, Jack. I can't, I can't make it out."

"That's okay, Pete. You're doing good. You're doing good. Is there anything else you can see? Is he wearing a wedding ring? Can you see his rank on his sleeves?"

Steve's stomach lurched as he ended the call. He bent over once again, willing his dinner to stay down.

"He's wearing stripes, Jack! He's got sergeant stripes!"

Steve's voice cut through the silence, startling them all. "It's Ron Wilcox."

Chapter 29

NEWS OF RON'S suicide flew through the ranks like wildfire. By the time Jack got Pete out of the water and sitting on the edge of the dive van, awaiting the chaplain's arrival, the entire Dive Team knew, the two River Patrol deputies on Boat One had found out, all the deputies on patrol had heard from Deputy Berg, and the rumors had spread over to Portland Police when one of their officers came down the ramp to see what all the commotion was about.

Nodding to Max, thanking her for watching over Pete, Jack walked back down to the water's edge and spoke quietly to Steve and David.

"Sirs, we've got ourselves a bigger situation here than you realize." He then spent the next few minutes filling them in on his suspicions of Ron's involvement in Jack's serial killer case. Mouths agape, Jack took the opportunity to continue, filling them in on Ron's upcoming interrogation and the warrants currently being served on his house and car. "We've got to get Larry and Manny down here ASAP. This car," he nodded his head toward the river's edge, "is now a crime scene. We've got to make sure that we don't lose any potential evidence when we get his body up and get the car out of the water."

He took a deep breath, taking a moment to look each of them carefully in the eyes. This next part wasn't going to go over well, and he wanted to make sure neither of them took their anger out on him. "And at some point, we're going to have to find out who tipped off Ron that he was about to be interrogated as our prime suspect in the serial murders."

"Son of a bitch." David pulled out his phone, reached in his breast pocket for his reading glasses, and eyed Jack. "I'll get Manny and Larry on the line, get them on down here. We'll want to get the detectives unit down here as well."

"They'll need to head over to his place, get the search warrant started."

"And over to the Hansen Building. Lock up his computer and empty out his locker. I can supervise that. How much longer will it take before you get that rig out of the water?"

Jack spoke to the water's edge, visualizing the upcoming mission. "First we need to get the body out of the water. Then I'll have to see what kind of evidence, if any, can be recovered under water before the car actually comes out. Then I'll take a good look around at the car and find out what kind of tow truck we're going to need. As long as the car isn't hung up on something under there, it won't take much time at all once we get to that point."

"I'd like to have the car towed over to the Hansen Building. I'll get my guys on it to start the evidence recovery once it's dried out a bit. Keep me apprised as to the timing." David turned on his heel and headed up the ramp, focusing on his phone and leaving the drowned car behind him.

The pained expression on Jack's face made Steve's stomach lurch again. Jack turned to talk to Max or Shea, and his eyebrows drew together when he realized they were no longer there; the only one left around him was Steve. "As soon as we get the body out of the car and get him identified, we're going to have to notify his wife."

Steve nodded his head. He hated death notifications as much as the next guy, but this case called for an extra light hand. "I'll take care of that." He glanced over his shoulder and spotted Pete, still huddled and dripping on the back of the dive van. "As soon as the chaplain gives Pete the once over, I'll take the chaplain with me over to Ron's house, break the news, and have him keep Ron's wife company."

Jack nodded, and turned his gaze back to the car.

"Who was he married to? Do you remember her name?" Steve flipped through his contact list on his phone, but hadn't yet reached the name of Ron's wife.

"Claire. Her name is Claire." The pain stabbed through his chest, his heart barely able to handle the pain. He cleared his throat and looked out toward the Gorge. "But she's not at home right now. She's uh, staying at my place at the moment."

Steve's eyebrows shot off into outer space, his grief momentarily lapsed by Jack's startling revelation.

"It's not like that."

Sure it isn't. Steve bit the inside of his lip to keep the smug smirk off his face.

"Her best friend was murdered tonight." Jack let the cruel words sink in. "By that sonofabitch." He nodded toward the car in the water. "And now that sick sonofabitch took the coward's way out and killed himself, leaving her to deal with *this* whole mess by herself."

"'Mmmkaaay. But that still doesn't tell me what she's doing at *your* place."

"Listen. It's complicated."

Steve fought the urge to roll his eyes.

Inwardly, Jack seethed. He could feel his face redden, and he gritted his teeth, forcing himself to calm down. "She and I are old friends. I had a Portland officer take her there so she could get some space from Ron, and some rest to deal with her grief." He sighed, thinking of the pain she must be going through, so very sad knowing that her pain would all too soon grow to immeasurable lengths. "She's fairly heavily sedated, and may not even be awake yet. You'll want a key to my place. I'll go grab it for you."

Jack walked slowly up the ramp and toward the dive van. Steve followed along in silence, letting the whole of the matter sink in.

240

After twisting his key off his key chain, silently thanking GranNini for insisting he carry multiple sets of his house key in his various work bags for emergencies, Jack pulled the chaplain aside to talk with Steve. That settled, Jack nodded to Shea and Max, and gathered his Dive Team together for an update. They quickly agreed that Jack should take over as lead diver, with Shea staying on com and Mason stepping in as safety diver. Hank "the tank," agreed to take on the video monitor. Now that the recovery of the dumped, stolen car had turned into a crime scene investigation into the suicide of one of their own, they would need to videotape the entire recovery as evidence. Max frowned her frustration at being left out of the good jobs. She swallowed her disappointment and volunteered to take over the search lines, and they headed down the boat ramp with an underwater recovery body bag in tow.

"Are we going to bag him under water? Or will we bring up the car with him still in it?"

"Given all considerations, I think we'd better bring him out first. Do it under water. We'll need some plastic bags to cover his hands. And some rubber bands to secure them at the wrists. But I'd like to make sure we don't get the car out of the water until sunrise. Make sure we don't lose any evidence in the dark."

Shea looked down at her phone, reading the time. "What time does the sun rise this morning?"

They all looked up, toward the Gorge, to gaze the lightening of the sky. "Probably around 6:30 or so. It should take me a while to get the body out,

241

investigate the car, and call in the tow truck. We've got plenty of time now."

Hank chuckled under his breath. "It's not like the body's going anywhere."

Shea and Max whipped their heads around and glared at him.

"What?!"

"Tank, you can be so incredibly insensitive some times."

"Yeah, well, it's true."

"Just because it's true, doesn't mean you need to say it out loud." Out of all the people on the Dive Team, Hank was the only one who really got under Max's skin. A huge, powerful man, built like a tank, with behemoth arm and shoulder muscles, and leg muscles that bulged out of his thighs, stretching the seams of his pants to maximum capacity, Hank intimidated nearly every person he encountered while on patrol. Most of the other patrol deputies loved having Hank as their back up on difficult or challenging calls. One look at that body in a County uniform sporting a duty belt with mace, handcuffs, a baton, taser, Glock, and a rifle in the back of his rig, almost everyone felt compelled to comply in an agreeable manner once he showed up.

Max, however, cringed every time he appeared. In her opinion, Hank bulked up too much, focusing too much time on the size and shape of his muscles, and not enough time on cardio or on how to use his muscles effectively in a good fight. Max's workouts included both weight lifting and cardio. Not only did she take regular self-defense and tactics training classes, but she also biked and ran competitively. She'd made it to the World Championships in the Duathlon, a run-bike-run race, six years in a row. But that wasn't even the worst of it. Hank's reputation as a womanizer disgusted her. She hated how he could simply smile at a group of blond chicks, and they'd all ooh and ah and fawn over his large arms. She found herself scowling at him, imagining him as a dumb blonde version of Gaston, from "Beauty and the Beast."

In truth, Hank bulked up as a self-defense mechanism, helping him to overcome his deep-seated fear of being thought of as an outsider, un-liked by his friends and coworkers. Hank's parents, both born and bread in Wisconsin, had splurged on a honeymoon trip to Hawaii. It was love at first sight. Immediately on returning home, they sold everything they owned, quit their jobs, and spent every last penny they had buying a place on Oahu. Even though he was born on the island, Hank's bleach blond hair and his bright blue eyes made him an instant outsider.

Painfully shy in his youth, he'd spent years in the gym as a teenager in Hawaii, using his knowledge of weight training to build up the nerve to talk to others, to urge them to like him. At home, he spent hours reading. He deliberately bulked up his muscles and dumbed down the conversations, trying to control others' perceptions of him. He excelled at calming down roughed up feathers, and egos, during stressful conversations. His strength, coupled with his size, made him an amazing asset for the Sheriff's Office. It was one of the main reasons Jack had recommended him for the Dive Team.

Hank equally excelled at agitating and irritating people around him. And Max was his favorite target. In private, he wanted to settle down. He longed for a long-term relationship with a nice, quiet, small woman. One who enjoyed working out and staying in shape, going to the movies, long walks through the neighborhood, having quiet nights in. He'd had a crush on Max since the first day he met her. Her spitfire attitude and killer body drove him crazy with admiration every day. But knowing she despised him irritated him to no end, making him want to exaggerate his oafish habits just to annoy her, like a nine year old bully pulling a girl's pony tail in school. The thought made him smile. His smile made her growl.

Chapter 30

SLIPPING INTO THE water, Jack tested out his com gear and then allowed his natural instincts to help him take over the dive. The car had settled in the boat basin. Luckily, there wasn't a current, pushing anything around. He looked down at his fins and tried not to stir up any of the sediment.

He allowed himself to get a long, slow look of the outside of Ron's car, avoiding looking inside for now. He knew the macabre scene that awaited him. No need to rush to it.

"There's no damage on the back of the car. Doesn't look like the car was pushed into river." Jack took the video camera and turned his high powered light toward the car. "Can you see this?"

Hank watched the car appear onscreen. He and Shea moved closer together so she could monitor Jack's progress visually as well. "Yeah, you're coming through just fine."

"Side of the car doesn't show any damage either. Back driver side window is closed."

Hank and Shea watched as the car appeared on the video monitor.

Keeping Ron out of the picture as much as he could, Jack pointed the camera at Ron's window.

"Driver side window is open a few inches." Jack tried, and failed, to get his arm with the video camera through the driver's side window. "I'll have to see if I can videotape the inside of the car from the passenger side."

"Got it. Okay, are you ready?"

Jack took a deep breath. "I'm ready when you are."

"Show us what you can then." Shea braced herself for the grim scene about to appear on the monitor. Her heart began to pound in her chest, just as it did every time she faced a dead person in the water. But the images came through as disjointed and disorienting. Then, with a jolt, the side of Ron's face appeared on camera, bobbing in the water. Jack panned the camera out, and gave them a better angle of the side of Ron's body, his arms floating forward, bumping up against the steering wheel in front of him.

"The airbag didn't deploy."

"He couldn't have been going more than what, 25 miles per hour then when he hit the water?"

"Or they just didn't deploy." Jack floated his camera back to the front left corner of Ron's car and kept the search going.

"The front wheels are hanging off the boat ramp's concrete slab. The car is kinda teetering off the edge."

"Got it."

246

He surveyed the front of the car. "Again, there doesn't appear to be any damage up here. I'm headed over to passenger side."

Max let out more of the search line, and Jack swam with his video camera over to the passenger side of the car. "No damage over here, either. Everything looks pretty clean."

"Got it."

He took a deep breath and braced himself for the worst. "All right, I'm going in. The passenger window is open, so I'm going to put my arm in there, see if I can get a good look around."

Everyone up on shore took a deep breath and awaited Jack's report. Extending out his arm, Jack pushed the camera through the passenger side window, and tried to capture the scene as best he could.

"Keys are in the ignition. But, I can't see from here," Jack grunted. "Can you make out what gear the car is in?" He pointed the camera toward the gear shift on the steering wheel, and waited to hear Shea's reply.

"It looks like," she looked up at Hank, who nodded his head. "Yep, from here it looks like it's in Drive."

Jack nodded his head, then felt instantly ridiculous. No one could see him under the water. "Shea, can you please remind me to videotape the boat ramp up top to look for skid marks? See if he at least tried to stop his car from hitting the water?

Obviously we'll need to have the mechanic check his breaks for tampering, just in case."

"Got it."

"I'm going to check out the rest of the car. See if there's any evidence floating around that we might want to take while it's still under water. I don't want to lose anything when we pull the car out."

"Got it."

Jack panned the camera toward the back of Ron's car, and noted that his rifle was still loaded on the rack. He peered into the back seat, but didn't notice anything other than a wadded up garbage bag from McDonald's floating around.

He took his time looking at the passenger side of the car and both the wheels on that side.

"I'm not seeing anything unusual on the car. No damage from here. I'm heading up."

"Got it."

Jack surfaced and pulled the com mask off his face. He handed his video camera to Hank. Mason, his safety diver, tossed him a small hand towel and he wiped off his face. When he opened his eyes, his whole team had zeroed in on him.

"Looks like we'll be able to hook the car up to the rear axle. Max, why don't you call for a flat bed with choker chains and a cable?"

She nodded and pulled out her cell phone.

"There's a really good pick point on the axle. Back around the rear well on the passenger side."

Mason nodded his head.

"You'll need a couple of choker chains since the car is pointed down."

"You gonna want me to hook it up to the tow truck?"

"We'll see. I'm getting pretty tired."

Mason patted the black bag lying next to him. "You still want to bag him under water?"

Jack nodded, taking a deep breath.

"You sure you want to do this? We can have Max suit up."

Jack shook his head, wiping his face down once more. "No. I'd rather take care of this. I want to make sure it gets done right."

Hank guffawed. "Mister perfectionist."

Max elbowed him in the stomach and he clutched his side, yelling, "Hey!"

"You about ready to do this?" Mason looked at Jack with cautious eyes, making sure Jack really was up to the dive. Ever the professional, Jack nodded his head, and reached for his face mask. Without a third diver in the water, they wouldn't be able to videotape the removal of Ron's body from the car under water, but Jack didn't think the video tape seemed necessary. Sometimes getting a body out of a sunken car could be a bit trickier than expected. Body parts could move in strange and unsettling ways while under water. Besides, he had already videotaped any evidence found in the car. He just wanted to get the body out of the car, bagged up, and landed on shore, safe in the hands of the M.E.

Looking around, he couldn't see the M.E.'s car. "Is she here yet?"

"Who?"

"The M.E."

Shea looked around, her eyes resting on the myriad faces and cars that had amassed in the Columbia River boat ramp's parking lot. "I don't see her." She turned and faced Jack. "But that doesn't mean that she's not here. I'll call up there. Make sure she's ready when you get the body up top."

Jack nodded his head, gave Mason a look, and slipped under water. Max squatted down next to Mason and slipped two smaller plastic bags into Mason's hand, and then secured them with two heavy rubber bands.

"These need to go over Ron's hands. Carefully place each plastic bag over his hand up to his wrist, and then keep the bag on his wrist by securing it with this rubber band. We don't want any potential evidence to get lost while you're moving him around."

Mason nodded his head. Although he had been on many dive missions before, he had only recovered a couple of corpses, both of which had been accident victims. He had yet to recover a suicide victim. Max patted the top of his head and headed back to the search lines, ever vigilant in keeping a careful watch on her divers while they were under water. Mason grabbed the body bag, and slid himself in. Before letting his head go under completely he nodded to Shea. "Wish us luck!" With

250

that, he slipped under and allowed the cold black waters to wash over his head.

Jack helped Mason unwrap the body bag, unzipping it entirely and making sure it was fully extended. "I can't get him out through the window, so I'm going to have to open the door. I'll get his head out first and float that toward you. Then you get him secured up to his shoulders and I'll work on his feet, okay?"

Mason nodded.

Jack turned and faced the car. The door was unlocked, making this process much easier, and he opened the door carefully, not wanting Ron's body to float out without having a good hold of him. As he positioned himself around the door frame, opening it slowly, he watched to see if anything new floated out. Pleased that he hadn't missed any potential evidence, he turned to Ron's body, not surprised to see that he had buckled himself in. It wasn't uncommon to find people who had committed suicide by driving into the river had buckled themselves in first. Perhaps they hoped the additional seatbelt protection would provide a layer of security, making it that much harder for them to escape should their bodies instinctively try to fight their way to the surface. Perhaps they simply buckled their seat belts out of habit. Either way the seatbelt wasn't a surprise.

"Don't forget these."

Jack looked over to see Mason handing him one of the small plastic bags for Ron's hands. With quick, practiced steps, Jack slipped the bags around

251

each of Ron's wrists and secured them with rubber bands. Mason slid back into position, stretching out the body bag, making sure it stayed prepped and ready.

Jack tried to reach over Ron's body to undo the seat belt clasp, but he couldn't reach without disturbing the body. Reaching up with his left hand, he held onto Ron's arm and shoulder while he pulled out his knife and sawed through the seat belt. As the seat belt released, the water began to pull and tug at Ron, and Jack had to hurry to slice through the lap belt, slipping the knife back into its sheath and grabbing Ron before he floated out of his reach and out the door.

Carefully watching the car door, Jack tugged and pulled at Ron's body, gently persuading it to float toward its awaiting body bag. Mason's deft hands made quick work of the project, and soon Ron's body found itself tucked gently into the zipped body bag. Jack rested his hands on top of the black bag, his heart heavy for Claire's loss, but his mind grateful for the end to this serial killer's brutal string of abuse and death.

With help from the rest of the Dive Team, they slid the black bag carrying Ron's body onto the shore. Jack's head ached with exhaustion. He could only imagine the media's flurry when they discovered the conclusive evidence that, not only were some of the rumors true — someone had, in fact, driven a Multnomah County patrol car into the Columbia River, and that the driver was an MCSO sergeant. Then he imagined their buzz when they discovered he hadn't survived his suicidal attempt to escape. He couldn't even imagine the tizzy they'd get themselves into when they realized that this same sergeant was in fact the Diamonds for Diamond serial killer.

Chapter 31

"WHO CALLED IN the fire trucks?"

Jack nodded to the two large trucks pulling into the parking lot.

"Mason. He figured they could position themselves in a vee shape, block the view from up above. Keep onlookers from Marine Drive and the press from over at the Sextant from getting a good look at him." Shea nodded down at the body bag.

As the trucks moved closer to the dock, Jack saw Mason stretching up, gesturing to the fire truck drivers as to where to park their rigs. He nodded, impressed.

The long-awaited tow truck followed the fire trucks into the lot, and Jack looked down at the body. "Guess we'd better move him up there." He nodded toward the river patrol office. "Give the tow truck driver some space."

Shea, Hank, Max and Jack hauled the body bag up into the parking lot, keeping it somewhat stashed away from onlooking gawkers. Hank and Max headed toward the tow truck driver to explain how they planned to hook up the rig. Shea stood guard with Jack until the M.E.'s truck pulled in a few minutes later. Reading the look that passed between

Jack and the M.E., Shea patted Jack on the shoulder and headed back down to the water's edge, meeting Mason along the way.

"So. Lots of rumors are floating around, Jack." Monday's hair glowed positively orange, back lit against the bright and beautiful sunrise. The Columbia Gorge truly was one of nature's most beautiful presents to the world. He took a moment to close his eyes against the rising sun, and took a deep breath, knowing that even the sun couldn't take away the rest of the day's responsibilities.

He pressed his hand against his forehead, shielding his eyes from the rising sun, and tried a small smile. It didn't take. "Well. At least it's finally over."

She nodded her head. "There is that. No matter how tragic it is when someone's life comes to an untimely end, there is some relief in knowing that a bad guy, especially someone who had committed so many wretched and deplorable sins as this serial killer here, won't be able to hurt anyone else ever again." Monday took a good long look at Jack while he had his eyes closed and she had the chance to look, really look at him. In all the years she'd known him, she had never seen Jack look so completely strung out. "You really ought to go and get some rest, Jack. You look terrible."

This time his smile lasted a bit longer. "Only you could get away with a comment like that."

She squeezed his arm. "Well, yes. Me and GranNini." Her soft smile left a warm spot in his aching belly.

255

"Yes. GranNini too."

Monday allowed the silence to envelope him for a moment, giving his body an emotional break before the next round of brutality. Death, though peaceful in theory, could be a very messy, brutal business. Even if the person had wished and wanted and prayed for it to come. "Let's get this over with, shall we? Then we can get you home and off to bed. Unfortunately, I have plenty of other cases I can work on today. After the preliminaries here, he can wait until later this evening, or even tomorrow morning, so that you can be there for the post mortem, should you wish to be there."

Jack nodded his head as waves of relief washed over him. Exhaustion coursed through his weary body. He honestly couldn't remember the last time he had been this tired. All he wanted was a quick shower, a nice long soak in his hot tub, a cup of GranNini's homemade soup, and bed. He wondered if it was too early to call her, to put in a request for chicken vegetable. He stumbled, and Monday's strong, firm grip steadied him. "You're worse off than I thought. Why don't you head on home now, Jack. You don't need to be here for this. I'll be in and out and done in just a moment. You've seen the worst of it. Go on home." She pulled her small knee pad out of her bag, covered it in plastic, and dropped it on the ground next to the body bag.

Sorely tempted to leave, Jack swayed in his feet, fighting the urge to finish the job he'd started. He watched her through half closed eyes as she slipped on her gloves and pulled out her digital recorder, stringing it around her neck and pressing the on switch. He listened with half an ear as she recited the date and time, described the scene around her, unzipped the body bag, and quietly began to outline her findings.

He closed his eyes and let his mind start to wander as he listened to Monday's voice describe the condition of Ron's hands and face, noting the amount of water logging his exposed skin had acquired.

He nearly jumped when Hank placed his hand on his arm. "We should really get that into a bucket of water."

Confused, Jack focused his eyes on him, trying to figure out what on earth he was talking about.

He nodded toward Ron's body. "His gun and his taser. The sooner we get those into a bucket of river water, the better off we are at holding off corrosion."

With a jolt, Jack realized Hank was right. He'd been so damn tired he hadn't even thought about Ron's gun and taser and the rest of his duty belt still strapped to his uniform. The river water, when combined with the morning air, would quickly corrode the metal in Ron's work tools. Keeping the tools in the water itself enabled them to hold off the corrosion process, and enabled them to process any fingerprints or gather any other evidence they'd need to acquire during their investigation into Ron's suicide. Besides, they'd need to count rounds of ammo and secure up the work tools not only for safety but also for the evidence log. He'd need Ron's uniform and bullet proof vest at some point, too.

"Hank, could you…"

"I've already got three big plastic tubs down at the boat ramp, sir. One for his rifle, one for his computer. We can use the other one for his duty belt here." Jack nodded his head, his ears having the grace to turn pink at the tips at his embarrassment for having forgotten something so vital.

He turned his head to watch as Hank trotted down to the boat ramp toward the plastic tubs. His Dive Team stood around the tow truck driver gesturing and pointing, trying to describe how they planned to bring up the patrol car. The young tow truck driver clearly disagreed with their plans. Even from a distance, Jack could see Mason's neck starting to turn red and splotchy. Just as he thought he'd better head over there to straighten things out, he came up short as he saw Shea gently urging Mason to the side. With just a few gentle touches, she had managed to calm Mason down and ease her way into the conversation as an authoritative source with which to be reckoned. She turned on the video monitor and saddled up to the tow truck driver, quickly and effectively showing him exactly what her Dive Team had planned for the hook up. Jack smiled in admiration as the young tow truck driver nodded his head, and all three of his divers smiled and shook hands with the driver.

So caught up in their interaction with the tow truck driver, Jack hardly noticed when Monday called his name.

"Jack, I think we have a problem here."

258

He whipped around, the smile dropping off his face the instant he saw the color draining off hers. In two quick strides he was at her side, kneeling down beside her.

"What is it? What's wrong?"

She took a long moment to gaze into his eyes, almost imperceptibly shaking her head.

A chill shivered down his back.

Monday let her eyes lead his toward her left hand. Looking back at him to make sure he was looking where she needed, she gently pulled aside Ron's collar where she had removed his clip-on tie and unbuttoned his top button.

"Is that...?"

Monday nodded her head.

Jack's heart rate quickened and a wave of nausea washed over him.

Monday pressed open the collar on the other side of his shirt, revealing the rest of the mark that had left her so troubled.

"Oh my God."

The bottom dropped out of his stomach.

Monday took extra care and unbuttoned another button, opening his collar even further and exposing the rest of Ron's neck. Under the folds of his neck, clear as if it had been drawn, a dark blue ligature mark had left its imprint.

"Is there any chance he could have done this himself?"

"It's highly unlikely, given that his shirt was buttoned to the top. And his tie was clipped into place. Did you find anything in the car that could have left a mark like this? Heavy wire? Covered twine?"

Jack ran through the images in his mind, watching the McDonald's bag float around in the back seat, seeing Ron's arms floating in front of him. "I don't believe so. I can run through the video again, just to make sure. And we'll go through the car, of course, once it's out of the water."

Monday nodded her head, her fingers deftly undoing the last button she could reach before getting to the top of Ron's bullet proof vest.

"Jack, I just have to look."

"Have to look where?"

"Under there." She nodded toward Ron's chest. "Can you please hold up his vest while I take a peek? I don't want to take off his vest here if I can help it. I'd rather wait until I'm in my autopsy suite."

Distracted by her request, Jack slipped his fingers into the rounded scoop at the neckline of Ron's bullet proof vest and tugged. With a sucking sound, the water-logged vest pulled away from Ron's chest.

"I can't quite…"

Frustrated, Monday slipped her fingers under the vest, and undid the last button she could reach. Then, like a child searching for a lost toy under the furniture, she peered inside and found the monster hiding under the bed.

"Oh, Jack." Her troubled eyes crushed his spirits.

"What? What is it?"

She held his gaze, her eyes misting over into tears. Not for her victim, but for Jack, whose already difficult day was about to become a horrible nightmare.

"What?"

And then it dawned on him, and he knew. A cold breeze blew down the back of his neck and he felt the shivers deep into the pit of his stomach. Unable to look away, he moved his head down toward the ground, pulled out a small flashlight, and peeked inside, peeked where Monday held open Ron's shirt, and watched in horror as a diamond shaped gap appeared in the middle of Ron's chest.

His world fell apart.

The real Diamonds for Diamond serial killer had struck again. This time, killing his one and only suspect.

Chapter 32

Jumping to his feet, Jack sprinted down the boat ramp to Shea. He ripped the com gear from her fingers and pressed the mic up to his mouth. "Stop! Don't pull up the car yet. Stop! Stop! Stop!"

Shea watched in horror as Jack's sanity seemed to disappear. "What on God's green earth did you go and do that for?"

He pulled off the com gear and sprinted up to the tow truck driver. "You've got to stop! Don't pull up the car yet. We're not done yet."

"Come on, man! I got shit I gotta get done, yo."

The glare that Jack poured onto the young man could have peeled paint off a dresser. The tow truck driver held up his hands. "All right! All right! I'll call my boss, tell him I'm gonna be here a while."

Mason held up the search line, waiting for Jack's explanation while Shea readjusted the com gear onto her head and asked her two divers to resurface.

Jack bent over, trying to catch his breath and find his center of balance once again. Discovering Ron's suicide a few hours ago had broken his heart for Claire, but had provided him with an enormous sense of relief. He'd found his serial killer, and he had desperately been looking forward to getting off the crazy carousel ride he'd been on for the last few hectic weeks.

But now, now not only was he back on the damned carousel ride, now the damned ride was spinning out of control.

Turning back toward the river patrol office, he saw Monday talking to Nick, quietly filling him in on her findings. He hadn't even known Nick had made his way down here. He rubbed his face with his hands, and ran his hands through his wet hair. Max and Hank popped their heads up out of the water, a mix of curiosity and annoyance on their faces.

"Come on, Diamond. Let's just get this done and out of here. We all want to go home."

He took a deep breath and braced himself. "Mason, I'm going to need you to get back to the dive van. Get out The Box."

Mason's mouth dropped open.

"The Box?" Shea's confused face searched Jack's. "But I thought this was a suicide."

"So did I." He rubbed his hand across his face once more. "But now it looks like he might have been murdered."

"Jesus."

"Holy shit, man."

Mason turned on the spot and trotted up to the dive van.

"Do you want to get back in the drink? Take the lead on this?" Max tried not to let the disappointment show on her face. She'd always wanted to take the lead on an underwater murder investigation, but had never had the opportunity. Now was her chance. She looked away and bit her lip, not trusting herself to look at Jack until she heard his reply.

"No. I'm no good any more today. Once you get the car up and out of the water, I'll walk you through it. That okay with you, Shea?"

Shea shrugged her shoulders and handed over the com gear. Max turned her head away and tried to suppress the grin on her face. Yes, she understood that this was, in fact, a serious murder investigation. And a murder investigation into one of their own. But it's not like Ron was actually a great sergeant, or anything. No one really liked him. Not that he deserved to die, she thought. But she didn't think anyone was really going to miss him now that he was gone. She started ticking through her mental checklist, trying to remember all the steps she'd need to cover while performing her investigation. She'd watched Jack do them many times, and she'd assisted with him once or twice under water. But now was her chance, and she wasn't going to blow it. Maybe she would even be able to find something to help them find the killer! She suppressed a smile once more, and watched as Mason brought The Box down toward them at the water's edge.

Chapter 33

ONCE THEY'D HOOKED up the rig, it only took the driver a few minutes to get Ron's car out of the river and into the parking lot. Mason had The Box prepped and ready, and Max flew into action. Hank and Shea held a mesh cloth beneath the driver's side door and nodded their heads. Max stepped just to the side of the driver's side door and slowly drew open the car door, allowing the river water to pour out of the car and down the sloped cement ramp, while any solid residue and potential evidence remained trapped into the awaiting mesh cloth. Once the flow of water eased, Hank and Shea stepped out of the way, taking their mesh cloth with them, and Max pounced. In a flurry of activity, she slipped inside the car and sprayed a wet mixture of small particle fingerprint reagent on the gear shift, the car keys, and the steering wheel. Mason slipped into the seat as she slid out, and he scanned for useable fingerprints.

Quick as a wink, she had the entire right side of the driver's door and window sprayed with reagent, and let out a squeal when she found two finger prints and a partial palm print on the window, right behind the driver's door.

"I suppose it could be Ron's." Max bit the inside of her cheek, her foot tapping impatiently on the pavement, waiting for Jack's opinion.

"Or, it could be where the bad guy held onto the side of the car when he pushed the car into the water."

Max grinned and whipped around. She pulled out the Dive Team camera from The Box, and took closeups of the prints. She passed the camera through to Mason who photographed the smeared and most likely unusable prints inside the car. Then, willing her adrenaline levels to ease up a bit and her shaking hands to steady themselves, Max pulled the prints off the driver's side door. She grinned like a kid on Christmas morning when the prints pulled off clean.

Mason shook his head, not wanting to look Max in the eyes. None of his prints came out. He wasn't too surprised. Theoretically, it is possible to get prints off of items that have been submerged for short periods of time. But he'd had no luck. He wasn't sure if his lack of success was due to the amount of time the car had been submerged, or, more likely, because either someone had wiped the steering wheel clean, or the prints had simply become smudged before the car had even been submerged. Either way, he hadn't been able to get anything off the steering wheel. He'd nabbed a wee portion of a print off the gear shift, but he doubted that it would be sufficient to successfully identify who had last touched the gear shift.

Max dashed to the passenger side of the car and frowned, disappointed when no visible prints popped up with the reagent.

"Is there any other place I should spray?" Like a small yippy dog, practically bouncing and salivating with the excitement before her, Max had come back around to get Jack's approval and sage advice. "Mason sprayed the gear shift, steering wheel and keys inside. He only picked up a partial on the gear shift. And I sprayed the passenger side window, door, and handle, and got nothing. The only good prints we got were on Ron's driver's side window."

"You might as well spray the back doors as well. Just in case."

"I already did." She chewed the inside of her cheek. She surveyed the car, looking for hidden nooks and crannies where she could spray her reagent and hunt down prints. "Didn't find anything."

"That's about it, then, for the fingerprinting." Jack stifled a yawn. He nodded toward the inside of Ron's car. "Don't forget to put his MDC and his rifle into tubs of river water. Get them down to the crime lab."

"Got it."

She caught Hank's eye, and nodded her head for him to follow her. She grabbed the two plastic tubs she'd collected earlier, and had Hank help her lug them up toward Ron's car after filling them with water. Max started bouncing on the balls of her feet, impatiently waiting for Mason to get out of the driver's seat so she could ease Ron's mobile data computer into the awaiting tub of river water.

Jack yawned again, and headed toward the M.E.'s truck. Monday's team had loaded up Ron's body. Monday stopped the truck, rolled down her window and waited for him. "Go home, Jack. Get some sleep. This," she nodded toward the back of her truck, "will wait until tomorrow morning." She couldn't resist the urge to rumple his already rumpled hair. "Seriously. Get some sleep. You're no good to us if you aren't back up to speed."

Jack nodded his head slowly, exhaustion making it next to impossible for him to reply. He tapped the window sill twice and watched her drive the rig up the sloped drive and pull out onto Marine Drive. Looking over his shoulder, he suppressed a grin when Max nearly pulled Mason out of the seat so she could continue with her investigation of Ron's patrol car. Shea caught his eye and nodded toward his rig. She mouthed the words, "We got this." Jack nodded his head in gratitude and headed toward the group of deputies milling about near the fire trucks.

"We pulled a couple of partials and a palm print off the driver's side door. Got another partial — probably useless — off the gear shift. I'll plug them into AFIS when I get back to the office, see if we get a match."

As if on cue, the whole group protested at the same time.

"Not on your life!"

"That's so not going to happen."

Jack looked up in surprise.

"Go home, Diamond. You look like shit. You're no good to us in this condition. Give me the prints. I'll take care of it." Nick reached his hand out to snag the lifted prints from Jack's grip.

"But I..." His protests fell on deaf ears. They all but kicked him toward the dive van where his civvies awaited him. Once again he tried to protest, and stopped in mid-sentence when he caught a glimpse of Manny's face.

His legs felt like lead as he made his way over to the dive van. Stripping out of his gear took him three times longer than normal when his body seemed unwilling to cooperate. Grief and exhaustion and frustration mulled together in a cacophony of emotions. He pulled his warm, dry shirt over his naked chest and missed the sigh of admiration as Shea appreciated the view from afar.

As he pulled into his driveway and slipped the car into park, he blinked, suddenly realizing that he had no idea how he'd gotten there. He had no memory of the drive home. He stumbled into the house, dropping his keys into the porcelain bowl on the little shelf by the front door, and mindlessly slipped his jacket onto the hook beneath. He ran his hands through his hair, dragging his weary feet toward the shower and his awaiting bed. He never even noticed the beautiful woman nestled deep in the blankets of his couch, already enjoying the blissful freedom of the dreamless sleep he so desperately sought.

Chapter 34

JACK AWOKE WITH a start. Something had banged, or dropped in the kitchen. Covered in sweat, heart racing, he grabbed the Glock out of his nightstand and slipped soundlessly down the hallway. In four quick sweeps, he'd ruled out an intruder in his office. Popping his head in and out of the bathroom, he'd quickly ruled that out too.

Bang.

The kitchen.

Pressing himself against the hallway wall, he slipped as quietly as he could the few remaining steps, and rounded the corner, his gun pointing the way.

Claire dropped the red bowl with a screech.

Jack sagged in relief.

Shards of porcelain skittered to the far corners of his kitchen floor, coming to a rest underneath cupboards and slipping beneath the refrigerator.

"Jack! You startled me!"

He stooped over, resting his hands on his knees, and nodded his head, his heart racing madly in his stomach.

She squatted down, scooping up the larger pieces. "I'm so sorry about the bowl." She glanced up, noticing for the first time his naked chest. His bare feet. The way his sleeping shorts hung low over his hips. So very low. She gulped, her face turning as red as the shards of porcelain in her hands. She turned away in embarrassment, not wanting to get caught ogling his chest. His muscular legs. The way he looked so damned sexy in his bare feet.

Glancing down at the gun in his hand, he, too, reddened in embarrassment. "I'll, uh, be right back." He headed back to his room to slip the gun back into its drawer.

Claire leaned forward and peeked down the hallway, admiring the retreating view. Blushing anew, she grew flustered and slipped her hand underneath the refrigerator to reach a few of the missing larger pieces.

Jack came around the corner just as Claire was stretching for a piece just out of her reach. The large tee shirt she'd borrowed from Jack's drawers had slipped over her shoulder and he could just make out the swell of her breast. The jolt of attraction and yearning shocked him. He looked away, just as she looked up. Reaching behind him, he pulled out the broom and a dust pan from beside the fridge, and began sweeping up the smaller pieces and crumbs.

"I'm really sorry about this." Claire held up the pieces and then dumped them into the garbage under the sink.

"Don't even worry about it." He swept up the mess and brought the dust pan to the garbage. She held the cupboard door open and then pulled out the garbage can for him, their bodies only inches away from one another.

Unable to resist, she slipped her arms around his naked chest and breathed him in. The smell of his skin, all warm from his nap, instantly brought back pleasant memories. Memories of feeling safe and warm, feeling protected and comfortable. She allowed herself the time to press her cheek against his chest, and sighed when he wrapped his arms around her, pressing her body next to his, the broom handle hanging at an awkward angle at her side, the dust pan clenched in the fingers he so desperately wanted to spread out against her back.

She resisted the urge to kiss his chest as she pulled away. For a moment she had forgotten where, and when, she was. It had always been that way for her — losing herself in him. That was the main reason why they'd stayed together for so long, and why she'd had to break it off with him in the end. As good as it felt, it was too easy to lose herself in him. She had wanted to do things with her life. Become someone significant, someone of value. She'd had ideas and dreams and wishes that she had wanted and needed to fulfill. And when she'd been with Jack, all of those needs and dreams and wishes flitted through the open windows. When she'd been with Jack, all she had needed was him. She shook her head, shaking out the memories.

She'd found herself. She'd created a good life for herself. An independent life. A life with a job she loved, work that fulfilled her, a husband who, well…

At one time, early on at least, things had been okay in her marriage. She allowed herself a moment to grieve over the loss of her little step-daughter. At least Ron had been, up until recently, fairly decent to her. Their marriage had ended, in all practical sense, on the day his daughter had died. But they had stayed married on paper out of convenience on her part, and she supposed out of loneliness, or laziness, on his. And now he was dead. And all the grief from early on in her marriage came flooding back. Grief and guilt. Forever intertwined. She couldn't afford to regret what could have been. Or what should have been.

She rested the top of her head against Jack's chest, closing her eyes, not wanting the moment to end, but needing to step away from the comfort and the closeness. She had made a mistake in leaving Jack. She knew that instinctively the moment she'd walked out the door all those years ago. But her stubbornness and her willful desire for success and life fulfillment had shielded her view from the possibility that perhaps she may have been able to have all those things and have Jack too. Only after she'd married Ron did she realize what a fool she had been for letting Jack go. No one had ever looked at her the way he had. No one had ever made her feel so loved, so safe the way he had.

Her tears began to drip onto Jack's feet. Hot splashes of grief raining down upon the floor. With an awkward twist of his hand, he let the dust pan drop into the kitchen sink, and rested the broom up against the kitchen counter. With a practiced and gentle hand, he pulled her into a full embrace, and allowed his hands to press up against her back.

The tears grew in earnest, flowing freely down the hairs of his chest. Within moments the tears turned to sobs, and the sobs eventually turned into silent convulsions. He stroked her hair, pulling it gently to the side away from her face, and allowed some of the cooler air to wash over her. As her weeping turned to hiccups and the hiccups turned to sniffles, he leaned them both to the right just enough to snag a tissue from the box on the counter and passed it to her with his free hand. She sniffled and wiped her tears and her nose, suddenly embarrassed by her emotional outburst. He pressed another tissue into her hand, and then another, and another as she wiped the flow of tears and moisture away from her face. She turned her head and kissed his chest, wiping the wetness from his chest hairs. A shiver of pleasure coursed through his body and he grew very still.

Letting her hair create a veil around her face, she spoke to his chest, apologizing for her outburst.

"You don't need to apologize."

"I've used up all your tissues." She hiccuped once again, sniffling into the wad of tissues she'd amassed.

"I'll buy more."

"I've gotten your chest all wet."

"It'll dry."

"Oh, Jack. I'm a mess." She pulled her head away from his chest and wiped her face off with the wad of used up tissues.

Tucking her hair behind her ears, he leaned down and kissed each of her warm cheeks. "You have never been more beautiful."

Her eyes pooling once again, she watched in wonder as he leaned forward and kissed her, ever so gently, on her swollen lips. Her heart fluttered.

He scooped his hands around her face. Her heart raced madly, beating roughly against her rib cage. She closed her eyes, leaning up into him. He held her face in his hand for just a moment and then dipped his head down, pressing his lips against each of her eyelids in turn.

Waves of disappointment, comfort, and thrill washed over her as he took a step back, then squeezed her arms and stepped away. She felt suddenly cold and at a loss.

"Let me make you some tea."

Feeling lost and abandoned, she nodded her head, chastising herself for wanting something that she had no right to want. Needing something she had given up because she didn't want to need it.

"I'll just..." Embarrassed, Claire stepped around the kitchen island and headed to the guest bathroom to dispose of her wad of used tissues and to recompose her face. She sat on the edge of the tub for several long moments getting a grip with herself. What had she wanted? For him to kiss her? For him to tell her, once again, all those lovely things he used to whisper to her in the dark quiet hours of their lovemaking? For them to get back together? A flutter of hope made its way through to her consciousness, and she sat up straight in awe. Maybe that's what she wanted. For them to get back together.

She blinked a few times allowing the realization to sink through. The flutter of hope turned into a gently galloping horse, and a burst of glee shot through her heart. She jumped to her feet, catching her reflection in the mirror in front of her.

Reality slapped her in the face.

Her puffy, tear stained face, even with the smile slowly fading from her lips, couldn't disguise her grief or the true purpose of how she came to be at Jack's house in the first place. In a rush, she felt ashamed of her previous feelings. Glancing down she seemed surprised to find the wad of used tissues still clenched in her fist. She opened the cupboard beneath the sink and dropped them into the small recycle bin. Suddenly feeling naked and exposed, she tugged the oversized tee shirt down, trying to cover more of her bum and her legs, but to no avail. A quick look in two of the drawers led her to a stack of clean, freshly laundered wash cloths. She let the cold water from the tap drench the cloth, and then pressed the cool cloth against her overly warm and swollen face.

What had she been thinking? Her husband was a cheater. A lying, cheating drunk who, up until a short while ago, the Sheriff's Office thought was a serial killer. She didn't know which was worse.

Knowing that they suspected him of killing all those girls, or knowing that the serial killer had turned the tables and killed him too.

Her cheeks burned with the memory of the the events from the night before. In a fog, having been rudely awakened from a drug-induced nap, she found herself sitting on Jack's couch, watching the chaplain's lips move as he slowly detailed her husband's exploits. The words barely registered as they moved sluggishly through the air. Like watching a movie play out in slow-motion, the distorted sound impossible to comprehend, she watched in wonder as the police officer received a phone call only moments later. Watched as his face registered surprise. Watched as he shook his head to the chaplain. Watched as he sat down and tried to explain the events of the night before. Watched them in silence as they explained their mistake. Watched as they told her that her husband was dead. Like her best friend. That both of them had been murdered.

She sank down to the floor and pressed the cold compress against her cheek. All of this was simply too much to handle. She didn't want to handle it any more. She just wanted it to all go away. Why couldn't it all just go away?

"Claire, honey, can I get you anything?"

His face was so beautiful. Her heart ached just to see him peer around the corner. But then his eyebrows furrowed together in worry and he stepped into the bathroom and squatted down next to her.

She could feel the heat from his chest. All she wanted to do was bury herself in his arms once again, and allow the grief of the whole damned day to wash over them both.

"I made you some breakfast."

Tears sprang to her eyes. Thoughtful. He was always so damned thoughtful. She pressed the wet washcloth against her eyes before he could see the new tears and she nodded her head.

"Peanut butter pancakes?"

"Of course."

She allowed herself the luxury of leaning in to him one last time. Then let herself be lifted to her feet. She carried his hand like a baby elephant following her mother, and allowed herself to be led down the hallway toward her favorite comfort food.

Chapter 35

DESPITE THE PEANUT butter pancakes, breakfast remained a subdued affair. Jack sipped his juice and scrolled through the missed messages on his work phone. Claire's attention wandered. The morning sun lit up Jack's front room, bringing in a cheerful morning glow, creating a sharp contrast to the harsh truth and grim reality of Ron's death. Her appetite gone, Claire stood and carried her dishes to the sink. She washed them quickly and, with efficiency, had the kitchen back to its original immaculate condition before Jack's attention lifted from his cell phone.

"You didn't have to do that."

Her brief smile didn't touch her eyes. "No, but I wanted to." She glanced down at the tee she was wearing and her bare legs beneath them. She blushed. "I need to get dressed."

Jack's eyes admired the lovely view of her bare legs, and his dimple popped out of the side of his cheek. He found himself unable to suppress a grin. "You look good all rumpled up and half naked in my kitchen." He winked at her and took a sip of his orange juice, pleased with the blush that grew deeper into Claire's cheeks. "But if you insist on getting dressed, I'll need to go fetch you some clothes."

Claire sighed and looked away.

Jack pushed back his chair and found his way over to her. He pulled her into his arms and allowed himself the luxury of comfort. Whether he was comforting her or himself, he wasn't quite sure. Probably a little bit of both. "Are you okay with staying here for a bit? Hanging out here until things settle?"

Claire nodded her head, looking down at the floor. She didn't trust herself to look up at him. Her feelings grew into a mangled mess of confusion and being so physically close to Jack only complicated matters.

"Tell you what. I'll head over to your place. Pick up a few of your things to make your stay here more comfortable."

She nodded her head, and then gave in to the urge and pressed her cheek against Jack's chest.

Mindlessly, he stroked her back. "After I drop off your things here, I've got to head into work for a little while. Get some things done. I'll call GranNini. Have her come by with a basket of muffins or something sinful. See if she can stop writing for the afternoon and come on over here and keep you company until I can get back here, okay?"

Again, she nodded her head, not trusting herself to speak. If she opened her mouth, the tears would start all over again. And she didn't want to embarrass herself further by having another sobbing festival in Jack's chest hairs.

He kissed the top of her head and tucked her hand into his. He led them both down the hall to his bedroom in the back, and sat her down on the edge of his rumpled bed.

"I'll just, uh…"

He bolted to the side of his bed and pulled the sheets and comforter up to the top. Then with a deft hand, he smoothed out the covers, straightened his pillows, and then tossed his two large throw pillows up onto the bed. That settled, he flipped on the lights to his enormous walk in closet and pulled out his old college sweat pants, a clean tee, and dug through his sock drawer until he found a pair of clean white socks without any holes in the heels. He spent a long moment contemplating his underwear drawer, wondering. But after an internal debate, he decided she'd probably be more comfortable in her own unmentionables, even if they were yesterday's clothes.

Setting the pile of clothes next to Claire on the bed beside her, oblivious to the amused smile growing upon her face, Jack headed out into the hall linen closet and pulled out two fresh towels, remembering that she liked a second towel to wrap around her hair. He thanked his lucky stars that he'd taken a few hours over the weekend before to catch up on his laundry and run a vacuum through his house. He'd have been mortified if she'd come over last week instead and seen the wicked state of his bathroom.

Bringing the stack of fresh towels, he pressed them into her lap and kissed her on her head once more. "Why don't you take the first shower. There are wash cloths in the bathroom cupboards. These are obviously way too big," he nodded to the stack of clothes next to him, "but I seem to recall you didn't mind wearing them back in college." What he really remembered was how insanely hot she looked wearing his sweats, and how great her ass looked when she'd wiggle herself into his sweat pants, teasing him mercilessly. He loved the way she let the much too large pants hang low against her hips, her flat belly aching to be kissed as she'd pull up her tank top, revealing the sexy bare skin beneath, to roll down the waistband.

Shaking the memories aside, he helped her up off the bed and scooted her off to the guest bathroom.

Once he heard the shower running, he hopped on the treadmill, forcing his pace faster than normal to try to run off some of the excess energy he felt building up inside. He pushed himself hard for the full twenty minutes Claire ran the shower, then allowed his body to ease up a bit when he heard the shower turn off. He kept his cool down brief, hopping off the treadmill a few minutes later. He kept his shower short and very cold. Taking a quick look around he tidied up his bathroom, taking an extra moment to run a Clorox lemon wipe across his sink and counter, and another across the toilet seat and bowl. GranNini had taught him well. For years she had chastised him never to let a guest see his bathroom or his kitchen in a disreputable state. He dressed quickly. Then, eying his closet, he tidied up there too, being sure to quickly pick up a few random socks that hadn't quite made it into his laundry basket.

He dug around the shelf in his closet where he kept his gun safe searching for a black mourning band. He found one, all dusty and grimy, hidden in the back under a plastic bag of bullets he'd brought home from the range. He hadn't had to wear his mourning band since Lieutenant Tom Sullivan had climbed out of the pool at the marine board Law Enforcement Academy. He'd just finished a survival swimming exercise training mission, took three steps, and keeled over dead from a heart attack.

Dusting the band off as best as he could, he wrapped it carefully around the Sheriff's star of his badge, and slid his belt through the badge holder, adjusting the badge and his gun at his side and buckling his belt in front. He'd use a piece of black electrician's tape to make a black horizontal strip across the star on his pocket badge when he got to work. Even assholes earned a moment of mourning when they died on the job.

He found Claire sitting on the edge of his couch, one foot propped up against the coffee table, the other foot wiggling its way into his much too large sock. He grinned. Squatting down in front of her, he took a good long look at her face. She looked tired, her face lined with grief and exhaustion, but she smelled clean and fresh, her hair still wet and wavy.

He resisted the urge to tuck a wet curl behind her ear.

"I hate to leave you here by yourself. You going to be okay for a little bit?"

She sat back against the couch and pulled her legs up to her chest, nodding her head. "It'll be nice to just have some quiet space, you know?"

He nodded his head. He remembered how good it felt to have a moment's peace after his mother's funeral and the whole mess with his brother. At the time, he would have given just about anything for just two hours of pure silence; a respite from the well-meaning good wishes from his mother's and brother's friends, what few of them they'd had. Sometimes it wasn't laughter, but quiet and silence that truly were the best medicine.

Jack leaned over, holding his tie against his chest so it wouldn't hit Claire in the face, and kissed her once again on the top of her head. Her hair smelled like coconut, and he smiled.

"I'll be back as soon as I can. Are you okay if I head to work first? And then go over and grab some of your things after?"

She nodded her head.

"Is there anything in particular you'd like?"

"I can't think of anything. I really just want to…" She glanced at the pillow at the end of his couch and reached over to grab the fuzzy blanket and pull it onto her lap.

Jack understood, and nodded his head. "I'll be back as soon as I can. Call me if you need anything."

She nodded, shifting her body around so that she could lay down and stretch out her legs.

"You know, Claire, you can always go take a nap in my bed."

"I know." She yawned and shifted her body so that she faced the back of the couch.

Looking around, he found his cell phone sitting on the kitchen table with his dirty breakfast dishes. He felt a stab of guilt as he carried his dishes and left them unceremoniously in the sink to wash later. He stuffed his phone in his pocket and turned, admiring the gentle way her body moved as she slipped into slumber. Sleep. Sleep and quiet, in his opinion, the two best ways to deal with grief.

He took one last look of her still form, grabbed his keys from the porcelain bowl, nabbed his jacket from its hook, and headed out the door and off to work before he could change his mind, drop his gear, and pull her into his arms.

Chapter 36

"SO, WHAT HAVE we got?"

Nick spun around, startled by Jack's sudden arrival.

Manny looked up and grinned. "Diamond! You're looking better! Not so much like death warmed over any more. I take it you got some sleep?"

He nodded. "A little sleep, a little food. It's amazing what the comforts of home can do to bring you back to the land of the living."

Nick thumped Jack against the arm and turned back to face the paperwork strewn across the conference room table.

"Did you get a hit off AFIS?"

"No...but we did get one off IBIS."

Jack grinned. "You're kidding me! So who've we got?"

Nick pulled out a black and white military photo from the stack of papers in front of him. "The finger prints and the partial palm print you got from Ron's driver's side door — and, by the way, your partial index finger print off the gear shift — all match up to one Richard L. Barrett. Thirty-six. Ex-army. Six foot even, one seventy five. Lives here in Portland."

"Does he have any warrants?"

Manny dug around in the pile of papers in front of him and pulled up a sheet of paper with yellow highlighter lines scattered throughout. "No warrants, but the guy is the suspect in a rape on a military base down in California about six years ago. Beat the woman half to death, roughed her up good while he raped her. There wasn't any semen, and no other DNA to tie him to the case. Her word against his. He, being an upstanding young man from the military with a clean record — give or take a few allegations of suspected excessive use of force as an MP. Never substantiated. And she having a rather more colorful track record down there... well, you know how it goes. Besides, she never got a great look at the guy. Couldn't narrow it down between him and another guy in the line up, so even though the other guy had a solid tight alibi, this piece of work got off scott free." He threw the paper down against the table so hard that several other papers scattered, and a few slid off onto the floor.

Jack leaned down and picked up the papers, setting them down with care on the conference room table.

"So what's next? When are we off to go get Barrett and bring him in for questioning?"

"Just waiting on the warrant."

"We've got two of our detectives out scoping his place now."

"And the plan of attack?"

287

Nick started stacking the papers into piles, reaching across the table to grab certain pieces of paper, and leaving others. Jack watched in fascination as Nick made order out of the chaos. "As soon as the warrant comes through, and we get the intel from our detectives on Barrett's comings and goings at his apartment, we'll have the detectives and a couple of our undercover cars come with us to serve him up with the habeas grabus, and we'll haul his sorry self back here to question him."

"Does any of your evidence tie our Mr. Barrett to any of the serial murders?" Manny looked up at Jack, then to Nick, and back again, a hopeful look in his eyes.

The two spoke at the ends of each other's sentences, as if they'd practiced this speech a dozen times before they'd been asked.

"Other than the rather damning fingerprints on Ron's car? No."

"We never did pick up any prints or DNA from the victims."

"But our evidence against Ron really was pretty tight. We had the PI's report placing Ron at the bars with each of the victims."

"And we had all those photos of each of the victims at the bars."

"And we'd found credit card receipts that indicated that Ron bought alcohol at each of the bars where each of the victims last visited before they were murdered."

"We went through his phone records…"

288

"And found that he'd talked to at least two of the women before meeting them at the bars."

"Our case against Ron was pretty solid." Jack's face reddened in his defense. Learning that Ron had become his serial killer's latest victim had thrown Jack in a tailspin. Their case against Ron had been so strong that had Ron lived, he felt confident that he would have been able to give the D.A. enough evidence to put Ron away for the rest of his life. Shame and embarrassment mixed with grief and guilt. He found it difficult to swallow.

"Yeah, well, that's all turned to rot in the pot." Manny cleared his throat. "So, we don't have anything to tie Barrett to any of the victims except Ron."

"Not at this time, sir. But I'm sure after we interview..."

"And the post mortem?"

Nick cleared his throat, grateful for the change in subject. "Dr. Willner from the M.E.'s office called about an hour ago, said that she could fit Ron into her schedule as soon as Jack and I were able to fit it into ours."

Jack whipped his head around to see Nick's face. Nick avoided his gaze. A second wave of embarrassment reddened his face. He hadn't realized he was holding up the autopsy. "We could head on down there now, while we're waiting for the arrest and search warrant for Barrett."

"No, the warrant should be coming through any minute now. Wait here until it comes through. I want to get this guy in our custody as soon as possible." He swallowed the hard lump trying to find its way up his throat. "Fortunately for us, Ron can wait a bit."

Jack bowed his head. Nick just looked away. Manny straightened up and gave Nick and Jack a full once over. "I want you guys to find something, something good. Something solid. Something that will tie Barrett to the rest of our victims. I want you to search his house upside down and backwards from Sunday. I want his car cleaned out and sucked dry of all evidence. I want his co-workers and his neighbors interviewed. I want his cell phone records and his credit card records and his elementary school report card gone over with a fine tooth comb. I want so much evidence found on this guy that even a third grader could tie him to our victims. I want him arrested, fingerprinted, tagged and bagged and into our custody today. Now. Five minutes ago, dammit! I want you guys to unfuck this situation ASAP! Do I make myself clear?"

"Yes, sir!"

"Absolutely, sir."

"We've got to get this slick sucker before the before press gets wind of our previous error. And I don't want any victims' mothers to come pounding down my door trying to find out why I haven't arrested the monster who did these unspeakable things to their daughters. And I certainly don't want Ron's wife to hire an attorney and sue the snot out of our department when she catches wind that we dredged his name and reputation through the mud, thinking her poor, dead husband was guilty of drugging, beating up, and sexually assaulting these women." He took a deep breath. "That's the last thing we need." He let his eyes glance over the stack of photos in front of him. "Those poor women."

Manny took another deep breath and allowed his gaze to pass between Jack and Nick, both standing at attention before him. "Go get him, fellas." He stepped around the side of the conference room table and opened the conference room door. "And don't let me down."

Chapter 37

UNLIKE IN THE movies, tires didn't squeal and screech as they turned the final corner into Richard L. Barrett's neighborhood. Dozens of patrol cars with lights and sirens blaring didn't surround his block, double parking on the narrow side streets. Uniformed officers didn't come pouring out of cars, guns at the ready. No one grabbed a bull horn, demanding for the accused to come out with his hands up. And certainly no one came running down the fire escape, daring to try to sneak out the back, eluding the police who surrounded the front, and only the front, of the building. In reality, arrests aren't usually so dramatic.

Because of Barrett's violent tendencies, and the rather vicious nature of the brutal rapes and murders of all the victims the Sheriff's Office now accused Barrett of committing, Jack and Nick took along back up. More back up than they normally took when picking up a potential bad guy. They brought along their two detectives who had previously scoped out Barrett's apartment. Then they brought along two unmarked patrol cars as well, and had those deputies park in strategic locations near Barrett's apartment, keeping an eye out for him approaching, or leaving, the apartment.

The two detectives who had scoped out the apartment beforehand had reported that they had seen no sign of Barrett coming or going. They had avoided talking to the neighbors or to the apartment manager for fear that one of them would tip him off. They didn't want Barrett to get the heebie jeebies and take off before they had a chance to interview him. Jack and Nick headed straight up to the third floor, while the two detectives persuaded the apartment manager to let them borrow the apartment key. Evidently the manager had no desire to pay for a new door and door frame, should somehow the door get broken during their attempt to interrogate the suspect.

Just like in the movies, Jack pulled out his gun, kept it close to his chest, pounded on the door, and kept his body pressed up against the wall, rather than standing in front of the door. Sometimes even the movies get things right. "Mr. Barrett? Can you please open the door? Sheriff's Office!"

When they heard no response, Jack pounded again. "Mr. Barrett? Are you home?"

Again, no response. Nick looked at Jack, and they nodded to one another. "Mr. Barrett, we're going to let ourselves in to your apartment now."

With that, Nick unlocked the door, let himself into the apartment with his gun drawn, and Jack followed right behind. It took only seconds for them to realize that the apartment was a ruse. The empty apartment clearly hadn't been used in quite some time. Dust covered everything. The electricity either hadn't been hooked up or had already been turned off. A few spiders had made sad, sorry attempts at webs in the corner of one of the curtain-less windows.

Just to make sure, they searched the entire apartment and found nothing. Jack flipped on the water tap at the kitchen sink, and the only thing that came out of the pipes was a loud groan emanating from deep down in the depths of the building. The pipes began to shake, and Jack flipped off the tap before something unpleasant could make its way upwards.

"Well shit."

Jack just nodded his head. What more was there to say?

They headed downstairs to talk with the apartment manager, while the two detectives interviewed the one neighbor who bothered to answer his door. Jack only caught a quick glimpse of the man, but he reminded Jack of Mr. Heckles, the downstairs neighbor from the television sitcom "Friends." He suppressed a grin and made his way down the stairs.

"Mr. Kaufman, can you tell us about the tenant who rented apartment 3B?"

"Who, Mr. Jones? Can't really tell you much. Paid six months' rent in advance. He was pretty quiet. Never got any complaints." He pushed his glasses up to the bridge of his nose. "Why, did he do something wrong?"

"Is this the man you refer to as Mr. Jones?" Jack showed him the military picture of Richard Barrett.

"Looks like him. But he's a bit older now, I'd say. And he's bald now." Mr. Kaufman scratched at the grey stubble on his chin, wiping away a bit of spittle that had acquired in the corner of his mouth.

"We'd like to talk to him about an ongoing investigation. Do you have any emergency contact information for him? Perhaps his application form?"

"Oh, well, um…" Mr. Kaufman turned his body to give his apartment a quick once over, then turned back, a look of resignation on his face. "You know how it goes. I'm sure it's in here somewhere, but I don't remember where I would have put it." Mr. Kaufman peered over his shoulder, glancing around his apartment once again with futility, then allowing his gaze to linger at the television screen where the showcase show down was about to begin. He sighed with longing. Stacks of newspapers swayed in a pile next to the door. Paperwork of all shapes and sizes littered every visible horizontal surface. Although not quite at the hoarding level, his apartment clearly could be deemed a fire hazard should the fire marshall ever stop by for a visit.

Mr. Kaufman pulled up his brown trousers, revealing a pair of mismatched socks and overly worn slippers. "Is there anything else I can do for you fellas?" He straightened his glasses and pushed them further up to the bridge of his nose, tilting his head back a bit to see through the bifocal portion at the bottom of his glasses. The nose hairs in his overly large nostrils caught Jack's attention. He found himself staring. The man's nostrils were truly enormous. Jack's mind wandered to the time he had to interview a young, almost beautiful woman who had a very sizable mole on her left cheek, which had the unfortunate mistake of sprouting a small, delicate brown hair out the middle. It was like a train wreck. He found himself unable to look away.

Mr. Kaufman's eyes glazed over for a moment, and he tilted his chin down to his chest and peered out of the top of his glasses this time. His gaze passed from Jack to Nick and back again.

"No, sir, I think that's probably about it. If you happen to run into this man again, could you please give us a call? Or if you find out that he's made himself at home up there? We'd really like to talk to him."

Mr. Kaufman held the proffered business card in his shaking hand, tilting his head upwards once again to read through the bifocals of his lenses. Jack caught himself staring, once again, at the man's nostrils. He cleared his throat.

They watched as Mr. Kaufman slipped the business card into his pants pocket, knowing that, in all likelihood, they'd never hear from him again. They thanked him for his time. Jack smiled as the man turned and shuffled back over to his barcalounger, swinging the door shut behind him.

Chapter 38

THEY CAUGHT UP with the two detectives from upstairs and exchanged information. Mr. Heckles, a.k.a. Fred Donovan, had never seen anyone in apartment 3B. The place had probably remained empty from the moment Barrett had rented the apartment.

"Can you guys please pull the utilities on the place? Just to make sure? It doesn't look like anyone's been living here, but let's make sure we didn't just miss him."

One of the detectives nodded her head, and jotted down instructions in her leather covered pad of paper. "We'll meet you back at the office. Let you know what we come up with."

Nick nodded. Jack waved and watched them cross the street.

"So what's next then?" Jack ran his fingers through his hair as he crossed the street toward their car. "I'm feeling completely dejected. Geez, it's like someone just swiped my feet out from underneath me." He stepped up and over the curb and stood by the passenger side door, waiting for Nick to unlock the car. "I'm not sure why, but I really thought we'd find him here."

Nick started up the car and headed back to the office. He glanced over at Jack, whose attention had been caught by the messages on his cell phone.

"Seriously?"

Jack looked over at Nick. "Well, yeah."

Nick laughed. "It's never that simple."

Jack smiled. "No, I guess not. It's just…"

Nick let the silence fill the car until Jack could collect his thoughts.

"Everything in this case has obviously been well thought out."

Nick glanced over at Jack, encouraged by his train of thought, but not wanting to interrupt his flow. He glanced back at the road and flipped on his turn signal, easing the car into a left hand turn.

"So this guy drugs, rapes, and murders all those girls. Cuts diamond shapes out of their chests. Stashes all of their bodies in water. He leaves no trace of evidence. No fingerprints, no semen, no hairs, nothing. He completely gets away with it. And then he kills Ron." He glanced out the window, seeing nothing. Then he turned his head back to Nick. "Why did he kill Ron?"

Nick looked at Jack, keeping his thoughts to himself, and then glanced back at the traffic in front of him.

"Seriously? Why did he kill Ron? He could have let Ron take the fall for this whole thing. We were so close to putting Ron away for this. We had enough evidence to put him away for the rest of his life." A wave of nausea washed over him, and he rubbed his face, trying to rub the guilt away. "So why didn't he just let Ron take the blame for it? Have Ron take the fall?"

Nick shook his head. "Maybe Ron figured out who the killer was, and got too close. Tried to kill Barrett himself."

A guffaw burst out of Jack before he could help it. "Ron? Figure out something on his own? Are you kidding me? The guy's a total waste of space. He was a drunk and an idiot. How he ever managed to get Claire to marry him, I'll never know."

Nick offered up a "hmmm," but kept the rest of his thoughts on the topic of Ron and Claire to himself. He'd seen Claire enough times at the office to know Jack was right. Whatever Claire saw in Ron, he certainly didn't see it. But this wasn't the time to debate Jack's bias on the subject.

Nick cleared his throat. "Okay, so let's talk theories here. Theory one: Ron figured out who the serial killer was. Who knows how he did it, but let's just say, for a moment, that he did."

"Okay."

"So maybe Ron thought we weren't doing a good enough job, who knows. Or maybe he decided he'd take the killer on by himself — like a vigilante or something. Or, or, or — get this, yeah, this makes more sense, — maybe he just wanted all the credit for taking him down. But then the killing went awry, and Barrett killed Ron before Ron could kill Barrett."

"Doubtful. Ron was too big of an idiot to figure it out on his own. Besides, I don't think he was even paying attention to our case. Frankly, I don't think Ron was even paying attention to anything other than hanging out at bars and flirting with blonde chicks."

"Well, hmm. There is some truth in that. Okay. Theory two: Ron got in the killer's way. Maybe Ron saw Barrett kill one of his victims, and therefore Ron had to be killed too."

"Hmmm. That makes more sense. But that doesn't explain how Ron ended up in his own patrol car."

"Well, let's not complicate things just yet. Can we both agree that it's possible that Ron saw Barrett killing one of the victims, and that our killer then killed Ron to avoid being caught?"

"Okay."

"Okay, so theory two is still in play." Nick stopped the car at a traffic light, waiting for the cars in front of him to move again. Traffic thus far had been pretty light, and they'd made quick work of heading back to the office. "Theory three: Barrett wanted to find out how close we were in identifying him, so he broke into Ron's marked police car, broke into our computer system, and tried to listen in on our investigation, and got caught by Ron in the process. A struggle ensued, and Ron ended up dead."

"Hmmm. Possible, but less likely. There would have been more signs of a struggle inside of Ron's patrol car."

"Unless he didn't get that far, and Ron caught him before he could break in."

"Okay. I suppose that's possible."

"All right. So theories two and three are still on the table. Any more ideas?" Nick turned into the parking structure, allowing his eyes to adjust to the dark before pulling the car around the corner in search of an elusive parking spot. One could rarely find a spot after nine thirty on a week day morning, but since it was coming up on the lunch hour, he had hopes he'd be able to snag the spot of someone heading out early for lunch.

"I can't think of anything. My brain is just fried."

Nick whooped with glee when he found an empty spot, tucked between two rather enormous SUVs. "Better get out here before I pull in. It's a bit tight."

Jack slipped out of the car and winced as Nick pulled his car into a space meant for a much thinner vehicle. How Nick managed to squeeze his oversized belly out of his car and still have room to lock the doors was a feat of physics he couldn't possibly understand.

"So. We have a couple of theories. But now we have no idea where this guy is. What's our plan?" Nick puffed a bit, trying to keep up with Jack's brisk pace across the third floor bridge leading from the parking structure back to their office.

Jack rubbed his face, slipped his key card out of his pocket, swiping it across the keypad, and then held the door open for Nick when the door buzzed open. "First, we go back to the office and run a credit check. See what he's been buying. See if that'll pinpoint his current whereabouts."

"What about his internet activity?"

Jack's brain started to kick in once again. "We can try to see if we can find out if he's searching for stuff online. Trace his IP address back to a physical location. Then we should probably task all our snitches."

"And what, offer up a hefty reward for any information on the guy's whereabouts?"

"Yep. It's what's worked in the past." Nick punched the button for the elevator and they waited, rather impatiently, for the elevator to arrive.

Jack nodded his head.

"First things first, though, we should put up a BOLO to all the other law enforcement agencies in Oregon, Washington, Idaho and California."

"BOLO?"

"Be On The Lookout."

"Ah." Jack felt his cheeks redden for not knowing the acronym. He turned his body to the side, stepping into the elevator, grateful for the elevator's perfect timing.

"Then," he sighed, "if none of that pans out..."

"Which it probably won't."

"Such an optimist you are. At that point, I think our only option is to circulate his picture out to the media. Let people know that he's a person of interest in an ongoing investigation. Have them call 911 if they see him. You know, the usual. Make sure we mention that he's considered armed and dangerous, and that they shouldn't try to approach him."

When the doors slid open, Jack felt a wave of fear pass over him. What if they weren't able to locate Barrett before he struck again? How many more women were going to be drugged, beaten, raped and murdered before they caught him? How many more diamonds were going to get carved out of how many more women's chests?

Jack shivered.

Chapter 39

NICK OPTED TO stay at the Sheriff's Office, working on pulling up Barrett's credit card reports, trying to hunt down any internet activity on the guy, and finding out anything else he could to help narrow down the search on where to find their latest suspect. Jack grabbed his jacket and headed over to the M.E.'s office to witness Ron's post mortem.

Watching an autopsy had never made Jack nauseous, like it did for some people. Nor did it hold a fascination for him, like it obviously did for Monday. She peered inside each and every one of Ron's crevices and orifices, documenting everything from his overly abundant ear hairs, to his apparent testicular atrophy. Without so much as a raised eyebrow, Monday noted in her oral dictation recorder that she believed his shrunken testicles were most likely caused by either excessive abuse of alcohol, or steroid usage. She made a note to herself to add steroids to her toxicology screening report. Then she added an aside to take an extended look at his liver to look for signs of cirrhosis. Jack kept his own theories as to Ron's shrunken testicles to himself, trying his best to keep his snickers to himself until he could laugh to his heart's content in the privacy of his own car.

Monday noted, for the record, the deep ligature marks across Ron's neck, from just below his left ear, down across the deep folds of his neck, and back up to his right ear lobe. The marks, created by a piece of twine or thin rope, were similar in findings from those marks found on each of the other victims in Jack's serial killer case.

She spent quite a bit of time analyzing the carving out of Ron's chest. "Like the other victims, a diamond, approximately seven centimeters in length and four point five centimeters in width has been carved out of the victim's chest. The diamond was carved out approximately two centimeters above the man's left nipple, in an almost identical setting to that of each of the other victims. The entire epidermal layer has been removed, revealing the reticular dermis tissue beneath. Again, these findings coincide with the findings of each of the female victims in these connected cases. In this victim's case, and in the case of all the female victims save for the first, I find no evidence of a tattoo removal, nor of any bitemarks near the area that had been removed."

"Bitemarks?"

Monday looked up, startled to remember that Jack had been standing beside her, observing and listening to her dictation of Ron's post mortem. She'd been so caught up in her investigation, and he had been so completely silent, she had forgotten that he was standing beside her. "Yes, bitemarks. You'd be surprised at how many aggressors bite their victims. It's typically seen as a sexual action of sorts.

So in cases of sexual abuse, I always take another look for bite marks. Or in NAIs in children."

"NAIs?"

"Non accidental injuries. Parents biting their children as some form of punishment."

Jack blanched. Out of all the horrific things his father had ever done to him or to his brother, not once had his father ever bitten either of them. He shuddered, grateful — to whom, he wasn't sure — that his father hadn't ever thought to do that to them. Another shudder passed through him, and he clenched his fists, willing his thoughts to move away from his past and back to the table in front of him.

"I also see no contusions — bruises — in the general area, that almost always accompany bitemarks. If he'd been bitten hard enough, some of the bruising would have shown up at this level." She pressed the tip of her instrument against Ron's body, and Jack looked on in morbid fascination.

"Furthermore, the size of this excising of skin is smaller than one would expect if Ron had been bitten by his attacker, and then the attacker tried to excise the evidence of the bitemark. I'd expect an area a bit larger and of a slightly different shape."

Jack nodded, following along.

"That's not to say that the perpetrator doesn't simply have a smaller jaw, or didn't excise a different shaped area to simply disguise the fact that he or she bit the victim." She looked at Jack to see if he was paying attention.

"I simply do not believe that this victim was bitten in this particular area. I see no abrasions — scrapes, lacerations — tears, erythema — redness, or indentations or any punctures in or around the area near this section that has been removed that one would expect to see, or could often be seen in bitemarks. So at this point I'm fairly comfortable ruling out the theory that this section was excised as a means to remove a bitemark."

Jack nodded his head, impressed with Monday's ability to carefully, clearly, and concisely state her findings. No wonder she made such an impressive expert witness on the stand. He smiled.

Jack's mind wandered as Monday made her way through the rest of the autopsy. He watched as she carefully cut through his rib cage and then systematically weighed and measured each of his internal organs, examining each of them carefully for signs of trauma or disease. His mind phased in and out as she spoke into her recorder.

"He didn't drown."

Jack looked up. She had a sizable chunk of ew in her hand and held it up to him. "His lungs are clean. They're not overinflated. Nor are they heavy with fluid."

Jack nodded.

"And there was no sign of foam in or around his mouth. There's no watery fluid in his stomach. Most drowning victims swallow at least a little of the water while they're struggling under water. So all of this, coupled with the petechiae in his eyes, the broken hyoid bone, and the ligature marks on his neck leads me to believe that the cause of death is most likely asphyxia due to garotting. I'll have to wait for the toxicology reports, of course, but that's what I'm leaning toward at this point."

Jack nodded his head.

Monday gave him a smile. "Let me finish up here. If I find anything else of any interest to you, I'll give you a call."

"Thanks, Monday."

"Bye, Ryerson!" Jack called across the room to Ned Quon, elbow deep into the chest cavity of a rather sizable gentleman on the other side of the autopsy suite. Ned looked up and nodded. Jack smiled and headed out to his car.

When his bluetooth picked up an incoming call just as Jack found himself merging into traffic, Jack answered without looking at the caller ID. "Monday! Calling back so soon?"

"Jack?"

"Monday?"

"No, it's Claire."

"Oh, sorry about that!" He glanced over at the caller ID on the readout and saw that the call, indeed, came from Claire. Just seeing her name sent a zap of electricity up and down his legs. "You okay? I haven't had a chance to get to your place to pick up your stuff. I just finished up..." He jolted. Claire really didn't need to know where he just was, and what he was just doing. He cleared his throat and started again. "I'm just now on a break, actually. I can head over to your place now if you'd like."

"Um, yeah. But…"

"Did GranNini every get over there?"

"Well yes, but…"

"Did she bring you some of her famous potato leek soup?"

"Yes, actually. It was quite delicious. But listen, Jack…"

"And some of her homemade bread?"

"Jack! Focus, will you?"

Her stern tone caught him off guard. "Are you okay, Claire?"

"Jack, I'm fine. Just listen to me."

"Okay, I'm listening!"

"GranNini and I were having a nice lunch. I had the television on for some background noise. You know how I hate it when it gets too quiet. Anyway, the news came on."

The smile that had been growing on his face, just at the thought of seeing her in just a little while slowly began to fade.

"They had a news flash about Ron's case."

"Claire, you know you don't need to watch that stuff. You shouldn't trouble yourself with watching the nitty gritty news crap about Ron's death. It's only going to upset you."

"Don't tell me what I can and cannot do, Jack. I'm not a little girl. And I'm not someone you can just tell what to do!"

A pump of adrenaline surged through Jack's chest. Claire had never talked to him like this before. She'd never needed to. Her strength, especially at a time like this, surprised him. She'd changed, and obviously for the better, since he'd been with her. She was right. He had no reason to treat her with such disrespect. A wave of guilt washed over him, and he wondered how many times he was going to feel guilty for his stupidity today.

"Claire, I'm sorry." He kept his voice low, hoping she could hear the honest truth in those words.

"I'm sorry too. I shouldn't have snipped at you like that, but you've got to listen to me. The news came on, and they flashed up a picture of a person of interest in the case."

Jack stopped at the traffic light, and glanced down at his work telephone, noticing for the first time he had five new voicemail messages, a dozen texts, and more than enough emails to keep him busy the rest of the evening. One of them was probably from Nick, letting him know they released Barrett's photo to the press, hoping someone would be able to identify — and help them locate — their newest suspect.

"Um, yeah. Nick said that if he wasn't able to turn up any new evidence, we'd put out a picture of our latest suspect on the news, see if anyone could identify him. See if anyone knows where he is."

"But why didn't you tell me?!"

He stammered. "You were sleeping when I found out. And right afterwards, I went straight over to..." He caught himself just in time from revealing his latest whereabouts. "Listen, I've been busy all day. And out of the office for most of it. I haven't even had a chance to check my messages, or to get an update from the office. Talking to you now is the first chance I've had to give you an update."

"So you've known this whole day that Shelly's boyfriend killed my husband and you didn't think to take a moment out of your day to give me a call? I had to find out from the news, Jack. The news!"

Chapter 40

"WAIT, WHAT?!?"

"You made me find out on the news. Why couldn't you have told me in person? Am I not worth at least that, Jack? After all we've been through?"

"Claire, honey, listen to me. You're talking in circles. I'm sorry I didn't get a chance to tell you that we got a match to the fingerprints off Ron's car. And I'm sorry I didn't get a chance to tell you in person. I swear I was going to. I'm actually on my way to you now. I'm only a couple miles away. But please, Claire, what does all this have to do with Shelly's boyfriend?"

"Shelly's boyfriend. You know, the P.I.? The one who gave me all those pictures?"

"Yeah."

"He's the guy in the photo on the news. But his name is all wrong. Shelly's boyfriend isn't named Richard L. Barrett. His name is Len. Len Barry."

Jack's stomach landed at his feet. He flashed back to the memory of looking at the PI's report, with the stacks of photographs showing Claire's husband at each of the bars with each of the Diamonds for Diamond victims. He flipped through his memory to the page of the PI's bill and saw the name, in his vision, printed at the bottom of the bill. Len R. Barry. A reversal of his real name. R. L. Barrett.

Then everything slowly began to click into place.

"Claire, honey, I've got to go. I'll get back to you as soon as I can. I've got to go take care of something."

Flipping an illegal turn on the overpass, Jack swerved his car back onto the I84 onramp and sped his way through the traffic, trying to make his way back to the Multnomah building as soon as humanly possible. Following as many traffic rules as he could, albeit at the very minimalistic way he could get away with, Jack made it back to his office quick as a wink. He parked illegally in a handicapped spot and flipped his temporary handicap parking pass up onto his mirror. He hated having to use his brother's parking pass for a work related matter, but in his rush to get up to the office to hopefully stop a serial killer before he could kill again, he prayed his brother would forgive him.

He took the stairs two at a time, foregoing the ever too slow elevators, and dashed through the halls, ignoring the stares of the coworkers as he ran, coat tails flying, through the maze of cubicles.

He rounded the corner to the conference room just as Nick was making his way back from the photocopy machine.

"Jack! Great news! We're already getting hits..."

"It's Shelly's P.I.!" He bent over, placing his hands on his knees, willing his breath to catch up to his body. Looking up, he focused on Nick's eyes. "Barrett. He's Shelly's P.I."

"You're not talking any sense, Diamond. Catch your breath, man. Who's Shelly?"

"Shelly Porter. Victim number six. Claire's best friend." His breaths were coming out more evenly now, and he straightened up, pulling Nick into the conference room with him.

"And Shelly's P.I. is…"

"Our suspect. Richard L. Barrett. Len R. Barry. Same guy." With a last sigh, letting the air whoosh out of his lungs, Jack sat down in the nearest conference chair, exhausted.

"Holy shit."

"It connects everything together."

"Everything makes sense now."

"He was right there. Taking pictures of each and every one of our victims."

"He had access to all of them."

"And he framed Ron."

"Cheeky bastard."

They both looked up and smiled. Then, sobering up, the glanced at the table filled with paperwork.

"How could we have missed this?"

"Did you ever get a chance to interview him?"

"No. Did you?"

"No."

"Son of a bitch."

"Manny's going to kill us."

"No he's not. Listen, we've got this. This case has been crazy fast. So much has happened, we never had a chance to get around to interviewing him."

"He's a PI, for Pete's sake! He's supposed to be one of the good guys."

Nick took a deep breath, looking around. "Not all of the good guys are good guys, Jack."

Jack lowered his head and ran his hands across his face.

"How'd you figure it out?"

"Claire called me. Saw his pic up on the news. Yelled at me for not telling her that I knew Shelly's boyfriend killed her husband."

"Oooh. That's gotta hurt."

"Yeah. Wait until she thinks things through the rest of the way and figures out that the bastard killed her best friend, too."

"Uh, yeah. That's not going to be fun."

They let the silence fill the room as they glanced at the files, pictures, and papers spread out on the conference room table in front of them. Then, jumping up, Jack touched a few of the pictures of the women in front of him. "So, now that we know who he is, let's go and find him!"

"Yeah, baby!" Nick slapped Jack on the back, and led them both back to Manny's office.

As the reached his office, Nick turned to Jack, whispering conspiratorially. "Take my lead on this."

Jack nodded his head and knocked on Manny's door.

"Got a sec?"

Manny pulled his reading glasses off his face and looked up from the papers in front of him. Unlike the conference room table, Manny's desk was immaculately clean. The epitome of how a proper functioning desk should look.

"Only if it's good news." He looked from Nick's beaming face to Jack's slight frown and furrowed his brows.

"We've got an alias."

"On our serial killer suspect?"

"Yep. Richard L. Barrett has been going by Len R. Barry."

"Huh. Kind of an interesting twist on the name. Did you find anything on him?"

"Some, not much. Turns out he's working as a private investigator in the area. And there's a connection between him and one of our victims."

"Two of our victims." Jack corrected Nick, and he took it in stride.

"Right. Two of our victims."

"Sounds interesting. Let's hear it then."

"So do you remember the P.I. who gave us all those photos linking Ron to each of the victims in the case? He's the sixth victim's boyfriend."

"The sixth victim's boyfriend."

"Yep."

Manny lowered his glasses and put them onto the desk in front of him. Then, slowly and methodically, he began to rub his almost bald head.

"Did you ever interview the sixth victim's boyfriend?"

"Well, no, but..."

"He was on our list to interview when..."

Manny cleared his throat. "So let me get this straight. What you're telling me is that we never interviewed a likely suspect in one of our murder cases."

Jack opened his mouth to explain when Manny glowered at him. He promptly shut his mouth.

"And furthermore, we've been sitting on photographs, taken by a private investigator, our Mr. Richard L. Barrett — a.k.a. our number one suspect *and* I might add, the same likely suspect from our sixth victim that *we never interviewed.*"

The blushes on Jack's and Nick's faces rose simultaneously.

"And these photographs, taken by our prime suspect, link our last suspect to each of the victims. Photographs which make one of our own, even if it is Ron Wilcox, look like he's connected to each of the victims."

"That just about covers it, sir."

"That doesn't even come *close* to covering it!!" Manny slammed the flat part of his hand down against his desk, making both of them jump.

"We've got photographs taken of each one of our victims. We've got photos of them eating and drinking in bars, the last bars they will ever set foot in. We've got photographs of each of these women, just before each of them was murdered, and we never even thought to interview the photographer?!" Manny slammed his hand down on each of the last three words. The neatly stacked papers jumped in response. Once. Twice. Three times. His pen rolled off the desk and onto the thick carpet below.

"It's not that we didn't think of..."

"Don't tell me what you did and didn't think of! I don't want to hear it! What I *want* to hear is that you now have this man in custody. That he's wearing a pretty set of steel handcuffs, and he's sitting down in my holding cell, awaiting an arraignment for his upcoming trial into the murder of seven people. *That* is what I want to hear! Are either of you here to tell me *that*?!"

"No, sir."

"Not yet, sir."

Manny's face turned several shades darker. He picked up his reading glasses with gentle fingers and placed them carefully onto the bridge of his nose. He straightened out the papers on his desk and began to read again.

A moment passed and nothing happened.

Peering up and over the top of his reading glasses, Manny's voice returned to its normal calm and soothing timbre. "Is there anything else, gentlemen?"

"No, sir."

"Then I suggest you get back to work."

They shut the door quietly behind them, and ignored all the curious stares following them back to their office.

Chapter 41

"CLAIRE? DO YOU happen to still have Mr. Barrett's — I mean, Mr. Barry's contact information?" Jack tried not to let his voice sound as much like the pathetic pleading whimper he thought it sounded like.

"If you think for one minute you can simply call me up and ask me for favors, today of all days, Johnathan Dixon Diamond, you've got another thing coming!"

"Claire, please! I'm..."

The silence on the other end of his call clenched his stomach. He pulled his phone away from his ear and glanced down. Call ended. Great.

He pressed the contact information to reach her again, but to no avail. The call went straight to voice mail. Grinding his teeth together, he waited for her all too cheerful voice to finish its standard message and end with a beep. "Claire, it's Jack. I'm sorry that I screwed up. I'll apologize to you in person a hundred times. But for now, we need to catch this guy. We've got to get to him before he kills someone else! Please!" He cleared his throat and forced himself to calm down. "Please, Claire. Call me. Or just text me the information. If you don't want to talk to me, could you please, at least, text the information to me? Please?" He pressed end call and placed his phone down, not as gently as he should have, on the conference room table.

Nick tried to keep the knowing look off his face. "No luck, huh?"

Jack shook his head. "She's pissed."

"She has a right to be."

"Clearly." Nick watched Jack run his hands through his hair and tried not to smile. At least he didn't have to deal with girl troubles. He suppressed a grin and rearranged a few things on the conference room table.

Jack pulled his phone toward himself and composed a text to GranNini. Maybe she could help. Just before he pressed send, he looked at his phone as if it had grown six legs. He wondered if he should really involve his grandmother in his battles. She had already helped out once today. He knew that she was pressed for a deadline on her latest book. But this was murder, after all. Murder of Claire's husband and her best friend, along with five other people. Changing his mind, Jack deleted the unsent text and called her instead. He hoped his grandmother's love and adoration for his ex-girlfriend, her favorite of them all, would create enough magic to help persuade Claire to help them out. He kept their phone call short and to the point, thanking her profusely at the end.

A second wave of frustration washed over him, and he pressed his cell phone against his forehead, willing the pounding to go away. Too much stress and not enough exercise. That always gave him a headache.

"So, where do we go from here?"

"We could go back to Shelly's place. See if we missed something."

Jack shook his head. "I went through her place with a fine toothed comb. Both her computer and her iPhone were stolen. She didn't have a contact list in her purse. I searched the place upside down from Sunday trying to find something — anything — that would lead us to our bad guy, and came up with nothing."

"Yeah, but..." an idea started to bloom. "But you were looking for evidence against Ron, weren't you?"

"Yeah, still, I found nothing that would lead me to Ron — or to anyone else for that matter. And besides, I gave up everything I found to the evidence team."

"So there's nothing else you think we could find from her searching her apartment again?"

"I seriously doubt it."

"Well, then let's go through the stuff you *did* find, and see if we can find something — *anything* — related to Barrett."

Thirty minutes later they were elbow deep into the evidence box bearing the contents of Shelly's apartment search when Jack's phone chirped.

"Who's it from?" Nick looked up, his curiosity getting the best of him.

Jack's eyebrows shot up in surprise. "My grandmother. She says that she couldn't get away to go and talk with Claire again, but that she persuaded Claire to send her the contact information." He pressed the link on his phone, and up came the contact information sheet for Len Barry.

His grin could have lit up the Portland Pioneer Courthouse Square Christmas tree. "Let's go ping us a bad guy!"

In a few short minutes, Jack stood at the edge of Nick's cubicle and watched at the ease in which Nick used one of his templates to whip out a search warrant to ping Barrett's cell phone, enabling the telephone company to quickly and easily locate the phone. He emailed the warrant to the on-call judge, and sat back, putting his hands behind his head. "Now all we have to do is wait!"

Jack grinned.

His grin faltered when he felt the stern grip pressing his shoulder. "Do you have any good news for me, fellas?" Manny's large body filled the cubicle.

Jack willed the clench of fear to leave his stomach. His father used to grab his shoulder just like that, before reaching for his belt — or the nearest hard object — to pummel him with. He couldn't help but feel the color drain from his face. Out of habit he cleared his throat, willing himself not to shake off Manny's hand from his shoulder. "Actually, yes, sir, we do."

Manny, never missing a detail and noting the discomfort on Jack's face, slipped his hand from

Jack's shoulder and folded his arms across his chest, leaning his large frame against the other wall of Nick's cubicle. His subtle move fooled neither Nick nor Jack, but Nick let it slide, and Jack let his lips lift in a small smile of gratitude before looking down at his shoes. Neither Nick nor Manny knew the severity of the abuse Jack had suffered as a child under his tyrannical father. Neither of them had gotten the nerve to read the sealed files. But after having read his nonverbal behaviors over the years, and from what little Jack had told them, they'd both had a fairly good idea of at least the general circumstances.

Nick spoke first. "We've been able to ascertain the latest cell phone number that Barrett has been using under his assumed name." He glanced up at Jack, but Jack's eyes remained focused on the floor, so he continued. "I've just sent out a search warrant request to the on-call judge. And as soon as that comes through, we'll have the telephone company ping Barrett's cell phone. That will give us his current location, and then the game's afoot!"

Manny nodded his head. "I'm pleased to hear you've made quick work of redeeming yourself this afternoon. Keep me apprised." He nodded to Nick, and then gave Jack's arm a quick squeeze. Jack glanced up and returned Manny's small smile.

They didn't have to wait much longer. Within minutes of the approved search warrant coming through, Jack had the telephone company on the line. Nick emailed over the signed search warrant to the telephone company's supervisor. In no time at all, the supervisor came back on the line with a set of coordinates.

"You do know that these coordinates only guarantee that the cell phone is within a quarter mile to a few hundred yards of the specified cell phone."

Jack nodded his head at her mechanical voice. She sounded like she had been reading off a form. "Yes, ma'am. I'm aware."

"And you are aware that this information does not guarantee that the person who owns the telephone and pays for the service of this telephone is actually in possession of said telephone at the time in which this information has been given."

"Yes, ma'am."

"And that the location that we have provided for you today does not guarantee that the telephone in question will remain in said location for any length of time, and furthermore, that said telephone may, in fact, not be at the location we provided to you at any other point in time other than at the specific point in time in which said telephone was pinged by us at your request."

"Yes, ma'am. Thank you so much for your help!" He disconnected the line before she could prattle on about the further logistics of pinging non-smart telephones. He laughed, turning in his chair to face Nick. "This would have been so much easier if Barrett had used an iPhone, and had turned on the "Find My iPhone" function in the settings."

Nick laughed loud enough that several heads popped over the cubicle walls. He pulled up an app on his iPhone, plugged in the coordinates they had been given, and waited for the app to narrow down the location and pull it up on a map. "Stupid internet wifi. Why does the connection always seem to suck inside the office?"

Jack laughed. "Probably to keep you from looking up porn while on the job." He grinned, then ducked as Nick tossed a paper clip across the aisle and into his cube. "I've got to go hit the bathroom before we head out. Back in a sec."

Nick placed his phone down on his desk and started the shut down process on his computer watching out of the corner of his eye as Jack made his way down the hallway. Nick flipped off his desk light, grabbed his keys, and picked up his phone. A blue flashing ball winked at him as the pieces of the map slowly started plotting themselves into place. "Geez, come on!" He wondered how police officers used to handle the exceedingly slow pace of search warrants before faxes and emails, before smart phones and internet connections. His fast paced mind demanded fast paced response times, and he grew frustrated just thinking of how bad it must have been for his predecessors.

As he pinched his fingers across the digital map on his phone, increasing the size of the map and forcing the map to show more detail, his heart rate started increasing. As the names of the streets starting appearing on the small screen, a wave of fear gnawed at the pit in his stomach.

325

Jack's grin faded as he returned, making his way back to Nick's cube. Nick struggled one of his arms into the sleeve of his jacket, his other hand holding his phone. All the color had drained out of his face.

"What? What's wrong?"

Looking up, Nick studied Jack's face for a moment, his expression grim. "Jack, you're not going to like this."

Nausea, thick and overwhelming washed over Jack. He was used to fear. Grew up with fear, three meals a day, three hundred sixty five days a year. He could recognize it a mile away, and could feel the ache of it for hours afterwards. He hated the feeling. Especially when it left *that* look on someone's face. Nick looked positively wretched. "What? Damn it! What's wrong?!"

Nick handed the phone to Jack, his hand shaking so badly the phone almost fell on the floor. Jack took the phone and looked down at the screen, and for the second time that week, his world fell apart.

Chapter 42

"How did he find out where I lived?" They jogged up the stairs two at a time, skipping the elevator altogether, racing up to the fifth floor and over to the bridge that led to the building's parking garage across the street.

"I honestly don't know."

"How did he know that Claire would be there?"

Nick wheezed, struggling to keep up. "Maybe he wasn't looking for Claire. Maybe he was actually looking for you."

Nick's statement caught Jack off guard. He stopped abruptly and turned to face Nick. "Me?"

Nick, grateful for the chance to catch his breath, merely nodded his head.

"But why would he want me?" He turned around and headed toward his car. He unlocked the doors and Nick flopped inside, rocking the car.

"Hello? Diamonds for Diamond? Do you not even read the news these days? Didn't you ever realize that he's doing all this to impress you?"

Jack raised his eyebrows and backed out of his parking space. "You're full of crap. The media made up that name, not him. Besides, there's no reason to impress me. I'm utterly unimpressed."

Nick raised his eyebrows. "Except for being impressed by how he was able to find out where you lived."

Nick flashed his pass to the parking lot attendant, flipped on his blue lights — but kept his sirens silent — and turned right. "It's not that hard to find out where someone lives."

"So sayeth the man who was unable to locate where Barrett lives."

"Shut up."

Jack stopped a bit abruptly at the traffic light, forcing the seat belt to cut deeply into Nick's large belly. "Hey, now!" His fingers missed their intended targets on his phone's keypad, and he had to delete the last two numbers.

Jack looked both ways, then ran the red light, adrenaline pumping through his veins. "Who are you calling?"

"Portland PD. We've got to get them rolling on this."

Jack glanced down at the clock, his heart racing. "Shit. You're going to hit the eddy."

Nick raised his eyebrows, his phone pressed firmly up to his ear.

"The eddy? Shift change? Getting a Portland officer out on a Code 3 during the shift change? Shit." Jack slowed at the next intersection, only slightly mollified by the traffic's compliance to state laws as they all, for some blessed, uncanny reason, seemed to pull over to let him pass. He flew through the streets, pausing at the intersections, and willing traffic to continue to comply. Half his mind listened in to Nick's conversation as he talked to the dispatcher, calling all available cars to Jack's home address. Nick's swearing captured Jack's full attention.

"What?!" Jack let his eyes flit from the road to Nick and back again. "What?!?"

"There's a gang shooting in North Portland. Three gangsters down, plus one little kid who got in the way. Most of Portland is tied up in that whole mess. Dispatch is trying to untangle someone to head our way. They'll have more officers available as soon as shift change is done. They'll hold people over. Hang on…"

Jack's heart raced as the streets of Portland rushed pass. He pressed the call button on his bluetooth willing Claire to answer her phone. When he got nothing but her voice mail again, panic started to set in. The closer he got to approaching his house, the harder his heart started to pound. He willed his mind not to visualize possibilities of what could be. He turned off the argument inside his head and focused in on the last few words of Nick's conversation with the dispatcher.

Nick ended his call and turned to Jack. "So, good news. Dispatch pulled two Portland officers from the gang shooting, and they're on their way. All other available cars are coming Code 2, no sirens." He took a deep breath, and then ventured a side glance over at his partner. "But they're coming from southeast."

Jack allowed the information to sink in as he turned the last corner approaching his neighborhood. Traffic had been a nightmare, even when navigating the streets with his blue lights blazing. At least he didn't have to worry about the local school traffic, and kids walking home on top of everything else. He tried, and failed once again, to reach Claire. With each stop sign and traffic light, his heart pressed harder against his chest. He couldn't lose her. Not now. Not after all this time. Not after she was finally free.

He turned the last corner and dropped his car to a crawl. It felt a bit like missing the last step on a staircase, going from Code 3 down to nothing, and his stomach lurched. He tried Claire again, only to get her voicemail. He clenched his fist, willing his hand not to bash the steering wheel.

"She's going to be okay, Jack." Nick eyed his partner, worried.

"You don't know that." He pulled his car behind Mrs. Patinkin's Prius, three doors down from his house. He knew they couldn't approach his house without back up, and his fingers drummed the steering wheel, anxious to pound down his door, pound down the face of Mr. Richard L. Barrett. He pulled out his cellphone and tried to contact Claire again. "Come on! Come on! Answer the damned phone already!"

A Portland Police patrol car screeched around the corner, followed almost immediately by a second car. Jack nodded — to himself or to Nick, he wasn't sure, and then stepped out of his car, pulling his badge off his belt and holding it up and out in front of him. In an instant, the two patrol officers had double parked their cars, in a tactical offset position, partially blocking all further traffic from entering down the tiny side street. The two officers stepped out of their cars in unison. The back officer raised his radio to his mouth and called in their arrival to dispatch. They made their way to the center of the street, meeting up with Jack and Nick.

The first officer nodded to Jack, his right hand pressed up against the butt of his gun, his left hand hooked into the loop on the front of his bullet proof vest. "I'm Meyer, that's Zimmerman." He nodded to the officer behind him, and gave Jack and Nick the once over. A weird tension tended to flow between officers from different agencies. Minor one-upmanship and territorial issues, combined with high alpha male testosterone levels tended to keep the officers sniffing around one another, subconsciously marking their territory as they engaged in a nonverbal battle to decide which officers would be lucky enough to take charge of which cases. Jack discovered, to his relief, that the older he aged, the less need he had to prove himself and his authority to other people. He left the squabbles to the other folks, and only fought for those battles in which he felt his fight was warranted. When it came to Claire, he would fight to the death.

"So, what've we got?" Zimmerman allowed his gaze to switch from Jack to Nick, over to Meyer, and then back again.

Nick pressed a button on his phone and slipped it into his breast pocket. "Portland PD has three more cover cars headed this way, Code 2, from southeast." He took a deep breath, and eyed the tension building between the three other men. "They should be here any time. This is Jack Diamond, I'm Nick Buchanan."

They all shook hands, but the Portland officer's palms immediately reached back and rested, once again, on the butts of their guns.

"This here is Jack's house. Jack and I have been investigating the Diamonds for Diamond case…"

"Ah! So that's why the name sounded so familiar." Zimmerman flashed a smile, and then sobered immediately. "Damn, is this about that case?"

"Exactly. We've received intel that our bad guy is currently holding up in Jack's house."

The two officers both nodded.

"He's probably armed. We know he's dangerous. He's already killed five women, and one of our sergeants."

Meyer grimmaced.

"The bad news is that he's probably got himself a hostage in there."

"Sheee-it."

Jack nodded, the knot in his stomach growing with each and every word. "Can we move things along?" This discussion was taking far too much time. He wanted inside his house, and he wanted inside right now.

Nick glanced at Jack, and then turned his focus back on the two officers. "We've got to get in there and clear the place, get the bad guy covered, and make sure our hostage is okay. You with me?"

They nodded. Jack sighed in gratitude at Nick's ability to take over the operations with no fuss at all regarding territorial debates. His body was amped, and Nick's calm demeanor helped him focus his nervous energy on the tactical plan in front of them. His mind raced through seventeen different potential scenarios, visualizing the possible outcomes of each one.

"How do you want to work this?" Meyer looked to Nick and then to Jack. Jack cleared his throat and spoke for the first time.

"Which of you is the better shot?"

Meyer looked at Zimmerman and nodded. "He is." A faint blush tinted Zimmerman's cheek, but he nodded his head.

"Okay. You," he nodded toward Zimmerman, "head to the back of my house. There's a gate on the left. The lever's on the back side, so reach over the top to unlatch it. Once you get to the back of my house, cover the French doors in the back. This guy could bolt, and I don't want him disturbing my neighbors." Zimmerman nodded, and jogged his way across the street.

"I'd like you to cover the front door with Nick. Clear the living room and kitchen. They're both in the front. There's a hallway leading straight back with doorways leading to the office, laundry room, and guest bathroom. My bedroom is in the back. I'll go in after you clear the living room and kitchen. Nick, I want you to clear my office and the laundry room. Meyer, you clear the bathroom. I'll head straight back to my bedroom. When you're done, we'll need to clear my bath and closet."

They both nodded. "Let's not let her get hurt, okay?" Nick smacked Jack on the arm, and they started making their way to Jack's front porch. Another Portland Police car screeched around the corner. Jack eyed the car, and then nodded to Meyer. "Go fill her in, then meet us up on the porch. We'll meet you up there. She'll need to cover the front of the house."

Jack crouched to a stoop and slipped his key into his front door's lock, and waited, heart racing, for Meyer to return.

"She's going to be okay, Jack. Just breathe."

Jack nodded his head, questioning the wisdom in being part of the entry team. But the longer he had to wait for Meyer to return to the front porch, the more antsy he became. He had to get in there. He had to protect her. It was his job. His only job. To protect the woman he loved.

Dismissing all protocol, Jack reached his hand up and started to turn the knob.

Nick hissed.

Startled, Jack looked up and spied Meyer, finally, crouching up the front steps. Meyer peeked into his living room window, and nodded the all clear to Nick. Nick peered in the kitchen window and nodded as well. Jack pointed his gun toward the

334

front door and nodded his head. He twisted the knob, and pressed the door wide open. He watched in slow motion as Meyer and Nick pushed their way into his living room.

Chapter 43

HIS HEART POUNDED so hard against his chest he found it difficult to breathe. He watched them as if in a silent movie clear his living room, then his kitchen, and head down the hall. Everyone moved in complete silence, one checking high, the other low, as Jack crept down the hall, his gun braving its way down the hall before him, heading toward his bedroom. The tinnitus in his ears began to ring loudly, blocking out all other sounds, as if cotton had been stuffed in his ears. He saw, but didn't see, the photos lining the hallway walls. A black and white menagerie of his loved ones; his mother, his brother, his grandfather, his beloved GranNini. And Claire. He'd always kept his favorite photo of her. Years after he no longer had a right to, he still kept her photo on his wall. A memory. A promise. A hope. Time slowed to a complete stop as he approached his closed bedroom door. The cotton muffled silence in his head amplified his racing heartbeat, amplified the tinnitus.

He felt, rather than heard, the two officers approach his side as he stood, paralyzed in fear of what he might find behind his bedroom door. He took a deep breath, raised his left foot, and kicked in the door.

In a rush, the sound turned back on. Jack winced as someone screamed, "Drop the knife! Drop the knife!"

Jack blinked, and watched in horrified silence as his eyes revealed the gruesome scene before him. Richard Barrett had been standing over Claire, using a large hunting knife to carve something out of her chest. Blood stained the sheets. Her body, on its side, remained still. Too still. Her blonde hair had tangled itself over her face, just like it used to when to when she slept next to him, back when they were in college. Blood oozed out of her chest, dripping down her side, her shirt torn, her breast exposed. A lump the size of a softball filled his throat. He couldn't swallow. The grief too big. The damage too great.

He tore his gaze away from her hair strewn face and found himself staring at her breast, her beautiful breast, its creamy white skin so soft, so tender. He remembered the first time he'd kissed her there, aroused by her sigh, the nearly silent coo she'd made as his lips had touched her lovely skin.

The sound of gun shots lurched his attention back into focus, his heart pressing painfully against his chest. He tore his eyes away from Claire's body just as his bedroom lamp exploded into a million pieces as the bullets missed their mark. He looked up at Barrett just in time to see him fling his bloody knife at Nick and duck behind the bed. Nick grabbed his leg and went down, his gun clattering on the hardwood floor just out of reach. More shots fired, and Jack watched in horror as the Portland officer went down beside him.

Jack shook his head, clearing the cobwebs, and aimed his gun at Barrett. He got three shots off before Barrett stumbled out the French doors, crashing down the steps and into his back garden. Jack ran to Nick's side. He heard the pop, pop, pop of bullets flying outside. He glanced over his shoulder, but couldn't see anything, his vision completely impaired by grief, adrenaline, and fear. Turning, he knelt down next to his partner.

"I'm okay." Nick's sickly pallor suggested otherwise. Jack stripped off Nick's belt and looped it around Nick's thigh. He pulled the belt tight, and then notched it closed.

"He got your artery." He pressed Nick back against the floor. "Whatever you do, do not try to pull out the knife. You'll bleed out before the paramedics can get here."

Before he could protest, Jack pressed his phone into Nick's hands. "Get the medics here now." He glanced up at the bed, and then back to Nick. "Take care of yourself first." Nick opened his mouth, but Jack glowered. "Then see what they can do to make her body less, um…" He fought back a sob, and put himself in check. He gave Nick a stern look, and nodded his head when he saw Nick pulling the phone up to his ear, listening for the 911 dispatcher's voice to click on.

Jack stood, allowing himself one more glance at the body of his love, and then stepped over to Meyer's body. One glance at the gaping hole in his neck and the rapidly expanding pool of blood pooling beneath his head told him the Portland officer had been dead almost before he had even dropped to the floor. Jack swallowed his pity, pulled out his gun, and stepped cautiously out onto his patio.

Jack winced at Zimmerman's body. He, too, couldn't have survived his injuries for more than a second or two after he'd been shot. But the blood trail leading out toward his garden convinced him that either he, or Zimmerman, had gotten off at least one good shot. He surveilled his yard briefly, then spied the smear of blood on a few of the boards of his back cedar fence. Heart pounding, he ran back to Zimmerman's body, and pulled his portable radio off his chest. "Officers down! Officers down! We need medical and back up Code 3. Suspect has taken off on foot East, toward 33rd Avenue." He rattled off his address. Holstering his gun, he took off, racing for his back fence.

Reaching over the tangle of branches, Jack pulled and tugged at the rusty gate latch. With a bit of effort, Jack pushed the gate open, wincing when the gate tore at his neighbor's blueberry bushes. He'd never opened the gate between their two yards before, and obviously it had been some time since it had last been opened. Jack pushed through decades' worth of blueberry bushes and chastised himself for taking what he thought would be the safer, quicker path rather than launching himself up and over his neighbor's fence. Bailey, Mr. Sandy's yellow lab, met him on the other side of the bushes and barked once in happy greeting.

"Some watch dog you are! Which way did he go?" Jack searched around, looking for more blood. Bailey ran over to the side of the house and barked again. Jack cocked his head to the side, and followed. Sure enough, a trail of blood inched its way across Mr. Sandy's concrete RV pad. "Good girl, Bailey!" Jack rubbed her head, then checked briefly around the back side of Mr. Sandy's garage and peeked into the filthy windows. He couldn't make out much, but it seemed to him that no one had been inside the garage for at least a month or two. He rattled the door handle, but it remained padlocked.

Keeping one eye on the bloody drips, growing more profuse with each few feet, Jack made his way down the side of Mr. Sandy's fence. Jack whirled around when Mr. Sandy opened the side kitchen door and stepped down onto the cement step. "Jack? Is that you? What in tarnation are you doing?"

Jack pressed his fingers to his lips. Bailey trotted over to Mr. Sandy and sat, panting a happy smile as Mr. Sandy caressed her head. Jack waved his hand, urging Mr. Sandy to go back inside. Seeing the look on Jack's face, his gun drawn, his neighbor inched his way back into his kitchen, pulling at Bailey's collar making sure she, too, stayed out of harm's way.

A rustling in the bushes behind him sent a dump of adrenaline racing through his system. He whipped around, and started heading toward the blueberry bushes when a piercing scream stopped him in his tracks. The scream came from the front of Mr. Sandy's house. Changing course once again, Jack raced down Mr. Sandy's driveway and peered around the corner. His heart skidded to a stop when the scene in front of him unfolded.

Barrett had a woman pressed up against his chest. Her Trader Joe's reusable bags scattered at her feet, groceries strewn everywhere. She screamed again. Jack winced as the small trickle of blood tripped down the inside of her blouse. She clawed at his arm tightening around her throat, wild panic in her eyes.

Jack aimed his gun at Barrett's head, blinking away at the sweat inching down his face. He'd always been a good shot. He'd trained hard to become so. But even so, shooting bullets at targets, and shooting paint balls or bean bag pellets at deputies pretending to be bad guys wasn't the same thing as shooting an actual bullet into the head of someone else. He'd never killed anyone before. He'd wanted to. A million times and again and again he'd wanted to. Dreamed of it. Prayed for it. He'd wished he could go back into his childhood and do it again and again and again, wishing it for so long it had become a part of who he was, a part of who he'd become. He would have given anything to be able to have traded his father's life for one more day with his mother. To take his life to save another's. He'd trained his whole life for this moment.

Jack pictured his father's face. It took no imagination at all to picture the woman he pressed up against him, knife at her throat, to be his mother's. How many times had he walked in on his

341

parents like that? Twenty? Fifty? A thousand? A thousand times he prayed he could have had a gun in his hand, just like he did right now. A thousand times he wished he could stand where he was standing right now, protecting someone from harm.

His voice rang out — cool, confident. A moment of pure clarity washed over him and peace filled his heart. "Drop the knife, Barrett. Let her go. Or I will fire this gun. Drop the knife now."

He let his eyes meet up with Barrett's. Allowed him a moment to make the choice. To decide whether to die, or to live. He watched the gears and cogs shift and click their way through Barrett's brain. And then Barrett's gaze shifted.

"Jack?"

Claire's voice caught Jack off guard. Taking his eyes off Barrett, Jack turned around, stunned to find Claire stepping out from around the corner of the fence.

"What?! How?!" Jack blinked, his mind not comprehending the vision standing behind him. She was alive! How had she survived? She was alive!!

"Jack! Look out!"

Jack whipped around to see a whirl of activity. Barrett's captive had taken Claire's brief distraction to stomp on Barrett's foot. Then, when he loosened his grip, she used her elbow to jab him in the solar plexus. Keeled over, the woman made a dash for it, running across the street and onto the porch of one of the nearby houses.

Jack holstered his gun as he ran toward Barrett and plowed into him, taking him down like a blindsided quarterback sack. Nick would have been proud. Barrett knocked his head against the cement. He shook his head back and forth, trying to clear his vision. Jack pounded his fist into the man's face, unable to resist the urge. He shifted his body weight around and grabbed the man's left arm, using his right hand to reach behind him to grab his handcuffs.

"Richard L. Barrett, you are under arrest for eight murders, and the attempted murder of two more."

He sat back for a moment, allowing his knee to dig into Barrett's belly. The sudden dump of adrenaline had left him temporarily breathless, and he took a moment to catch up. Clamping the handcuff around Barrett's left wrist, he began again. "You have the right to remain silent." Using his weight to his advantage, Jack shifted his knee out of Barrett's belly, and began to flip the man over, so that he could place the other handcuff on Barrett's right wrist.

In a flash, Jack's elbow came crashing down upon the cement, sending shooting stars of pain into Jack's head. His vision clouded as he heard the "crack!" of the bone echo through his body. With a flick of the wrist, Barrett shifted his body weight around. Jack found himself caught at an awkward angle, his one hand trying desperately to hold onto the handcuffs attached to Barrett's wrist, his broken elbow sending screaming zingers up his shoulder, blacking out his vision with each pounding of his heart.

As Jack's consciousness ebbed and flowed, Barrett managed to wiggle a knife out of his pocket. With a flick of his wrist, he jabbed it into Jack's side. With a sickening "thuck," he pulled out the blade and flung it at Claire. He smiled when he heard her scream as the knife took hold.

In a surge of rage, Jack kneed Barrett in the side, shifted his weight around, pressed his foot down on Barrett's handcuffed wrist, and then slammed the side of his left hand into Barrett's neck. He felt the satisfying crunch of bone beneath his hand. The shocked look on Barrett's face brought a brief smile of appeasement to Jack's. As Barrett choked and gasped for air, the broken hyoid bone in his neck making it harder and harder for him to breathe, Jack sat back on his haunches, panting.

When the last of Barrett's raspy breaths grew silent, Jack turned his head, daring to brave the gruesome scene behind him.

She sat on the sidewalk, her pale face watching him with a look that could only be described as awe. Blood from the gash on her forearm started to seep through the grey sweater she'd wrapped around her arm. A bloody bandage on her chest also oozed with the dark red of her blood. Her hand rested on Barrett's bloody knife on the ground beside her.

Whimpering his relief, he stood, lilting only slightly when his vision blurred. He caught his foot on Barrett's leg, and tripped — skipping and hopping a few steps until he righted himself. Looking down, he noticed for the first time the gash in his left side. He pressed his hand to the gash, and looked in amazement when it came away bloody. He faltered for a moment, then pressed his hand back to his side, hoping to staunch the bleeding. Forever and a day later he finally reached Claire's side. He wiped off the blood from his hand onto his pants, wincing as the movement jostled his shattered right elbow. He looked her over, searching her face, her chest, her legs for further signs of injury. A wave of relief surged through his body that she seemed to be all in one piece. Overwhelmed with joy, he stifled a sob. When his eyes reached hers, his heart stopped completely, and tears spilled over. Dropping to his knees, he pulled her to his chest and vowed never to let her go.

Chapter 44

JACK BLINKED AT the dim light, rubbing the sleep from his eyes. He glanced around, disoriented for a moment. The monitors behind him silently charted every beat of his heart, numbers flashing his blood pressure, oxygen saturation, and respiration stats. The nurse had closed his curtains before he'd drifted off to sleep, and from what little light that poured through, he couldn't make out the time of day.

His gaze landed upon the pretty bouquet of flowers that his neighbor had brought over late last night. His lips turned up in a half-grin, pleased by the sentiment. She and her husband had stopped by to thank him for saving her life. Her husband had cried more than she had. She still had that look of numb shock across her face, her hands trembling when she'd squeezed his fingers, her lips shaking when she'd leaned over to kiss his cheek. The small bandage across her neck only showed the small outward scar left from the trauma she'd endured where the bad guy had held the knife up to her throat, when he'd used her as a hostage shield. The inner scars would take much longer to heal. Inner scars always took longer to heal.

Jack glanced around his hospital room. The county Chaplain had stopped by too, leaving another bundle of flowers. The Dive Team had brought by a basket of fruit. GranNini's cookies, what little were left, were tucked under a rumpled layer of plastic wrap.

Jack closed his eyes, allowing the feelings to wash over him. He'd killed a man. Just saying the words brought a stab of pain to his heart. Behind him, the monitors registered the drastic change in his body's autonomic responses. He turned his head to the side, squeezing his eyes shut, trying hard to swallow the lump in his throat. He'd actually killed a man.

Jack had always praised himself at having been able to stay in control, to protect the good guys and get the bad guys, and never have to lose control. He replayed the scene in his head, for the hundredth time, watching in slow motion as Barrett's blade kissed the woman's throat. The wild terror in the whites of her eyes, the man's glee in his own. He heard Claire, behind him, calling out his name, remembered feeling such a jolt of electricity at discovering her alive! Hearing Claire scream his name, watching Barrett go down, wrestling the man into handcuffs, feeling that sense of panic himself when he found himself pinned underneath. Feeling the crack of his elbow breaking, the sickening wave of nausea as the blinding pain threatened to take over, fighting to keep himself from losing the fight, losing the battle, losing the war. Feeling that warmth of a surge of energy as he flipped Barrett over, and then the satisfying, sickening crunch of

Barrett's neck breaking, hearing the last raspy breaths of his time here on Earth.

Tears flowed hot down his face. Jack wiped them off with the back of his hand, embarrassed, devastated, pleased, crushed. He'd never killed a man before. As much as he had always wanted to, he'd never done it. And now he was one of those. Someone who had taken the life of someone else. What kind of man did that make him?

Jack swiped at the tears that kept flowing. And now he was facing an inquiry into the investigation and the man's death. It may have been standard procedure for Internal Affairs to look into his lethal action, but it felt more like an impending punishment — the kind his father used to dole out when he and his brother were kids. He could hear the leather strap, slapping against his father's hands as he awaited his father's punishment. He could smell the sweat and the beer. He could practically feel the glee in his father's eyes, knowing he was going to exact his punishment for whatever nonexistent crimes his father planned to punish him for. No matter how innocent Jack had been, his father still found a way to twist his words into something worthy of punishment.

Jack hated being punished. And now he was facing the inquiry. A wave of nausea washed over him. Guilt and nausea roiled together. And yet, he knew in his heart of hearts, that his actions had been justified. Jack had killed a man, yes. But the man had murdered five women. And Ron Wilcox. The man had critically injured his partner. He had murdered two police officers. And when he was finally cornered, Barrett had been holding a knife to another person's throat — using her as a human shield, threatening her life as well. Then he had flung a knife at Claire, trying to kill her. Barrett had broken Jack's elbow, and then had stabbed Jack in his side, trying to kill Jack. Jack had killed Barrett out of self-defense. Jack had killed Barrett, while protecting two other people. Jack had killed Barrett, a man who had murdered eight other people and injured four others, including himself. Jack's actions were completely justified.

Jack closed his eyes. He took a deep breath, and allowed himself a moment to keep focusing on the positive side of things. The good things. He'd saved his neighbor. He looked at the flowers across the room. He'd saved Nick. His mind flashed to the belt wrapped around Nick's leg. And he'd saved Claire. Jack's heart clenched. He wiped the last tear off his face as he turned to look at her, sleeping in the chair beside him.

With perfect timing, almost as if it were scripted, Nick knocked on the door and peered inside. Jack pulled his gaze away from Claire and smiled at his company. He squeezed Claire's hand and her eyes flitted open. Her face broke into a broad grin, and she stifled the yawn that threatened to embarrass her in its grand size and enormity. She excused herself to use the rest room, giving Nick a kiss on the way out the door.

Jack grasped Nick's hand in an awkward handshake. Left-handed handshakes always felt awkward, even if they were essential. He winced when Nick jostled his hospital bed, scooting his wheelchair right up against the foot of Jack's bed. Despite the doctor's advice and well-wishes, Jack still refused anything stronger than over the counter pain medication. His decision had left him at the mercy of another night's stay at the hospital. The doctors wanted to keep a close eye on his abdominal surgical incision as well as on the first few days of his recovery with the pins and screws in his broken elbow if he was going to continue to refuse pain medication.

"Brought you some porn. And some cigarettes. And a bottle of whisky."

Jack blinked at the brown paper bag that Nick held in front of him.

The bubble of laughter caught him off guard. "Man, you should see the look on your face!!"

Jack grinned, reaching out with his good hand for the bag. "So what's really in here?"

"A rutabaga, some kale, and a bottle of that fancy bottled water you drink."

Jack blanched, his fingers poised above the folds of the bag. "Are you kidd—"

The peels of laughter were contagious, and Jack found himself joining in. Giving Nick a sideways glance, he peered inside, almost afraid of what he'd find. He grinned when he viewed the contents. Pouring them out onto his lap, Jack smiled. Nick had brought him a book of sudoku puzzles, a crossword puzzle book, a murder mystery novel, and two blue pens.

"Something to keep your mind sharp while you're waiting to get back to work. Any idea when that's going to be?" Nick raised his eyebrows, trying to avoid looking at the pins sticking out of the weird contraption attached to Jack's right arm.

"Six, seven weeks." He sighed. "How about you?" He nodded down to Nick's leg.

"Oh, me? I'll be out of here in an hour or so. Just got my walkin' papers." Jack grinned.

"And recovery?"

Nick sobered for a moment. "Not too long. Desk job for a week or so. Then I'll get my stitches out and I'll be good as new, with a brand new scar to woo the ladies."

Jack snorted. Nick and Chris, his better half, had been together for so long even their habits had grown together.

"How's things?" Nick nodded at the door, his gaze resting on the chair next to Jack's hospital bed and the woman who had recently left it.

A rush of heat spread through Jack's cheeks and down his chest. He smiled, ducking his head. "Good." He glanced up at Nick, and then looked away. "Things are good." He couldn't help the smile that grew across his face, and glanced back at Nick. His laughter grew contagious.

"So I've got some good gossip for you on our Mr. Barrett. The guys back at the Detectives Unit have been keeping me entertained by filling my ears with all sorts of good shit on Barrett while you've been over here sleeping off your belly wound and coddling your elbow."

Jack's eyebrows shot up. "Really? Like what?"

Nick pulled his wheelchair up a bit closer to Jack's head and lowered his voice. "Turns out Mr. Barrett's not so good at getting rid of evidence." He turned and glanced out the door, and then looked back at Jack, lowering his voice another level. "He left all sorts of crap in his car. We've got cell phones, purses, all sorts of crap from each of his victims."

Jack's jaw dropped to the floor. No one, absolutely no one was this stupid any more when it came to evidence. "Are you kidding me?"

"I shit you not. Furthermore, Mr. Richard L. Barrett even had the tire iron, with blood to match, from your Larch Mountain chick."

"Good grief!"

Nick nodded. And then he gave Jack a pointed stare, quirking his eyebrows.

"What?! What else did you find."

The twinkle in Nick's eye made Jack laugh. "What?! Come on now, I'm injured! I need details!"

"I'm injured too!"

Jack blushed. "Geez, Nick, I'm sorry. You know I didn't mean…"

His laughter peeled out again. "Just joshin' with you. You know that." He squeezed Jack's leg and left his arm to rest on Jack's bed. "So it turns out, our

Mr. Barrett's military past came back to bite him in the butt."

The confused look on Jack's face urged him on. "Remember how Barrett was accused of raping that woman down in California?"

"Yeah."

"So it turns out that Barrett fancied himself a job at the Sheriff's Office."

"With us?"

"Mmhmmm. Turns out Ron Wilcox was on the hiring committee when his application came through. Ron personally called the nice folks in California to get a background check on Mr. Barrett. And when his past came to light, Ron unilaterally obliterated Barrett's chances of ever working for the Sheriff's Office. Or, pretty much, any other police force in the Pacific Northwest."

Jack whistled.

"Evidently Barrett took offense." He tapped his hand on Jack's bed, fidgeting. Jack winced at the sudden movement, but Nick didn't seem to notice. "Turns out he stalked Ron, and Claire, for that matter, for a while. He found out who Claire's friends were, followed Ron around and studied his bad habits after work. Then he put his plan into action, framing Ron for the murder of all those women as retribution. From the evidence we've recovered, looks like he'd been planning this whole thing for quite some time. That's how he came to be Claire's best friend's new boyfriend. Set himself up with a fake ID and fake credentials as a private

353

investigator. Looks like he may have even been planting ideas into Claire's head, using his 'girlfriend' to pass along suggestive hints that Ron was having an affair."

Jack's stomach twisted, thinking of how invasive Barrett must have been to get so far.

"Of course Ron made it easy for him, already being a bit of an ass and all. Chasing skirts and being a drunk..." He blinked, suddenly realizing to whom he'd been preaching. "Sorry, man."

"It's okay. I'd rather know all of it, and get it all out in the open now." He swallowed the bile in his throat, and reached over to take a sip of water. "So. How much of this does Claire know."

"None. How much do you want her to know?"

"All of it. I want her to know everything. I don't want there to be any secrets between us."

Nick wiggled his eyebrows, a grin sneaking out of the corner of his mouth. "So it's 'us' now?"

A rush of pure joy raced through Jack's stomach, sending his heart pounding, his cheeks flushing. His face broke out into an enormous grin.

Just then, Claire opened the door and her eyes reached his. An irrepressible smile spread across her beautiful face.

"It's...complicated."

The End

Acknowledgements

FIRST AND FOREMOST, I'd like to thank the Multnomah County Sheriff's Office and all the good folks who work there. Even though this book and all the characters within it are completely fictional, I appreciate the ability to be able to write about the MCSO, their facilities, and about all the hard work those people do to help keep the county and its inhabitants safe. I'd like to thank the real Jack Diamond for giving me the permission to use his name. It's an awesome name, and my Jack Diamond is very grateful. I'd like to thank my kids who allowed us to have very strange and unusual discussions at the dinner table regarding dead bodies and whatnot. They never complained about the weird looks their friends gave me when I drove them home from school, still thinking of and talking about Jack Diamond and his adventures. I'd like to thank my sweet Shea who is the most amazing editor and cheerleader. May she always be willing and able to read my Jack Diamond manuscripts, giving me sage advice and criticism, all the while encouraging me with such heart-warming enthusiasm. Squee!

I'd like to give a special thanks to my friends and loved ones who supported and encouraged this dream of mine. I'd like to thank all the people in my life who so generously donated their names for various characters. I never really realized just how many names go into a book until I found myself naming character after character after character, and rapidly running out of names to give them.

And most of all, I'd like to thank my Harry, who spent way too many hours allowing me to pester him each and every day for months with a million bajillion questions about law enforcement, about procedures and equipment, and what's it really looks like to discover a dead body underneath a waterfall. Harry's one of the good guys. And I'm so very lucky I still have 46 years left on my lease.

About the Author

WHEN SHE ISN'T plotting new ways to kill off fictitious victims for her *Jack Diamond* series, Kay Nimitz Smith can most often be found in her kitchen, baking her way into the hearts, and stomachs, of her friends and family. Smith, a retired college professor, lives with her husband in the beautiful Pacific Northwest, raising their two children. Married to a career law enforcement officer, Smith uses her creative imagination to integrate real crime scene investigation strategies into her mysteries. When she's not mulling over book plots, she enjoys reading, being crafty, watching films, avoiding housework, and, of course, perfecting her culinary skills.

For more information about the author, visit her blog at kaysmithbooks.blogspot.com

✳ ✳ ✳ ✳ ✳